Harper St George was raised in rural Alabama and along the tranquil coast of northwest Florida. It was this setting, filled with stories of the old days, that instilled in her a love of history, romance and adventure. At high school she discovered the romance novel, which combined all those elements into one perfect package. She lives in Atlanta, Georgia, with her husband and two young children. Visit her website: harperstgeorge.com.

MARRYING HER VIKING ENEMY

Harper St George

MILLS & BOON

First Published in Great Britain 2019
by Mills & Boon, an imprint of HarperCollins*Publishers*
1 London Bridge Street, London, SE1 9GF

© 2019 Harper St. George

ISBN: 978-0-263-26896-6

MIX
Paper from
responsible sources
FSC C007454

This book is produced from independently certified FSC™ paper
to ensure responsible forest management.
For more information visit www.harpercollins.co.uk/green.

Printed and bound in Spain
by CPI, Barcelona

With sincerest thanks to
Laurie Benson, Nathan Jerpe and Tara Wyatt,
for their friendship and guidance
while I was writing this book.

Prologue

'Traitors will be punished.' Rolfe's words rang out over the gathered crowd, punctuated by the roar of the newly set fire at his back.

A black cloud of smoke rose high in the air, filling the village of Banford with its acrid scent as tongues of flame licked hungrily at the hut's thatched roof. It was engulfed like kindling, half-burned to the ground by the time a blaze flickered to life on a second one. Tightening his hold on his stallion's reins to be ready should one of the Saxon warriors dare to attempt to fight him, Rolfe ignored the sharp ache in his shoulder from yesterday's battle. He refused to show weakness before these people, especially when he had to make certain that his words were heard.

'We found one of your neighbours among the Scots we battled yesterday. Durwin was there as a friend to them, giving information to our enemy, and he raised his axe to us in battle.' Durwin had been a simple farm worker with no sword to his name. He'd had no cause to meet with the Scots. No cause save the wounded pride that many of the Saxons seemed to share when it came to the Danes. On his cue, his men cut Durwin's blanket-wrapped body down from a horse and laid him respectfully on the ground.

Rolfe and his men had come directly from that confrontation to this village on Alvey lands where the traitor lived. Cnut, Rolfe's man in charge of the Saxon village, had quickly led them to Durwin's house. Thank the gods that it had been empty. Rolfe didn't relish the task of making women and children homeless.

'But what of his brother Osric?' An old woman's voice rose from the people who had come from their homes to watch. They all stood huddled together, a few with blankets over their shoulders to guard against the snow that had started to fall. The flakes hissed when they touched the flames that engulfed the second hut. 'Was he there, too?'

Cnut stepped forward. 'They've been suspected of fraternising with the Scots for months. Osric hasn't been seen in days. Can anyone vouch for his whereabouts?'

Of course no one could. Rolfe knew in his gut that Osric was fraternising with the Scots. Everyone in the village knew it, but no one would give up that information. It was why Rolfe had given the order to burn both of their houses. It was the only way to send the harsh but necessary message that traitors would not be tolerated.

'You are people of Alvey.' It was a simple fact that should need no reminder. 'You were born here and your loyalty should lie with your lord and lady.'

A few in the crowd nodded along with his words, but many only stared at him. Pockets of rebellion had broken out since his Jarl, Vidar, had married their Saxon lady, Gwendolyn. Rolfe was hopeful that the melding of their people would continue, but it was inevitable to face some resistance. Their only choice was to catch it early. It was particularly disconcerting in this case because the village of Banford was the closest to the Scots who lived just north of their border. A rebellion here could have devastating consequences should they join with the Scottish army, which was why it was particularly important that he squash any seeds of uprising now. 'Lord Vidar and Lady Gwendolyn will not tolerate traitors. Anyone known to be giving information to the Scots will have their belongings seized and risk execution.'

A grumble of unease ran through the gathered crowd, prompting his dog, who had been lying beside the horse, to get to his feet, his ears forward. 'Easy, Wyborn.' Rolfe kept his voice low and the mongrel settled while still keeping alert to the possibility of danger.

'Consider that we Danes have not butchered your people. We have not taken your land from you. Will the Scots, who have haunted you for generations, be so fair? Will the Scots allow your women to choose their own mates? Will the Scots extend silver to the families who marry their warriors?'

He paused to look over their faces, hoping that his words rang true for them. The people murmured, but not one of them stepped forward or offered comment. This brooding rebellion was merely misplaced pride. If sense prevailed, they would come to understand that. For real peace to be fostered and to thrive, they would have to accept that the Danes were here to stay.

'Your lord and lady have offered you all of these things. We have come to live in peace and to unite our people. The Scots will not offer you that. They will befriend you, only to enslave you.'

Rolfe gave a final nod and swung his horse around to walk to the edge of the village. Cnut and Wyborn walked beside him. 'Are any other men missing besides Osric?'

'None from the village.' Cnut nodded in the direction of the fields and the farmhouse set with several outbuildings on the outskirts of the village. 'I couldn't say about the farm. Since I've been here Godric keeps most of his people to himself, but I will question him.'

The wheat field was fallow now with the arrival of winter and, though most of the trees were bare, a hill hindered a clear view of the house. Godric was known to dislike the Danes, but so far had done nothing that would cross the line to outright treason. However, Rolfe had been gone from Alvey all summer—first visiting Jarl Eirik to the south and then Haken up north where he'd come across Durwin meeting with the Scots—and things might have changed. He'd need to speak with Vidar before doing anything in that quarter.

'Thank you, Cnut. Send word if Osric returns or you have more information.'

'Aye, immediately.'

Rolfe set his heels to his horse and led the way from the village, some of his men falling in line behind him. The rest of his army had been left to return home in the longships, while he detoured to Banford. Wyborn ran out front as if he sensed they were going home. The wound from the spear Rolfe had taken to his shoulder the day before ached with every jolt of the horse. It would take over a day of hard riding to make it home to Alvey. He'd been gone for months and was ready to be home. He only hoped this show of treachery wasn't a sign of things to come.

Chapter One

❧❦❧

Bernicia, northern Northumbria—winter 872

'The Danes are a fearful sight, are they not?'

Elswyth could not find the breath to answer her sister's question. It had lodged in her throat where it held until her lungs burned. The Norsemen came out of the forest on horseback, filtering into the clearing in a stream of warriors that didn't seem to have an end. There were thirty...forty, but even more followed behind. Several mongrels in various shades of brown and grey ran in their midst. She imagined them as bloodthirsty wolves from the tales she had heard growing up, with teeth dripping the blood of their enemies and snapping jaws clamouring for more.

The sun hung low behind the trees, a stray

beam glinting off their armour and the hilts of their sheathed swords, casting their faces in the shadow of a cold nightfall. The earth rumbled from the beat of the hooves as the horde moved closer. Her heart echoed that beat of distant thunder. It knew that the days of calm were over. These men were why her father had sent her to spy on Alvey.

It was an objective she meant to carry out, not only to prove her loyalty to her family, but also to bring hope to their small village of Banford. Banford needed hope that a reprieve from the Danes would soon come. She was to bring that hope to them in the form of information about the Danes' plans for the future.

'Aye,' she finally whispered when she could draw breath. 'They are quite fearful.' The frigid stone of the fortress wall bit into her palms as she stared down at the men approaching. The warriors were merely coming home and not here for battle, but her instinct was to reach for the short-handled axe at her belt as fear pounded through her veins. They were Danes, which meant they were her enemy.

''Tis good they are attractive, then.' Ellan grinned, her eyes calculating as she looked them over.

Elswyth smiled, for once grateful that Ellan

was never serious about anything. Though only scarcely more than a year separated their births, Elswyth sometimes felt far older than her often frivolous younger sister. 'Why do you care if they're attractive?'

'Because I would not care for an ugly husband.'

The horde forgotten for the moment, Elswyth swung her head around to stare at her sister in shock. 'You are not seriously considering marriage to one of them?' Ellan surely wouldn't, especially after the way their mother had run off with a Dane, abandoning the whole family to take up with the heathen. But something in her sister's expression made Elswyth's breath catch.

'And why wouldn't I?' The wind caught the cloak covering Ellan's hair, forcing her to take it in hand. Her cheeks were pink from the frigid air, while her eyes were fierce with challenge. 'What husband is there for me once we return home to Banford? Shepherd? Farmer? I'd much prefer a warrior.' Her gaze returned to the Danes below. 'You have to admit they're far more attractive than the men at home.'

Still in shock at her sister's blasphemy, Elswyth's gaze found the man leading the warriors. He sat proudly on his stallion with broad shoulders. His shirtsleeves had fallen back as he rode to reveal the defined muscles of his forearms flexing as he held the reins. His fur cloak hung low behind him, exposing the strong sweep of his cheekbones and his bearded jawline to the light cast by the wall's torches. She couldn't make out details, but she could tell—with some regret—that it was a handsome face. Much to her surprise, his gaze was fixed on the two of them. If she wasn't so accomplished at keeping her thoughts to herself, she might've reacted, giving away how her heart pounded against her ribcage. Instead she levelled her gaze and stared back at him, too proud to let him know how afraid she was.

'Rolfe!' A boy near the gate called out to him and he forgot her, his mouth splitting in a grin as he surged forward, clearly happy to see the caller.

The warrior was attractive, but she would never admit that to her sister or anyone. It felt deceitful to acknowledge that attribute in her enemy. So instead, she focused on his hair. Ropes of the dark blond mass had been pulled back from his forehead and were secured at the crown of his head and left to fall well past his shoulders. No self-respecting Saxon man wore his hair in such a barbaric fashion. Her father would say that it was proof of their deviltry. She didn't think it was quite so sinister, but neither was it civilised.

Pitching her voice low so she wouldn't be overheard, she said, 'I would be careful what you say, Ellan. You wouldn't want word getting back to Father that you're thinking of aligning yourself with our enemy.'

The ever-present mischievous spark in her sister's eye glowed when she said, 'What will Father do precisely? Come and take me back?' Her arms widened as she indicated the thriving fortress around them. 'The great and terrible Godric may rule Banford, but we are in Alvey now and this is where I plan to stay. Besides, the Danes are not our enemies any more. Lady Gwendolyn has made certain of that with her marriage to the Jarl. Father is only bitter because of what Mother did. He lives in years that have long since passed. You can go back home if you want. You always did enjoy work on the farm more than I did.'

Elswyth refrained from pointing out that she didn't enjoy it as much as someone needed to care for the family after their mother's abandonment. Instead the sight of the Danes flooding through the gates, filling the yard of the fortress as friends and loved ones came out to greet them, held her captivated. Lady Gwendolyn had married the Dane Vidar nearly two years ago. Since then the pair had been doing their best to make certain the Saxons and Danes in their corner of Northumbria lived peacefully together. There was no doubt that the Danes only allowed the peace because they had taken lands, silver and women in return.

Saxon lands, Saxon silver and Saxon women.

The Saxons were slowly being replaced by the invaders, or so her father claimed. She could understand his fear as she looked down at the powerful warriors below. They were formidable.

Elswyth and her sister had spent the autumn in Alvey at the request of Lady Gwendolyn, helping with her household. Elswyth had seen first-hand how the people co-existed within these walls. The Danes and Saxons could get along, but only here. Outside in the farms and villages there was still strain. Every week brought more stories of the Danes' brutality to the south of England. Even in Alvey lands there were stories of men fighting over the women, who numbered too few to meet the demands of every Saxon and Dane warrior. Then there were women like Ellan—women like their mother— who willingly chose the Danes over the Saxons. Many Saxons were bitter about that.

A fight was likely to happen soon. Lady Gwendolyn might refuse to see it, but Elswyth had heard the discontent with her own ears. Her own family, with the exception of Ellan, it seemed, would champion a fight.

'You speak blasphemy. Father would never agree to you marrying a Dane.' Elswyth crossed her arms over her chest and met her sister's eyes which were green like the waters of the lake back home. Sometimes it seemed their eyes were the only thing they had in common. Instead of hair as dark as her own, Ellan's was striped with honeyed tones. Her sister had always been happy and free from the worries that plagued the rest of the family, while Elswyth had assumed the mantle of responsibility. Ellan was like their wayward mother in many ways and it was worrisome.

'As I said, Father doesn't have to agree. I'll choose my own husband, thank you very much.'

While Elswyth was certainly fine with Ellan choosing her own husband, their father and brothers would not agree to a Dane. Danes were not to marry.

'I think it best to get below,' she said, giving her sister a dubious look. 'Lady Gwendolyn will need extra hands for tonight's feast.' Elswyth led the way along the rampart to the steps set into the corner of the wall. The fires had been burning all day in preparation for the men arriving, so that the air was filled with the aroma of roasting meat and vegetables.

Ellan's eyes were alight with an infuriating glow as she looked over the crowd below. 'I wonder which of them I shall marry.'

Elswyth rolled her eyes. Tired of arguing, she said, 'You've had months to ponder that with the Danes left behind while these were out raiding or whatever it is they were doing. Why haven't you chosen one of them?' She had known that a large group of warriors led by a warrior named Rolfe were due to winter here, but she had not been able to find out what they had been doing over the summer months. She was certain it was information her father would covet.

Ellan giggled. 'Because these are *new*. Why limit myself when there are so many to consider?'

'You haven't the faintest idea how to choose a proper husband, Ellan. I fear for your future,' Elswyth teased and stepped on to the hardpacked ground to make her way to the great hall, careful to stay near the wall and away from the arriving warriors. They were creating such an uproar with their celebratory shouts and bellows that they seemed as wild as the beasts in the forest.

'You make it sound difficult. You simply pick a man with a pleasing look and a disposition to match and there you have a good husband,' Ellan explained.

'Ah, well then, I pity the task ahead of you. None of these wildlings have good dispositions.' As if to lend weight to her words, a man was thrown free from the crowd to land with a crash against the stone wall before them. He settled on his bottom with a hard thud before standing and shaking the wild mane of dark hair from his face. Muttering something in his harsh language that made his friends howl with laughter, he tackled one of them and the two rolled on the ground in a skirmish. The rest of their group shouted encouragements and circled around them. Elswyth resisted the urge to roll her eyes again. She would never understand the Danes.

Ellan hurried to catch up as Elswyth stepped around the group. 'Certainly not one of *those*. But there are some. Lord Vidar is acceptable. I thought I might make a search through the men closest to him.'

It was true. Lord Vidar was acceptable, as Danes went. In the months they had lived in Alvey, Elswyth had come to greatly admire

Lady Gwendolyn. Where her family saw Lady
Gwendolyn as a traitor to the Saxons, Elswyth
had come to see how well she and Lord Vidar
got along. He was crude and sometimes boor-
ish, but he treated his wife well and had gained
the respect of the people in Alvey, even the Saxons. She'd seen how he could be fair and reasonable. Their marriage had brought two groups of
people together while avoiding the bloodshed
of battle. Elswyth still pitied Lady Gwendolyn,
but perhaps in this one instance marriage to a
Dane had been necessary.

Still, the subject hardly bore considering for
her and Ellan, but there was no use arguing
with her sister. The girl did what she wanted
and always had. Elswyth had no doubt that an
ill-considered marriage with a Dane would send
her running back to the farm within a year. 'I
wish you luck sorting through that madness. As
for me, I'll remain unwed for the time being.'

Ellan snickered, but she took Elswyth's hand
to soften her words. 'Father won't like that any
more than he'll like me with a Dane. You know
he'd see you wed to Osric.'

'Osric?' Elswyth laughed.

'Aye? Why is that funny?'

'Osric is… Osric. He's a dear friend, but I'd
never marry him.' Though she had to admit

that it would be the natural choice. He was her father's trusted man on the farm and they had been friends since she was born, but he wasn't what she wanted in a husband. She couldn't name what it was that she wanted from a marriage except that it was to be more than a farmer's wife.

'I expect Father will disagree.' Ellan sniffed and took the lead.

'Nay, he won't like it, but he cannot force me to wed.' Lady Gwendolyn would never stand for it.

'I haven't found proof, but my gut tells me that Godric is in league with the Scots.' Rolfe tightened his grip on his tankard of mead and tossed back a swallow, savouring the honeyed sweetness. The stench of treachery might have soured his homecoming, but at least there was mead.

Vidar cursed under his breath and shook his head. 'Godric has that entire village in his grip. Either he knew of Durwin's treachery or he won't believe it. The only certainty is that he will demand blood in return for the man's death.'

Rolfe ground his molars as he remembered the fight with the Scots, anger at the Saxon's presence there still burning hot within him. 'They *have* blood in return. I wanted to take Durwin alive, but he fought, cleaving two of my men before he was felled. He'd gladly have killed us given the chance.'

'Are they well?'

'Aye, one will bear a nasty scar, but they'll both recover.'

Vidar nodded and leaned back, turning his tankard absently between his palms. 'We'll keep Durwin's death quiet for now. I'm certain the news will make its way here in time, but there's no sense in announcing it.'

Rolfe was in firm agreement. Many of the Saxons within Alvey's walls had already made peace with the Danes, but there were some holdouts. He wouldn't have them using this whisper of rebellion as a reason to fight. 'I've already talked to my men. They'll hold their tongues about him.'

'Good. How were the talks with Haken?'

'He has agreed to align with us should the need arise. He has nearly two hundred men on Alba's west coast. Says there were a few skirmishes, but he rarely sees more than twenty Scots at once. I doubt we'll have need of his men.' Rolfe took another long drink.

Aside from the matter of Durwin and his

brother, Osric, the summer campaign had been a success. After spending most of it to the south with Jarl Eirik, Vidar's eldest brother, Rolfe and his men had taken their boats north for the autumn. The meeting with Haken, the Dane Jarl to the north, had gone far in creating an alliance between his camp and Alvey.

Vidar nodded, but his eyes were troubled. 'We cannot underestimate the Scots. They've been a nuisance to Alvey for ages and with our numbers increasing, they're bound to be agitated. In the morning, after you've had time to refresh yourself, we'll discuss plans for what to do with them. It's time we meet and end this once and for all.'

'You think a meeting is necessary?'

Vidar gave a short nod of his head. 'The rumours of Banford turning to them get stronger and this could very well push Godric into it. I'd like to think they are only rumours, but we can't take that chance. Godric is difficult. I fear we have no choice but to put an end to any potential alliance before it gets worse.'

'You two look serious. Is there news?' Lady Gwendolyn approached with baby Tova in her arms. Wyborn rose from his place at Rolfe's feet, tail wagging as he greeted them both, giving the baby an enthusiastic sniff that made her babble gleefully.

'Aye, some,' Vidar said, shifting on the bench so that she could sit beside him. He indicated the sacks of coin on the table that Rolfe and his men had lifted from the Scots. 'Rolfe encountered the Scots and this is what we have for the trouble.' A smile lit his face as he took the baby and sat her on his knee.

Rolfe grinned, always happy to see the woman who had given Vidar his much-needed comeuppance. She, along with Tova's chubby cheeks, were enough to brighten his mood. Now that Wyborn had moved back to his place at Rolfe's feet, the baby stared at him, her blue eyes round in curiosity. 'I see you've had a busy summer. She's grown.'

Lady Gwendolyn settled herself on the bench beside Vidar, a soft expression on her face as she glanced over at her husband and child. 'Very busy. Not yet a year old and she's already trying to walk.'

'Ah, she's a determined one, like her mother.' Lady Gwendolyn smiled, so he shifted his gaze to Vidar as he said, 'I feared the babe would look like her father, but the gods have smiled on her and only given her his wheaten hair. She looks more like you now, Lady. She is beautiful.' And indeed she was. Her cheeks were plump and rosy, her eyes bright and inquisitive.

Lady Gwendolyn gave him a playful glare while Vidar chuckled and the babe looked away, the sound of her father's deep laugh drawing her gaze. An unexpected ache swelled in Rolfe's chest at the scene. There was no doubt that his homecoming was victorious. Despite the traitors in their midst, he should feel pleased and content for a job well done. Instead, watching the little family before him made him aware of what was missing from his own life. It was a peculiar feeling, when he'd been content with his life for a while now.

To distract himself he reached forward and stroked Tova's silken hair, stifling a grunt of pain as he pulled at the wound on his shoulder. 'She'll rule this place soon.'

'You're hurt, Rolfe!' Lady Gwendolyn exclaimed. She rushed around to his back and pulled at his tunic. He grimaced as the blood that had dried to the linen under-tunic pulled at his wound and looked across the hall to distract himself as she prodded.

He'd been vaguely aware of the woman he'd seen atop the wall working across the hall this whole time. He found her now, trying her best to not appear as if she was curious about him as she filled cups with mead, all the while she kept stealing glances at their small group. Her expression was filled with the same wariness and grim determination he'd seen on her face outside. A thick braid of dark hair fell over her shoulder, across her lush breast and nearly down to her waist. She hadn't been in Alvey when he'd left and he couldn't help but wonder who she was.

'There's a good amount of blood,' said Lady Gwendolyn and he grimaced as she poked the tender edges of the wound. The woman had many skills, but sensitivity to his pain didn't appear to be one of them.

'A spear tip, compliments of the Scots. It's fine. It wasn't very deep.' It burned like fire, but a fever had yet to set in.

'What happened?' she asked and he gave her an abbreviated version of events.

'A minor skirmish.' He shrugged when he'd finished. 'There were less than twenty of them.' He'd leave it to Vidar to tell her about Durwin's betrayal.

As she moved back around him to retake her seat, she followed his gaze to the girl across the hall. Giving him a knowing smile, she said, 'Go upstairs and I'll send someone to tend you.'

He thought about objecting, but the idea of

possibly having some time alone with the girl was too pleasing to pass up. Grabbing a bag of loot that would be his portion from the stash on the table, he rose to his feet and sought his chamber.

Chapter Two

Elswyth hadn't thought that she would be attending the warrior named Rolfe in his bath. Yet there he sat in a tub of steaming water. His chest was thick and broad, roped with muscle above the rim of the tub which was too short for his large frame. His knees were bent, sticking up out of the water so that she could see the cords of muscle that shaped his powerful thighs. Water clung to his hair, making it a few shades darker than the blond it had been earlier. It hung free from its constraints, but had been pushed back to better reveal the chiselled planes of his face. His nose was a bit too prominent, his brow line too defined, his lips too hard, but somehow taken altogether those features were almost pretty on him. A masculine pretty that took her aback.

And that was before he looked at her. His

eyes were the purest blue she'd ever seen. Not piercing, but intense and so vivid the colour almost didn't seem real. There was a kindness lurking in their depths that helped her to step farther into his chamber and draw the door closed behind her. Lady Gwendolyn had made it clear to all when they'd arrived that she and Ellan were not here for the men's pleasure. But this man was new and she didn't know if he'd been advised. Wounded or not, he was powerful enough to do what he wanted with her and, though she could fight him, her axe was best thrown from a distance.

A soft growl from the corner warned her to proceed with caution, as a large mongrel with grey fur rose to his feet. 'Down, Wyborn.' The dog responded immediately to the warrior's command and lay back down, but his ears were standing up as he watched her.

Casting her wary gaze from the mongrel to his master, she said, 'I've brought herbs for your shoulder, Lord.'

'I'm no lord.' His voice was somehow smooth and rough all at the same time and pitched so low that the timbre of it was quite pleasing. She was surprised at how easily he spoke her language with barely any accent at all. His gaze dropped to the axe on her hip before he turned back to the task she had interrupted and splashed more water over his head, though he only used his right hand.

His chamber was larger than she'd thought. Shelves and chests lined one wall and a table and bench occupied the corner. Behind the dog, a bed was set into an alcove that could be curtained off from the rest of the room. It was larger than the one she shared with Ellan and piled high with thick furs. In the middle of those furs a red stone set amid pieces of silver and gold glinted back at her in the candlelight. She carefully averted her eyes from that treasure. It was stolen from a Saxon, no doubt. The thought gave her the surge of anger she needed to rediscover her courage.

'What's your name, girl?'

She set the tray holding the poultice, linens and herbs down on a chest a little harder than she'd intended to. So hard that he paused in his administrations and looked over at her. 'I'm no girl,' she said, mimicking his words to her. Whenever men wanted to keep her in her place they liked to throw that word around. It made them feel stronger and she found herself disappointed that a warrior such as him would feel the need to use it.

She expected him to let those unnaturally

vivid blue eyes sweep down her body. To take in the curves of her breasts and hips. To make it clear that he understood that she wasn't a girl after all. Her body could only belong to a woman who could only be here to please him with those very same curves. But he didn't break eye contact except to take in her expression. Finally, he gave a brief nod and a tiny smile lurked around the corners of his mouth, hinting at a dimple in his cheek.

'Nay, you are no girl. I can see that now.'

Those words felt like a compliment. In a life that had been short on compliments of late, it was most welcomed. Her cheeks burned and she looked down at the tray to make herself appear busy.

'What are you called?' he asked.

'Elswyth.'

'I'm Rolfe,' he said and held out his hand.

She stared at it, half-expecting it to hold some danger, which was silly. It was simply a hand, calloused and rough looking with a complement of various nicks and cuts. However, men did not generally offer a hand to her, especially in her current capacity as servant. It was suspicious for its eccentricity alone. With a glance at his bare chest and the water lapping at his hips, she gave him her hand in a brief touch before quickly turning to secure a scrap of linen for a bandage. This man had unsettled her from the first. The sooner she could be done with this task the better.

'You weren't here when I left in the summer. Who are you?' He, too, seemed content to go back to the task at hand and continued to sluice water on his body.

'My mother was a distant relation of Lady Gwendolyn's mother. My sister and I have served here for the past few months at the Lady's invitation.'

With a gentle hand on his shoulder, she pushed him forward to take a closer look at his wound. His hair nearly covered it, so she was forced to take the thick mass in hand and move it aside. It was wet silk against her palm, smooth, yet strangely rough, too. The heaviness of it sliding against her skin seemed too personal. Everything about this seemed too personal. She should have very little to do with this man who was her enemy, yet here she was tending to him in his bath. He was naked beneath the water and her entire body burned in awareness of that fact.

Forcing a deep breath, she leaned in closer to examine the puncture. He was lucky that it hadn't festered yet. The edges were slightly pink, but they weren't swollen and angry. It was clear that someone had tended it after it had happened. Plunging the linen into the water, she gently ran it over the gouge to clean out the dried blood. 'Sorry,' she whispered, though he hadn't flinched.

The mongrel came forward, curiously sniffing around her as she worked on his master. She tried to ignore him, somewhat confident that the warrior would intervene should the mongrel overstep his bounds. Reassured that she meant his master no harm, the mongrel went back to his spot beside the bed and plopped down. Putting his front two paws out in front of him, he dropped his muzzle on to them and watched her, his deep brown eyes glittering in the candlelight.

'Are you a healer?' Rolfe asked.

'I know enough to clean wounds and mix common poultices. It is one of my tasks back home.' Satisfied that she'd done her best to remove the dried blood, she grabbed a bit of soap from the bowl that sat on the floor beside the tub. He clearly wasn't able to use his left arm well, so his back was still marred with smudges of dirt and old blood from the wound that he hadn't reached. With gentle strokes, she washed his back, the linen moving over his skin in a soft caress that allowed her to feel just how hard he was beneath his skin. His strength was powerful and could have been intimidating, but he merely hummed softly in approval of her touch and dropped his forehead to his knees, lending an odd peace to the moment.

When she was finished cleaning, she laid the linen across the rim of the tub and dipped a dish into the bucket of steaming hot water that had been left beside the tub, careful not to burn her fingers. 'This may hurt a bit.'

He smothered a groan as she trickled the hot water over his wound. The water left streaks of reddened skin down his back. 'I'll need to do it once more to make certain the wound is clean. It helps the healing.' He nodded, leaning forward a bit more to give her better access. This time he didn't make a sound save for a swift exhalation of breath as the scalding water slid over him. 'There. It's done.' The wound had reopened, but only a little blood seeped from it. It was a good sign that there would be no festering.

'You've been sent to exact Saxon vengeance. Admit it.' His blue eyes gleamed at her over his shoulder, that same almost-smile hovering at the edges of his mouth.

'I'll admit nothing,' she quipped, squeezing

out the linen and indulging this strange urge to tease with him. 'But if a Saxon gave you this scratch, 'tis my duty to make it hurt more.'

He laughed and sat back against the rim, his eyes stroking her face. 'Then I'm forced to disclose the truth. It was no Saxon, but a Scot. Are you under the same allegiance to the Scots?'

She had to force herself not to take in a breath or show any sort of reaction. He was teasing, but it was as close to the truth as anyone had come in the entire time she had served Lady Gwendolyn. *She* was not in league with the Scots, but her father very well might be by now. There had been rumours that he'd met with them before she'd left.

'Not to my knowledge.' She gave a shrug, hoping the comment sounded flippant and a part of the game.

'That's good to know. Otherwise I would worry about your axe.'

'You're not worried about it regardless? Saxon vengeance, as you said.'

His eyes fairly sparkled with merriment and she found herself unable to look away from them. It was as if someone had found a way to dye them the most vivid shade of blue she had ever seen. He slowly shook his head, a drop of water running down the side of his face. 'It's an interesting choice of weapon.'

She stared down at the axe attached to her belt because she had to look away from him. 'It's more tool than weapon. It's useful on the farm and I've grown accustomed to wearing it.' She didn't mention that she was more accurate than any man when it came to hitting targets with it. 'Lady Gwendolyn has been kind enough to give me archery lessons while I'm here. Perhaps you should worry about that tomorrow on the practice field.'

This made him grin and that dimple in his cheek shone. He was so handsome when he smiled that she had to look away again. He was likely to think she was a fool like Ellan with how she seemed suddenly unable to hold his stare. There were many ways that this man unsettled her. What was happening? Was he flirting with her? Was this teasing usual for the warrior?

Enemy, enemy, enemy, the mantra repeated in her head.

'I'll look forward to seeing that.' Something about the way he said that, so firm and exact, made her believe it. It also made her chest swell with pride. Despite herself, it pleased her that a warrior of his renown wanted to watch her skill.

'Is that where you were all summer?' She busied herself by sorting the items on the tray and preparing the poultice. 'Fighting the Scots?' She told herself that she was asking out of curiosity, but the words of her father wouldn't leave her. They made that feeling of unease churn deep in her belly. Any news about the relations between Danes and Scots would be useful to him.

'Not all summer, but a fair bit of it. They've been active, but are so far no threat to Alvey.'

'My home is to the north. Should I be worried about them?' It was a fair question. She had spent many nights in her bed worrying about the Scots to the north and the Danes to the south, and her tiny village caught between them.

'Nay, no need to worry yet. And, Elswyth...' She nearly dropped the poultice when he reached out to touch her shoulder. His eyes were deep and solemn with concern. The warmth from his touch moved down her back to settle deep in her belly, wrapping itself around that knot of unease. 'We'll protect you from them if the time comes.'

And what if we are the reason the Scots have come? What if Father has done something that has brought them to our door?

She didn't ask those questions, though. She would not give her family away. 'How do you know they won't be too powerful?'

He smiled again and let her go. His teeth were straight and white, making his smile far too pleasing for a warrior such as him. He should be fierce, with a fierce smile to match. His expression turned to pure masculine arrogance when he answered, 'They'll never be too powerful for the Danes.'

She scoffed and made a show of finishing her work with the poultice, mixing the herbs in the bowl before readying a bandage with a length of folded linen. However, deep in her heart, she feared that he was right. She'd been impressed with the Danes who had spent the summer in Alvey. She'd been even more impressed by the sheer power of the army that had marched into Alvey hours ago. Tomorrow she would see them in practice, but she really had no need to see them to know that they would be fierce. Their reputation preceded them there.

'You Danes are all alike. Too full of yourselves for your own good.'

'It's not conceit if it's true. I've never lost a fight.'

She found it very easy to believe him. He sat in that humble tub like a king, his powerful arms stretched along the rim, his eyes shining with confidence. In that moment she had to wonder if it was possible for anyone to best him.

His eyes had gone slightly hooded as he watched her, an indolent quality coming over his face. 'I toured the north after Lord Vidar married Lady Gwendolyn. I don't remember meeting you.' He said it as if he would've remembered.

God knew that she would have remembered him had they met before. He was too vibrant and too formidable, equal parts terrifying and fascinating.

'Nay, we never met.' She remembered their visit well, though her father had kept her and Ellan hidden away inside so that she'd never actually seen Rolfe. It was no secret to anyone that Father distrusted the Danes. She suspected it had been one of the reasons Lord Gwendolyn had sent for her and her sister. The woman was ever trying to make peace, but it seemed no matter what she did, Father wouldn't approve.

He despised the fact that his own wife had run off with one of them. It ate at him constantly. Before it had happened, he'd always been stern and quiet, but something had changed in him in the years since. He brimmed with anger and bitterness. Lady Gwendolyn marrying a Dane had brought it all to overflowing. He hated that she'd married Lord Vidar and he hated all the Danes in Alvey that came as a result of that marriage. There would be no peace as far as he was concerned.

Elswyth had been surprised that Father had agreed to Lady Gwendolyn's plan, but his reasoning had become clear on the morning of their departure. He had approached her horse where she was saying goodbye to her younger brother Baldric. Ellan had followed their older brother, Galan, out of the yard, giving them a brief moment of solitude.

Pitching his voice low, he'd said, 'Keep your eyes open, Elswyth. We need to know what these Danes are really up to. I'll expect your account upon your return.' She'd stared at him in shock, but he'd only slapped the horse on the rump and called after her, 'I'm depending on you!'

He had meant for her to spy. A lump of unease had been present in her belly ever since. Rolfe's presence only made it worse. While everyone knew that Lord Vidar was in charge, he would not dare to lead warriors against people he was sworn to protect. Should an uprising occur, it would be Rolfe sent to dowse it. Rolfe commanded the warriors. Rolfe would raise his sword against her village and her family if it was ordered.

Knowing all of that, she couldn't understand why he fascinated her so. She should despise him. Because of men like him, her mother had abandoned the family. Elswyth had been forced to take over her duties when she'd scarcely been able to carry a pail of water on her own. She had spent the formative years of her childhood wondering how she could have prevented her mother from leaving, questioning if she had been a better daughter would her mother have stayed and even secretly thinking that perhaps she herself was unlovable.

Yet, even with that history giving her plenty of reasons to hate him, she couldn't keep her eyes from him. From beneath her lashes, her gaze swept over his broad shoulders and the cords of muscle that defined his arms. 'You'll need to get yourself dry so that I can put the poultice on your shoulder. It shouldn't get wet.'

Without giving her a chance to prepare herself or even avert her eyes, he stood in the tub. Water sluiced down his strong body in rivulets, reflecting gold in the soft glow of the candles. The solid muscles in his back tapered down to a narrow waist and a pair of buttocks that might have been carved stone. His thighs were corded in muscle, thick as tree trunks and just as strong from the looks of them, with a light sprinkling of dark blond hair. In the slit of light visible between them, the weight of his manly parts hung—a gasp tore from her throat when a sheet of linen blocked her view, making her realise that she had been staring. Not once had she even attempted to avert her gaze. He had been decent enough to not ogle her the entire time she'd been in his chamber, his eyes had never left her face as they'd talked, but she couldn't find the decency to look away from his nakedness. Her face burned in shame as she forced her attention to the poultice.

He stepped out of the tub on to a rug made of rushes and tied the sheet around his waist. Grabbing another sheet of linen, he wrapped it around his shoulders, though he did it awkwardly with one hand while keeping his left arm against his torso. She would have helped him had she not been too astonished at her own bad behaviour. Instead, she waited for him to get settled on the bench before bringing the tray over to set it on the table next to him, her face—indeed her entire body—still flaming with embarrassment. Slowly and with as little touch against his bare skin as possible, she used the sheet to dry off his back.

Working with efficiency, she managed to apply the poultice on to his wound and wrap linen around his shoulder. The light sprinkling of fur on his chest teased her fingertips on the first pass, sending cinders of curious sensation running down her arm. This man was nothing like she had imagined. He wasn't a monster, or even particularly unpleasant. He was simply a man, made of warm, solid muscle and bone. Yet, that realisation somehow made him more dangerous to her. Tying off the end of the bandage, she stood back, making minor adjustments to the wrapping. 'I'll make you a sling. You should wear it to keep your shoulder braced until it starts to heal. You don't want it to break open again.'

'I'll try.' Wearing only the linen slung low around his waist, he walked to a chest at the foot of his bed and pulled out an under-tunic. 'Would you help me put it on?'

With a wordless nod, she took the folded linen from him. She was tall for a woman, but he was so much taller he had to stoop down for her to put it over his head. A tightening of his jaw was the only indication he gave that he experienced discomfort as he shoved his left arm through the sleeve. She didn't even give him time to rummage through the chest for trousers, knowing that she couldn't handle the embarrassment of watching him discard the linen sheet to put them on. Instead, she immediately grabbed the material for the sling and stepped up to him.

He smelled good. Clean like the soap, but also like evergreen needles in the forest mixed with a rich masculine scent that was very pleasing. He was quiet as she fitted it, knotted it and then slipped it across his chest, but she could feel his eyes on her face. They seemed curious and that damnable kindness lurking in their depths made it impossible for her to summon the anger and hate that she meant to feel towards him.

'When do you go back home?'

The question made her heart stutter. Satisfied with the sling, she lowered her arms from his shoulders and forced herself to take a step back from him. Distance seemed very good at the moment. 'My father is meant to come before the next full moon.'

'A fortnight, then.' He nodded as if the information pleased him somehow, as if he was mulling something over and that worked nicely into his plans, when she shouldn't fit anywhere into his plans.

Her heart picked up speed and she turned to

quickly gather up the tray of medicinals that she'd brought. Never mind that her hands shook for some odd reason or that her knees were so weak she felt certain they would follow suit. *Distance.* The single word replaced the 'enemy' mantra in her head because she no longer believed that to be true. Or worse. It was true, but it was no longer enough to keep a wall between them.

'Good evening.'

'I look forward to seeing your aim on the practice field in the morning.' His voice followed her out.

Chapter Three

'That's twice I've bested you. If these swords weren't wooden, you'd be dead by now.' Aevir deftly swung away, leaving several feet between him and Rolfe.

Rolfe doubled his assault, ignoring how his arm smarted where Aevir's training sword had hit as he pushed his friend even farther back in an attempt to wipe the smug smile from his face. Rolfe had spent the entire morning running the men through their paces and taking playful digs from some of them about his sling. It was time they realised that having his left arm in a brace wouldn't slow him down. 'You must be jesting. You've yet to best me once.'

Aevir scoffed, 'I would've drawn first blood had the sword been metal.' He lunged forward again and Rolfe rolled to the side, leaving Aevir off balance.

'And when do we ever battle to first blood?' Rolfe asked.

'Had the blade drawn blood, you would have cried out in pain and broken your stride, leaving yourself open so that I could skewer your gullet.'

'You live in your fantasies.' Rolfe laughed and renewed his attack. The truth was that he *had* been distracted in their sparring match, but it hadn't been because of his wound. Elswyth had come out on to the other side of the field with her bow and a quiver of arrows and was currently shooting at targets. His gaze had been caught by her form in profile, equal parts slim and lush as she had notched an arrow and pulled back the string. He'd been waiting to see if she'd made her target when Aevir had hit him.

'Go easy, Aevir.' Vidar's voice interrupted their sparring. 'He's an injured man. I wouldn't have you making his injury worse.'

Rolfe groaned silently. Vidar meant well, but he'd only make the teasing worse.

Aevir grinned and lowered his sword. 'The Jarl has saved you, my friend.'

The sling on Rolfe's left arm restricted his balance a bit, but his wound was hardly in any danger. 'Nay, let's finish.'

Aevir raised his sword to accept the challenge, but Vidar stepped between them. 'We have other things to discuss this morning, now that you've both had some rest.' The three of them walked to the edge of the practice field. The clang of steel on steel and splintering wood as the warriors continued to practise filled the air around them.

'As long as it's the Scots and not wives we're discussing again,' Aevir said in a dry tone.

'Wives?' Rolfe asked.

Vidar gave him a telling glance before looking towards his own wife, who had made her way to them across the sparring field where she'd been leading a group of archers in practice. Lady Gwendolyn was quite possibly the most accomplished archer Rolfe had ever seen. She smiled at them as she approached, but trepidation lurked in her expression, a rare moment of uncertainty for her.

'Good morning. How is your shoulder?' Lady Gwendolyn asked.

After assuring her that he was on the mend, he asked, 'Am I being offered up as a husband?'

She had the grace to look sheepish. 'I admit the lack of marriages among the Danes and Saxons concerns me. We've had a few families take us up on the offer of coin in exchange for marriage to the Danes, but most are reluctant.' It had been their hope that after their marriage others would follow suit. They wanted to unite the Saxons and Danes in Alvey through marriage and avoid as much bloodshed as possible.

'It will take time.' Vidar ran a hand down her back in silent support.

She nodded before continuing. 'We would like it to be known that our highest warriors... including you...are looking for wives. I think an offering of higher-status marriages would ease some reluctance.'

Rolfe laughed, but it was a hollow sound. The very thought of marriage made the skin on his neck tighten uncomfortably. 'You *are* offering me up as husband.'

Her cheeks reddened, but she didn't back down from her stance. 'You have to admit that many would say you are a desirable husband. Your word among the Danes is second only to Vidar's. You are known as a great warrior with great wealth.'

'It's true,' Rolfe said, mulling over her words and making Vidar laugh out loud.

'It's good to see you're still humble, Brother.'

Ignoring him, Rolfe said, 'I can see how this would be helpful for harmony.' It would not, however, be helpful for his peace of mind. He tried not to think of the woman he'd nearly married back home, but her face came to mind anyway. Hilde had been beautiful. He'd convinced himself that she was kind and generous, everything he'd thought he'd wanted in a wife. He'd learned too late—after her thievery—that her beautiful outside had hidden a traitorous core. She'd only used him for her own gain.

Lady Gwendolyn's smile brightened, encouraged by his words. 'I resisted my father's way of thinking, but I understand now how marriage to further peace is best for everyone.' Vidar smiled at her, his eyes full of gentleness and admiration.

Rolfe wasn't entirely surprised by the plan and it certainly spoke to that odd longing for a family he'd felt upon his homecoming last night, but he didn't relish the idea of marrying. The amount of trust inherent in such a union was not something he was comfortable with. Of its own volition, his gaze landed on Elswyth. The same short-handled axe from last night was hooked on the belt around her waist, leading him to wonder if she wielded it as well as the bow and arrow.

Glancing back to Lady Gwendolyn and then Vidar, he could practically feel the noose of matrimony tightening around his neck. He wouldn't shirk his duty, but neither would he welcome it. His only choice was to make certain of the only thing he could control. 'I would choose my own wife.'

'Of course,' Lady Gwendolyn was quick to acquiesce. In a softer voice she added, 'But you would have to choose someone beneficial to uniting our people.'

He gave a nod, his gaze once again shifting over to Elswyth of its own volition.

The victorious glance that passed between Vidar and his wife wasn't lost on him. They had already discussed his marriage, it seemed.

'Thank you, Rolfe,' Vidar said. 'You'll be well-rewarded for your duty. With things to the north unsettled, it goes without saying that sooner rather than later would be best.'

'Aevir will be called to marry as well?' Rolfe and Vidar had known Aevir for several years. He was a renowned warrior who had fought in the south as the battle had been waged for East Anglia. He'd gained a reputation there for his fearlessness in battle and had gone on to fight for Jarl Eirik for the past couple of years. Yesterday when he'd ridden in with Rolfe had been the first time he'd set foot in Alvey. Rolfe knew the man had vowed never to settle down because of some trauma from his past, so he lived a life that was never settled, always moving from place to place looking for the next fight. Rolfe liked him and respected him, but he found it hard to believe the man was ready for marriage.

'For the right woman it could be well worth it.' Aevir shrugged. 'But it's too early in the day to speak of women.'

'The right woman?' Rolfe asked, unable to believe his ears. Aevir was actually considering marriage.

Still smiling, Aevir shrugged. 'The right lands and riches to be more specific.'

That sounded more like what Rolfe had expected. Still, the idea of marriage without affection was hard for him to accept. He had pledged his loyalty to Jarl Vidar and would do it if his duty called for it, but it wasn't what he would choose for himself. Aevir had no such pledge holding him here. 'And what of the woman herself? Her face?' *Her heart.* Rolfe didn't say that part, but he could not imagine sharing his home and future children with a woman who was cruel or less than honourable. Someone like Hilde.

'What does a face matter in the dark of night?' Aevir laughed, but when he glanced away there was a hollowness in his eyes. It was the same empty resolve he brought to battle that made him a great warrior. Rolfe didn't think it would work so well in marriage. 'Her lands and wealth will suit me much better than a fine face.'

Rolfe shook his head, but he hadn't expected anything else from Aevir. The man would sell his hand like he sold his sword, it seemed. He wouldn't be the first man to do so. Once more he found Elswyth across the field. This time he watched her arrow fly and stifled a smile at her hoot of triumph when her aim proved true. She fascinated him and their banter the night before had come easily and naturally. She wasn't afraid to challenge him. He had no idea if she'd be suitable based on Lady Gwendolyn's requirements, but she was the only one who had stirred an interest in him in a while.

'Do you need to find your nursemaid to check your wound?' Aevir teased, following Rolfe's line of sight.

'I'd forgotten how insufferable you were,' Rolfe growled, which resulted in Aevir's bark of laughter.

Vidar had walked away to speak with his wife, but stepped up to them now, his gaze roaming across the field to where his wife's charges practised. 'Godric will arrive in about a fortnight and I hope to negotiate his blessing for a marriage. I've already allotted the silver needed.'

Elswyth had just landed another arrow in the target while a girl he assumed to be her sister cheered her on. Aevir's face shone with interest as he watched her, and Rolfe felt the hair on the back of his head bristle in warning. Aevir's interest in Elswyth alone would have raised his ire, but to have Godric's name spoken in regard to her did not bode well for Rolfe's intentions.

'The sisters will be available?' Aevir tipped his head towards Elswyth and her sister.

'Aye, but only one of them need marry... Elswyth is the eldest. I'd prefer it if one of you marry her. The match will go far to ease our troubles in Banford,' Vidar added in a low voice.

Rolfe froze, his hand clenched tight around the hilt of his sparring sword. The girl was Godric's daughter. When she'd said she was from the north, she meant Banford. She meant the very village he'd put a torch to only two days ago. The very village that seemed to turn out traitors one after the next.

'You would give the traitor silver and allow him to keep his lands?' asked Aevir.

Vidar's brow furrowed. 'Traitor may be harsh. Remember that we only have rumours that Godric's been in contact with the Scot King. We've seen no evidence. We *do* know that it will be in our favour to tie him to Alvey with his daughter's hand. We need him on our side.'

The very idea of giving tolerance to the man who was likely at the centre of every conspiracy with the Scots didn't sit right with Rolfe. 'You can't deny that Durwin's presence with the Scots is strong evidence. Everyone knows how close he and his brother were to Godric.' He knew in his gut that the connection was there. Rewarding Godric's tricks with a fortuitous marriage for his daughter would not solve their problems. Indeed, such a marriage could be disastrous for all parties involved.

'Aye, it's a strong indication, but not evidence. We'll see how he feels soon. He'll arrive in a fortnight and give his permission for Elswyth's hand unless he'd prefer to insult his Lady,' said Vidar.

'Is that why his daughters are here?' Rolfe asked. Now that he knew who Elswyth was he was shocked to find Godric's daughters within the confines of Alvey. Shocked because if the man had truly gone against Alvey, his daughters would have been locked within her walls and at the mercy of the very Danes he claimed to despise. The man had to be a fool and she had to be a spy. There would be no other reason for Godric to allow their presence here.

'They're distant relations of Gwendolyn's on her mother's side. Gwendolyn hoped to gain the girls' co-operation by inviting them here. I'd hoped that since he allowed them to come here, he had accepted that we are here to stay. She hasn't mentioned marriage to Elswyth yct, but she will now that you're both here.'

Both. Thinking of her with Aevir didn't sit well with him, but he pushed the thought aside to consider the issue of Godric. Sending his daughters to work for his Lady could have been a very solid offering of truce. Or it could have been a very clever way of appearing contrite while using them for his own gain. If Rolfe had to guess, he would assume the latter.

'Which other brides are we to consider and which lands come with them?' Aevir asked.

'We'll discuss the properties and dowries tonight. It's only fair that you know beforehand to help you decide which girl to win over.'

Aevir shook his head and laughed. 'Is enticing her necessary? The girl will marry who her father says she will marry, will she not?'

Vidar grinned. 'That's not how Lady Gwendolyn would prefer the marriages to happen.

She wants the women to have a say in their choice of groom.'

'It's only a bride, Jarl.' Aevir shrugged. 'What does it matter if she approves or even if I approve of her? Isn't it merely an arrangement for loyalty and coin?'

Rolfe and Vidar exchanged knowing glances. They'd had a very similar conversation when it was Vidar arriving to wed Lady Gwendolyn. Vidar had been of a similar opinion.

'The girl must approve of her groom,' Vidar said again and, like lightning drawn to the highest point on a plain, Rolfe found Elswyth again with his eyes.

He tried to see her through the eyes he'd had the night before. Eyes that hadn't known her parentage. The belt around her waist emphasised her lean figure, and the curve of her hips. She was soft in all the places a woman should be soft. The blush on her face last night when she'd gazed upon his nudity confirmed her interest in him as a man. If she *was* a spy, perhaps he'd have better success seducing the admission out of her.

Once realised, the thought took up residence in his head and refused to leave. As arousing as the idea of having her beneath him was, the task left a bitter taste. If she were a spy for her father, then it would confirm Godric's intention. And Rolfe would have lost the only woman to challenge him in a long time.

She let another arrow fly and this time hit the target dead centre. Despite himself, pride swelled in his chest. It was unreasonable that he should feel anything for her already, but there it was. He told himself it was lingering affection for the woman who had tended him last night, the woman who had sparked his interest before he'd learned her true identity. The wind tugged at the hair in her loose braid, sending a few dark strands to fly free across her face. It was actually a very lovely face, with soft lips and gently sculpted cheekbones. When she brushed the strands back, she looked up and caught him watching her, but the distance was too great for him to discern her thoughts.

Lady Gwendolyn had walked back to the sisters and started working with the other, drawing Elswyth's attention. Free from her stare, he caught Aevir watching the sisters. 'Leave her be, Aevir.'

'I rather like looking at the pair of them.' His friend grinned.

'They haven't the land or the riches you desire.'

Aevir stared at him in shock. 'You're declaring yourself already, man?'

Rolfe shrugged. 'Nay.' The word sounded weak. He had enough riches from his years of fighting at Vidar's side to see him well into his old age and he didn't particularly need or want lands. For whatever reason, he'd liked Elswyth last night before he'd found out who her father was. If she was here with honourable intentions instead of as an emissary for her father and he had no choice but to wed...why not let it be to her?

'Let's not quibble over women,' Vidar said. 'There are more than enough to go around. Besides, Aevir, I need you to go north. Watch Banford. Our skirmish with the Scots is bound to have an effect. If Banford is co-operating with them, they'll be communicating now.'

'I can go,' Rolfe offered. He felt responsible for the situation and he would see it through.

'Nay, stay and recover. Right now we're only watching. You need to be well for the fight, if there is one,' said Vidar.

Aevir nodded. 'Of course.'

'You'll leave tomorrow. We'll talk more tonight.'

Aevir agreed and then left them to finish sparring with some of his warriors.

Vidar chuckled when they were alone. 'It's good that you want her. I only hope she feels the same.'

Regret twisted inside him. He liked her well enough, aye, but why did she have to come from Banford? Some men married and were able to keep their hearts out of it. Rolfe didn't think he was one of those men. A few moments with Elswyth last night had already touched him far too deeply. Rolfe knew himself well enough to know that if he allowed himself to become infatuated with her, then his judgement could be compromised. If it had happened with Hilde, it could happen again. 'Do you not suspect her of being a spy?'

Vidar was quiet as he pondered that for a moment. 'Until last night she had barely deigned to speak to a Dane—aside from me—the entire time she's been here. It seems her father's attitudes have indeed been ingrained in the girl. I pondered early on in her visit that he'd sent her to poison us with the meals she helped prepare and was gratified when that didn't come to pass.' Then he shrugged as if her being a spy was nothing. 'Let her tell him of our warriors and our power. Perhaps the information will spur him to our side.'

'I would find out the truth of her intentions before marrying her.'

Vidar was quiet for a moment before finally nodding. 'How would you do that?'

Rolfe hardly thought Vidar would agree to seduction. Elswyth was his wife's relation and under his guardianship, spy or not. 'I'll ingratiate myself to her…see if I can get her to open up to me.'

'She'd hardly be a good spy if a little kindness gets her to spill her secrets,' Vidar said as if he suspected Rolfe's plan.

'She's a farm girl. She'll hardly be experienced enough in spying to mislead me.'

'And if she's innocent?' Vidar's voice was even and quiet.

Rolfe paused, nearly choking on the words he was about to say. 'Then I'll marry her. But if she's not, then we have proof of Godric's treachery.'

'It's a solid plan.'

'I'll have your word that she'll be mine and you won't offer her to Aevir.'

Vidar grinned. 'She will be yours, though you'll have a fight on your hands if she ever finds out about your actions in Banford.'

Vidar was right. If her loyalty to her family and village was even half as fierce as Rolfe suspected, then she would hate him for what he had done. 'Then we have no choice but to make certain she never finds out.'

Chapter Four

Notch the arrow. Pull back. Focus on the target. Let it fly.

It was a ritual that quieted Elswyth's mind and one that she'd come to appreciate. It allowed her to ignore the very real possibility that, with threats from the Scots and possibly the Danes, she'd have to use her newly acquired archery skills in the near future. Lady Gwendolyn and Ellan had moved farther down the field to work on her sister's aim, leaving Elswyth to her ritual. Ellan was enthusiastic, but lacked the interest required for hours of daily practice. Elswyth, on the other hand, loved losing herself in the steady rhythm of repetitive training.

She wasn't surprised that Rolfe came to a stop near her after the women had drifted away. He'd been watching her from across the field for nearly the entire practice. Her traitorous arm trembled at his nearness, forcing her to take in a deep breath to steady herself. He had a large presence and it wasn't simply due to his size, though that alone would have been intimidating. There was something about him that announced his arrival without him even having to say a word, as if he commanded the very air around him the way he commanded his men.

She let the arrow fly and it landed just to the left of the centre of her target. It wasn't perfect, but it was good. She had placed the sack fifty paces out, so she'd count it as her furthest success so far. 'Good morning, Dane.'

'Saxon.' She didn't look at him, but the smile was evident in his voice. 'You're very good. How long have you been an archer?'

The next arrow made a soft whooshing sound as she drew it out of the quiver on her back. She took her time notching it, letting her thumb brush over the roughly carved wood as she pondered his question. It was simple enough to answer, but she couldn't help but wonder why he was asking. Did he suspect something of her? What exactly did he want with her? Had she imagined the way he'd talked with her last night had been a sign of something more than benign friendship he was offering? Was she even capable of leading him down that path in the hopes of gathering more information from him? She wanted desperately to prove her loyalty to her father, but she wasn't very good at artifice.

Last night Rolfe hadn't come out and said anything inappropriate. If anything, *she* was the inappropriate one. But there had seemed to be something more. Even across the field this morning, when he'd looked at her, there had been an intensity there that hinted at an interest that was more than friendship.

Why her? Pulling the arrow back, she let it fly to land in the sack, but still outside the target. Evidence of how he unsettled her.

Dropping her arm, she finally turned to look at him. He was dressed casually today in trousers with a simple tunic, leaving his muscled arms revealed even though the morning air was quite brisk. His dark blond hair was pulled up again in the barbaric style he'd worn yesterday with ropes of it pulled back from his face and secured at the crown of his head. The dimple in his cheek shone when he smiled at her and it nearly hurt to look at it. How could a man so potentially dangerous to her family appear so attractively virile? The ever-present knot of unease tightened in her belly. 'I've been practising archery only since Ellan and I arrived in Alvey.'

He raised his chin a notch and gave her an approving nod. 'You're a quick learner.'

He said it as if the trait met with his approval and that approval filled her with pride. Instead of commenting on his statement and facing that emotion, she asked, 'How is your shoulder?'

Part of her had wondered in anticipation if Lady Gwendolyn would direct her to tend to him again that morning, while another part of her had been busy coming up with a bevy of excuses that would get her out of the task. In the end it hadn't mattered, she'd left the little alcove she shared with Ellan at the same time a serving girl had emerged from his chamber. The white hot flair of jealousy she'd experienced had been quickly extinguished and tucked out of sight. What did it matter to her if someone else tended him? It particularly did not matter that the girl had emerged with mussed hair, making Elswyth wonder exactly how long she'd stayed in Rolfe's chamber and to which part of him she had attended.

'It's sore but improved.' His honesty impressed her. Most men she knew would not admit to any ailment. Her older brother Galan had once walked on a broken foot for three whole days before it had swollen so large that his shoe had to be cut off. Only then had he admitted he 'might have twisted it a bit'.

'Is there any inflammation? Heat?'

He gave a quick shake of his head. 'Not any more than there was, but I'm nearly out of the salve you left. Can you can bring more tonight?'

She stared at him, weighing the risks of agreeing to help him again. There was no denying the fact that helping him would give her a chance to gather information for Father, but her sense of self-preservation warned her away from him. He unsettled her, making her feel interest when she shouldn't. Yet, she understood that to refuse would rouse suspicion, so she nodded and said, 'I'll prepare more for you.'

'Do you wield the axe as well as you do the bow?' The abrupt change in topic startled her, prompting him to nod towards her hip where her axe was secured.

'Better. I've been using it for years.'

'Would you show me?' He gestured towards the piles of wood a bit farther down the field past where Ellan and Lady Gwendolyn were practising.

'Do you not know how to use one, Dane?'

Through his close-cropped beard she could see the dimple in his cheek when he smiled and shook his head. 'The sword is my weapon.

I can swing an axe in battle, but I can see how a smaller one for throwing could be useful.'

No man had ever asked her to show him how to do anything before. At the farm, she and Ellan ran the household and helped with the animals when it was needed. No one asked them for advice or sought them out, though that hardly deterred her from offering her opinion on matters when she saw that it would be beneficial. Still, she couldn't stop the pleasure that welled in her chest that this warrior would ask her for a demonstration. Unable to find her voice, she nodded and set down her bow before unstrapping the quiver of arrows from her back. When she was finished, he stepped back to let her lead him farther afield.

Finding a nice, round stump, she rolled it to a clearing farther away from the practising warriors and set it in place upright. Satisfied with its position, she walked back to him and withdrew the axe from her belt. 'As with your sword, I imagine, the trick is to keep your blade well tended. It need not be so sharp that it nicks your clothing, but it shouldn't be dull.'

'Do you sharpen your own blades?' He took the axe from her and held it up, running the pad of his thumb across the edge of the blade.

'Aye, it was necessary at home. Father didn't

approve of my use of it so forbade anyone to help me. Of course, here the blacksmith has been kind enough to see to the task.'

Grinning, he handed it back to her handle first. 'But you didn't let your father's disapproval stop you.'

'Nay, of course not.' In some ways his censure had spurned her onwards. Her father was a difficult man, equal parts kind and stubborn. After her mother's abandonment, he had seemed to look upon both her and Ellan with suspicion, as if they were somehow waiting to betray the family as well. That suspicion drove her now to prove to him that she could be relied upon. Growing up, it had meant that she had been forced to grab at her every freedom. Fortunately, he'd allowed her to keep them once she'd wrested them away.

'I can tell you're related to Lady Gwendolyn. Independence must run in your line.' He said it with pleasure, as if it was something to be celebrated instead of criticised. An opinion in direct opposition to her father's...and most of the men in her life, now that she thought about it. Lord Vidar was the only man she'd known to tolerate his wife's eccentricities as he had.

Still, for all the delight it gave her, it made her feel rather like a horse. Her attributes weighed and measured against the line of her ancestors. 'Does independence run in your line as well, Dane?'

He laughed, a deep and rich sound that was entirely more pleasing than it should have been. 'You could say that. I have four older sisters, each one more independent than the next.'

She tried to imagine a young Rolfe with four older sisters badgering him about, but she couldn't do it even though she liked the idea of it. She could only see him as the powerful man that he was. Every man in a position of power over women needed at least one woman in his life to answer to.

Instead of responding, she gripped the axe by the handle and held it high over her head. Aiming for the centre of the stump, she let it go, hitting her mark dead on with a smooth popping sound as the tip of the blade embedded itself in the wood.

'That's good. Do it two more times and we'll call it skill and not luck.'

He was teasing her, and she couldn't help but laugh. Twice more would be no trouble at all. She had been throwing axes since she was a child. Retrieving it, she went on to show him two more times how accurate she was. Each throw landed within a finger width of the one before.

'Now you try.' She grinned as she walked back to him, holding the axe out. 'Let's see how *lucky* you are.'

'The difference, Saxon, is that I never claimed to be skilled.'

'Now you're retreating? Interesting. I took you for a man of courage.'

He chuckled and took it from her, his fingertips grazing her palm and making goosebumps move up her arm. Only when she stepped back to give him space to throw did she realise that they had drawn a small crowd. Being with him had made her forget everyone else and she would have sworn it was the same with him. He didn't seem to care that his warriors watched them. In fact, he only seemed to have eyes for her. When she spoke his gaze never strayed from her face and, every time she'd thrown the axe or shot an arrow, she had felt his study of her. Being the centre of his attention was a heady thing, but no matter how important or valued he made her feel, she must remember that he was the man who would be sent to destroy her family if the need arose.

He finally looked away from her to study the stump, bringing the axe up to gauge the distance. She worried that he wouldn't get leverage without the use of his left arm for balance, but when he threw it the axe sailed through the air, easily reaching the stump. He probably could've thrown it much farther. It sliced into the wood deeply, landing roughly a hand's width below the gouges she had left.

'Not bad,' she said as he walked to retrieve the axe, and she couldn't stop her treacherous gaze from roaming down his backside when he bent over to pull it out of the stump. The sight of his nude body, muscled and unquestionably masculine, was still vivid in her mind. A tiny flicker of awareness joined the tension in her belly. It gave her pause, because she'd never felt that for a Saxon man.

Had she been secretly harbouring a core of wickedness like her mother all this time? Last night she'd been able to assuage her guilt by convincing herself that her feelings had been a natural result of seeing her first nude male body. But that wasn't precisely true, she realised now. It was him. The Dane clearly made her feel wicked things.

His next throw was a bit wide, barely clipping the stump on its right side. His third attempt was true and hit where her first blade had touched to the cheers of the small group of warriors watching them. He gave a simple nod of acknowledgement to them.

'You're very good for someone who doesn't know how to throw an axe.' Honestly, she would have been amazed had he been terrible. The man was probably good at everything he tried.

'Not as good as you,' he said, bringing the axe back to her.

'Nothing a little practice won't cure.'

Holding it out for her, handle side out, he said, 'You've mastered the axe. You're progressing at archery. How would you like to try learning the sword? Or am I wrong and you mastered the blade as a child?'

She smiled at his question and shook her head, taking the axe to affix it to her belt. 'I've never held a blade. My father forbade it and a sword was too costly for me to acquire on my own.'

'Do you want to learn?' He asked it as if it were a simple thing.

'From you?' Why did her heart pounce in anticipation?

He nodded. 'Unless you're afraid of disobeying your father.' There was a challenge in his eyes as he said that. 'But you never let that stop you before, have you?'

Actually, she had let that stop her. Since her

mother left, she'd been doing everything she could to prove to her father that she wasn't like the woman. That meant that, aside from a few indiscretions such as the axe, she had done everything to find his favour. Father would not want her spending time with this man, yet she was very tempted to accept the offer.

Rolfe's voice had been pitched too low to be overheard, but she still took a look around to make sure. Lady Gwendolyn casually glanced over at them from where she was still instructing Ellan, curiosity burning in her features. The warriors, assuming correctly that the entertainment was over, were slowly going back to their own sparring. That more than anything decided her. She couldn't bear their audience as she practised. Slowly shaking her head, she said, 'I cannot. I'm afraid that my pride couldn't bear the scrutiny of an audience.'

'There's a clearing to the south. It's not far from the walls of Alvey, but far enough for privacy. I could teach you there in the mornings.'

He spoke so earnestly that she almost forgot to be suspicious. Almost. 'Why would you teach me?'

He took in a breath, his chest expanding with the effort as he thought over his answer. 'Because you want to learn and I can see that no one else will teach you.' She didn't know what she had expected from him, but it wasn't that.

She did want to learn. Every day at home felt like a threat with the Scots and the Danes on each side. The more she learned the better chance she had of protecting herself and her younger siblings. Of course, she also had purely selfish reasons. She was good at learning how to fight. She liked the training. 'What would be the point if I'm to leave in a fortnight?'

'You're right. It's not nearly long enough to master the skill, but it's enough to give you basic knowledge.' He paused, but she sensed that he wasn't finished. 'Although I understand if you're too afraid.'

'I'm not afraid,' she said before she realised that he'd baited her.

Grinning, he said, 'Then I'll see you in the morning.' He walked away and she was curious enough about him and what the morning would bring that she let him go without arguing. One morning with him wouldn't change anything.

Chapter Five

'What are you smiling about?' Ellan surprised Elswyth by following her outside the great hall later that evening.

They had finished the evening meal, so Elswyth had come out for a bit of fresh air and to clear her head. The warriors were crammed inside to capacity, but despite the crowd, she'd been aware of Rolfe's gaze on her all evening. 'Was I smiling?' Elswyth frowned.

'Aye. It was quite strange watching you all night because you hardly ever smile. What has you so cheerful?'

'If I was smiling—' which she really didn't think she had been '—it's because we'll be leaving soon.' Her thoughts of Rolfe were so new and unexpected that she wanted to keep them to herself for a while. Maybe for ever. Nothing could ever come of them.

Leading the way, she meandered with no particular destination through the various cook fires that flickered in the yard. Several men huddled around each one, talking and not paying the sisters any attention. It seemed that Lady Gwendolyn had mentioned to the newcomers that they were to be left unmolested.

'Hmm... I thought you were smiling because a certain Dane couldn't keep his eyes off you all night.' Ellan grinned and, even in the deep shadows of twilight, her eyes sparkled with merriment.

'He couldn't, could he?' The words were out before she could stop herself. Once she said them it was a relief to have someone know. 'I must admit that these warriors are different than I thought they would be. I suppose I was expecting barbarians and, while some of them fit the description, most of them are...tamer than I anticipated.' Would her father believe her if she told him that? Even saying the words felt like some sort of betrayal to him.

Elswyth had never met the group of Danes that her mother had run off with. They had camped along the coast, a little bit north-east of Banford. Her mother had come across them on one of their trips inland. That trip had led to several others until one night Elswyth had heard her parents arguing. She'd heard enough to realise that Father had found their mother in a compromising position with one of the Danes and had fought the man. At home that night he'd given her an ultimatum: repent and face punishment or be banished. She had chosen banishment. The next morning she'd left to meet her Dane and they'd never seen her again.

To this day, Elswyth didn't understand what could prompt someone to leave their family behind. She had struggled with the question for years, but wasn't any closer to coming to an answer. The only conclusion she'd come to was that she needed to try extra hard to prove her loyalty. If that meant despising the Danes, then that's what she did. Only now that didn't seem so simple to do.

A Dane at the nearest cook fire threw back his head and laughed at something his friend, a Saxon warrior, had said. Father would have her believe the Dane and Saxon warriors were constantly at each other's throats, but that didn't seem to be the case. Not here.

'You *like him*, don't you?'

Elswyth's ears burned. 'Shh.' She glanced around to make certain that no one had overheard her sister's dubious claim. 'I don't like him, not the way your tone implies.' *Liar*, a tiny voice in her head accused. 'I merely think he is kind and not nearly as ruthless as I had thought.'

Ellan didn't believe her. She wore a smug smile that made her eyes gleam victoriously. 'Time will tell.'

Elswyth opened her mouth to argue. She didn't quite understand her need to argue, she only knew that she needed to emphatically deny any interest in the warrior so that her sister would understand that in no way did she favour the man. She was not like their mother and she would not abandon her family for one of them.

'Elswyth!' The voice came from nowhere, but it drew every eye in the area. The men at the nearby fire briefly stopped talking to look around, but went back to their meal when no culprit could be found.

Her heart clamoured, taking a moment to gather itself before trying to beat free of her chest when her gaze landed on a flurry of movement in the shadow of the granary. Someone stood there motioning to her, the hand white in the inky black that surrounded it.

'Who is that?' Ellan asked, following her gaze.

'If I didn't know better, I'd think it was Galan,' she whispered. But that couldn't be.

Their older brother was at home on the farm, not here sneaking around among their enemy, especially not alone.

The longer she stared into the shadows, and the more urgently he waved her over, the more convinced she became of his identity. If it was he, it could only mean that there had been trouble at home. Father! Dear God, what if something had happened to him? 'Stay here. I'll go see what he wants.'

She made her way around the perimeter of the open area, not going directly towards the granary. No one seemed to notice her as she turned in that direction. Galan—or who she assumed to be her brother—whirled when she approached and retreated farther through the fortress, moving with ease through the night. His cloak was up around his head to shield his identity. He could have been any number of the Saxon men who wandered through the village at this time of night. But he wasn't and her heart pounded from that knowledge as she followed him. He finally stopped in the shadow of the wall—the gates were swung wide open which is probably how he'd got inside.

A small village made of tents had been set up outside because Alvey wasn't big enough to hold all the warriors within her walls. A sea of fabric fluttered in the cold winter gusts as far as the trees. This was the first time she'd seen them and the sight nearly stole her breath. More of the warriors had returned from the south than she had anticipated. Despite what she'd said to Ellan and how she felt about Rolfe, the spectacle of them made her shiver with the reminder of how precarious this all was. War could come any day. If her family chose the wrong side... She couldn't even allow herself to finish the thought.

Stepping carefully into the shadows, she approached her brother. The white of his smile was barely visible in the twilight and she was seized by the need to hug him and shake him all at the same time. She decided on hugging, closing her eyes in thanks for his safety when his arms went around her. It only lasted a brief moment, but it was enough to reassure her that, aside from being thinner than she remembered, he was whole. She released him when he pulled back, but only to grip him by the shoulders and look up into his dirt-streaked face. 'What are you doing here? Have you come alone?'

'Aye. I'm by myself.'

Between the Scots, the Danes, unknown Saxons and travellers, it was foolish to travel alone. 'But why? It's too dangerous. Any number of catastrophes could have befallen you on the way.'

His smile fell to become a scowl. 'I can take care of myself, Elswyth. Besides, I didn't come all this way to have you scold me.'

'Why are you here? Has something happened to Father?' In her excitement it was hard to keep her voice low so that any of the Danes coming in and out of the gates wouldn't hear.

'Nay, Father is well, or at least I assume he is. I haven't been home yet, I've come straight here.' He hesitated and her chest tightened. 'It's Baldric. He's been taken by the Scots.'

'What?' That was the last thing she had expected him to say. Their younger brother was only fourteen winters and he had no interaction with the Scots, or he hadn't when she'd been home. Galan had been their father's accomplice in advocating for joining their ranks. He'd ridden with Father last spring to their secret meetings with the warriors. She had hoped that the winter would bring an end to that, but it seemed her hope had been in vain. 'How is that possible?'

Galan had the grace to look guilty. The cloak had fallen back a bit and he ran the heel of his hand over his brow and couldn't seem to meet her eyes. 'He went with me to our meeting with them.' Ignoring her gasp of outrage, he continued, 'While we were there a group of Scots met up with some Danes who were on their way to Alvey, we believe. They destroyed them, Elswyth. Every last one of the Scots were killed.'

She tried not to imagine the carnage that sort of battle involved, but the images flashed behind her eyes anyway. Rolfe had taken a Scot's spear a few days ago. Could it have been him and his group of warriors? She shuddered at the violence she had known him capable of. 'You were not involved in the battle?'

He shook his head. 'Nay, we were at their camp. The group of Scots were on their way to us, but obviously they never made it. A scout found the carnage left behind and came to let us know. The Scots suspect that Father was somehow involved in revealing their location to the Danes.'

'That's preposterous! Father would never betray their location.' Whether or not she agreed with his madness in attempting to drive the Danes from their land, she knew that he was an honourable man. He would never betray anyone he considered a friend or ally.

'We both know that. They, however, want proof of our loyalty.'

'How does kidnapping a child prove anything of loyalty?'

'Baldric is hardly a child. He will be fifteen winters very soon.'

She sniffed in disagreement. The weight of Baldric's hand in hers was still vivid from all the nights she had lain in bed with him after Mother had gone, telling him stories when he couldn't sleep or was ill. He wasn't old enough to be brought into this madness. 'He is a child and he should never have been there. How could you have taken him with you?'

'He demanded to come and he's old enough to make his own decisions now.'

She strongly disagreed with that, but arguing that now wouldn't get them anywhere. 'What does Baldric have to do with proving Father's loyalty?'

'Because the Dane bastards…' He paused to spit as if the word was foul on his tongue.

'Shh.' A quick look around assured her that no one had overheard him.

'They stole a small fortune from the Scots they attacked. It was a stash of coin and jewels meant for the mercenaries at our meeting.'

'Mercenaries!' This time it was Galan's turn to shush her. 'Have things progressed so far already? They're hiring mercenaries to attack the Danes?'

Galan took her arm and led her farther away from the gates. In a whisper he explained, 'There are Danes on their western coast. They are preparing to fight those. At the moment there are no set plans for Alvey.'

That was a relief, but it was only a matter of time, she feared. Somehow in all of this, hating the Danes had come second to keeping her family safe.

'I don't know the details,' he continued, 'but one of the jewels that was taken with the coin was a bloodstone. It belongs to King Causantín's family and has some ceremonial importance to them. That is what they want us to recover. If we can deliver it to them, then they will consider Father's loyalty proven and release Baldric. Do you think you can do it?'

She still didn't understand their idea of loyalty. Wasn't it possible for Father to despise them and yet return the stone to free Baldric? Sometimes she failed to comprehend the logic of warriors. 'You want me to find the bloodstone?'

'Aye. They believe that Rolfe led the band of Danes that took it. He's here?'

She nodded, because her mouth was sud-

denly too dry for speech. Last night Rolfe had
sat with Lord Vidar and Lady Gwendolyn in the
hall, sacks of coin between them. Later, when
she'd patched his wound, she had noticed a red
stone on his bed set amid some silver. Could
that be the one?

'Good. Then the stone is likely here as well.
You must find it, Elswyth. It's the only way to
save Baldric.'

'But how will I know which one it is?'

He shrugged. 'All I know is that it is the size
of a walnut and is set in gold on a chain.'

'I may have seen it.'

Galan grabbed her shoulders in his joy. 'Have
you truly?'

'Aye.' She nodded. 'I saw the warrior Rolfe
with a red stone. I don't know if it was set in
gold or on a chain. I only had a glimpse.'

'Do you think you can find it and relieve
him of it?'

Shaking her head, she said, 'I'm not certain.
It's possible.' It would mean she'd have to make
a search of his chamber, because he hadn't worn
it on his person today.

'But you will try?'

'Aye, of course I'll try. We must save Baldric.'

'Thank God.' He let out a breath and pulled

her close, his shoulders slumped in obvious relief. 'Can you make a search tonight or tomorrow? I must get back to Baldric soon.'

'If I hurry, I can make a search of his chamber tonight before he retires.' As she spoke, the reality of what she was about to do set in, making her heart pound. Dear God, war really was coming and their family could be right in the middle of it! With a hand on her chest, she took a step back from Galan and struggled to take a deep breath. The air raced through her lungs as quickly as her thoughts raced through her mind.

Sensing her panic, Galan touched her cheek. 'You can do this, Elswyth. I believe in you.'

Stories of the Danes haunted her. They were ruthless and brutal when crossed. There was one story that her father liked to tell of a man who had stolen a coin from a drunken Dane in some unnamed southern village. He'd gone about his evening, thinking that he'd got away with the crime, only to wake up as his hand had been cleaved from his body. They gave no quarter or mercy. What would happen if they found out she'd stolen something as precious as a jewel?

Rubbing her wrist, she held her hands against her belly. Would Rolfe be that brutal and unforgiving? She was having a difficult time reconciling the gentle Rolfe from last night in the bath with the warrior who had cut down an entire troop of Scots. Even this morning, he'd been kind and teasing with her. How could he be a ruthless Norseman as well?

'But what if he finds it gone before morning? What will happen?'

'They'll make a search for it, I'm sure, but no one will be able to connect you to the crime. Keep it hidden. You'll need to bring it to me as soon as you can.'

She had to do this for Baldric. He needed her right now more than she feared for her future at the hands of the Danes. 'I'm due to go south in the morning with Rolfe. There's a clearing there where he's to teach me swordplay.' She didn't have to see Galan clearly to sense the tension in his body that her words had caused.

'You will be alone with him?'

'Aye, we'll be alone. If I'm able to find the stone tonight, I'll bring it and leave it for you at the base of a tree.'

'But why would he teach you swordplay?'

'To be honest, I'm uncertain. He seems to have taken an interest in my axe. I demonstrated my skill with throwing it and he offered to teach me the sword.' He was quiet for so long that his very silence lent a significance to her words that wasn't really present.

'Be vigilant with him,' he finally said, letting out a disappointed breath. 'I would tell you not to be alone with him, but we must do this.'

'Oh, Rolfe wouldn't hurt me…not yet, anyway.' She knew that Galan's fears were unfounded, but that would change if her thievery was ever exposed. 'Once we have Baldric back you and Father must stop this madness. No more secret meetings.'

In an instant, his ire was back. 'The Danes need to be run out of here once and for all. We were once the proud people of Bernicia.'

'You sound like Father.' His eyes flashed with hatred that was so familiar to her. Her father ate that hatred with his porridge every morning and spent his days with it coursing through his blood.

He drew himself up taller, shoulders back and his voice a harsh whisper. 'Northumbria has given herself over to the Danes, but we won't follow suit.'

'So you'd rather we join the Scots? Give our homes over to them?'

He shook his head. 'It won't come to that. They only want things to go back to how it was with Alvey a buffer between the north and the Danes to the south.'

'You must tell Father to stop this madness. The Danes cannot be defeated so easily.'

He stared at her as if she'd become the lowest of traitors. 'How can you say that? They must be!'

'Shh!' she again warned him to keep his voice low. 'Do you see the warriors in their tents? The warriors walking around Alvey? There are even more in the great hall. He is wrong to think that the Saxon warriors will rise up and defeat them. I've seen with my own eyes how they work together with the Danes. They will join forces with the Danes and together there are too many of them.' She knew her words bordered on treachery, but she needed him to understand the truth of the situation.

Galan shook his head manically. 'There are still loyal Saxons in the villages who would take our side.'

'Our side? We don't have a side. They would be forced to take the side of the Scots and the Scots have been our enemies in the past just like the Danes.'

'Not like the Danes,' he argued. 'The Danes are worse.'

Taking a deep breath so the argument wouldn't

escalate, she clenched her jaw and spoke through her teeth. 'Be that as it may, they are still too powerful. Tell Father that he needs to stop this madness at once. We could all die if it comes to war.'

'Some of us would rather die than make peace with them.' He glared at her and his body stiffened. She knew that he was about to make a run for the gates, so she put a hand on his arm to stop him.

There was no use in arguing at the moment. Perhaps Father was right, or perhaps they had no choice but to accept the Danes. Whatever the answer, it wouldn't be decided between her and Galan tonight. 'This arguing won't get us anywhere. I'm sorry.' Only slightly mollified, he shrugged out of her grasp.

Closing her eyes, she forced herself to swallow past the lump in her throat. It did nothing to dispel the heaviness of her heart or her disdain for what she was about to do. 'In the morning try to hide near the clearing so you can see where I leave the jewel. I'll try to leave the ground disturbed just in case you can't see me hide it.' She had no idea how she would accomplish this task she'd set for herself, but she'd figure that out in the morning.

'You won't even know I'm there, unless he tries to hurt you. If he does, I'll kill him.'

His crooked smile softened the harsh words. It was the same smile she always remembered when she thought of him. A wave of affection washed over her and she pulled him into an embrace. He put his arms around her again and squeezed. 'I've missed you,' he whispered.

An ache swelled in her throat, making speech impossible for a moment. 'I've missed you, too,' she said when she could speak. 'Please be careful. Please take Baldric home safely and don't venture north again. Please.'

He pulled back and grimaced and she knew that he had no intention of following her order. With a nod of goodbye, he disappeared into the deep shadows cast by the wall. Dread made her steps heavy as she walked back towards the great hall. She had no choice but to steal from Rolfe, a man who had been nothing but kind to her. Baldric's life was worth more than a blasted bloodstone. For a moment she imagined telling Rolfe why she needed the stone and in her fantasy he was understanding and gave it to her. But it was only a fantasy. If she confessed all to Rolfe, then she'd have to confess what Father and Galan had been up to. Somehow she didn't think he'd be so understanding about their dallying with treason.

She told herself that it didn't matter she was stealing from him. He was their enemy. He'd have no qualms about doing what must be done if he found out about Galan's talks with the Scots. Besides, hadn't he merely stolen the jewel from the Scots anyway? It wasn't even really his to keep.

None of those arguments seemed to make a difference to the guilt gnawing at her.

She would have to steal from Rolfe.

Chapter Six

The tray felt heavier in her arms than it had the night before. Or maybe it was the weight of her intentions making it seem that way. She had tried to talk herself out of the plan at least a hundred times in the past hour, but Baldric's life was worth more than her misgivings. Putting her body against Rolfe's door, she nudged it open with her shoulder. The bowl on the tray wobbled, but she managed to right it before any damage was done. Once inside, she pushed it closed with her toe and waited there in the dark silence, quite certain that someone would come in and know her for the thief that she was.

After a moment, the pounding of her heart in her ears settled enough that she was able to hear the revelry still going on below. The men had finished their supper, but the deep voice of a skald could be heard, regaling them with some adventure in their own language, his words punctuated by cheers and heckles at various times. Elswyth had only picked up a few words of their language, not nearly enough to follow along. Because her own Saxon tongue was important to Lady Gwendolyn it was the one spoken the most; the Norsemen only spoke their own language among themselves or on nights like this when a story must be told.

She hoped the entertainment would keep Rolfe below for now. When she'd left the main hall, he'd been deep in discussion with the lord and lady and some warrior she thought was named Aevir. Wyborn had been busy chewing a bone under the table. She only had a few moments to herself before they would both come up to retire for the evening.

Placing the tray on the small table, she set a taper to the single candle burning low on the table and lit several more so that she could study his room. Her gaze immediately went to his bed where she had last seen the stone, but of course it wasn't there anymore. Her steps were slow and shaky as she walked over to run her hand over the furs just in case. Rolfe's scent rose from them and she couldn't help but think of him lying beneath them. The flutter in her belly at that thought was so visceral that she jerked her hand back.

She had to get on with this or he would surely find her. A chest was set against the wall near the end of the bed, but she recognised it as the one he'd pulled his under-tunic out of the night before. Probably not that one. There was a smaller one next to it, so she made quick work of tossing open the lid. A cloth-wrapped bundle lay on top. She unwrapped it gently so that he wouldn't know she'd disturbed it to find that it was a child's doll. It seemed rather old and worn, but it clearly meant something to him if he had kept it with him these years. Bringing it to her nose, she confirmed that it, too, bore his scent. She imagined him taking it out from time to time and the image did not match the ruthless warrior that Galan had described. It did match the man who had smiled at her with his kind blue eyes and a single dimple.

Suddenly she felt worse than a thief. Who was she to have access to this man's memories? She had no right to set her eyes upon something so personal to him, yet she wanted to climb into the chest and stay there. She wanted to savour any knowledge she could find about this man who was so mysterious and fascinating to her.

Wrapping the doll back up very carefully, she

set it aside. No matter how she chastised herself, she couldn't help her curiosity when it came to him. The things in this chest were little pieces of him and she found that she wanted to know more about him—not for Father's sake, but for her own reasons. Underneath the doll, she found several things that she imagined he'd brought home from his travels over the years: a wooden coin with the crude carving of a nude lady on it, a volume of strange writing wrapped in leather, a piece of amber. At the very bottom was a bottle of wine laid on its side, but no jewel. Something gleamed at her from the darkened corner, the flicker of candlelight picking up the trace of metal. Cool iron met her fingertips and she lifted the slight weight. It was a key. Her heart gave a slight leap of joy. Reverently, she placed everything back inside except for the key and closed the lid.

Her gaze made a search through the rest of his room, looking for the lock that it matched. His shelves proved fruitless as did another large chest which was unlocked in which she discovered some of his chainmail and leathers. She was beginning to despair, having almost decided that he kept his valuables locked in the armoury, when she fell to her knees beside his bed and put her cheek to the floor. The light barely reached there, but it was enough to reveal the latches of two small chests, the metal of the clasps winking at her.

Stifling a hoot of triumph, she pulled the first one out. It was heavy and what sounded suspiciously like coins tinkling against each other met her ears. The key slid in easily and turned. The lock released and the lid popped open. There was a small fortune of sacks filled with coin inside. Along with the coin she suspected to be in the other chest, there was enough to buy an entire army of mercenaries if he needed them.

She couldn't stifle the shiver that ran through her body as she reverently touched the sacks, the coins hard and cold beneath the coarse fabric. This was only Rolfe's personal stash. It didn't include the larger chests in the armoury and whatever else might be hidden. The Danes were never leaving. This confirmed it, but she knew even with this knowledge Father wouldn't reconcile himself to their staying. She knew that with a certainty that was a physical pain through her body.

Footsteps walked briskly past the door outside, making her remember how tenuous her current position was. She made quick work of searching the chest, feeling the contents of each bag through the fabric. Finally, one of the sacks on the bottom seemed to hold something other than coin. It was heavy and there was a bulge larger than a coin, so she dumped the contents into her hand. She could hardly believe her eyes when the bloodstone sat in her palm, winking at her in the candlelight. It was set in gold filigree and attached to a golden chain which hung down through her fingers. It had to be the jewel Galan had told her about. It was about the right size and she was almost certain that it was the one she'd seen on Rolfe's bed.

Deciding it would have to do and that she didn't have the time to search through the other chest, she put everything else back inside and dropped the key into the corner of the chest where she'd found it. Then she pushed the entire chest back under the bed before tucking the stone between her breasts. Briefly, she considered staying and applying the poultice to his shoulder again so as not to rouse suspicion, but she knew that there was no way she would be able to keep her composure with his blue eyes staring her down. If she didn't crack under the strain and admit everything, she'd make a fool of herself as her fear got the better of her. She honestly didn't know if she'd be able to look the man in the eyes, knowing the stone rested against her skin.

It was best to leave and let him make of that what he would. It was better than her giving herself away. She wasn't made for thievery and deceptions. Opening the door, she glanced out to make certain that no one noticed her and then made her way to the alcove she shared with Ellan. Once inside she let the curtain fall down, hiding her away from the world.

The next morning a harsh shake woke her. She opened her eyes to see Rolfe staring down at her. He was a shadow above her, the only light coming from the fire below in the hall, but there was no mistaking his powerful form. She gasped. Her first thought was that he had found his bloodstone missing and come directly to her. It had to be obvious that she had stolen it. Her hand immediately went to her waist where the bloodstone rested against her stomach. She had tied a purse there beneath her clothes and around her waist where she kept the stone hidden.

'Please understand that it was necessary.' Her voice was husky with sleep.

He knelt down, balancing on his heels and leaned close, presumably so that he wouldn't wake Ellan who was snoring lightly next to her against the wall. 'Wake up, fair lady. It's time for your sword lesson.' There was laughter in his voice.

He didn't know. The relief that overcame her was so powerful that it left her muscles weak, her body sagging into the straw mattress. She couldn't speak, couldn't move.

'You don't wake easily.' The smile stayed in his voice.

'I never have,' she said, though it was in no way an explanation for what she had almost confessed, and it came out rather garbled. Pushing herself up, he moved back to give her space.

'Come, I'll be waiting outside for you with the horses. I have food you can eat on the way.'

She nodded, too surprised for speech as he turned and left, his broad shoulders nearly filling up the opening of their little alcove. She was caught off guard that he would see to those things for her. She was essentially a servant. She had served the lord and lady last night and he had sat next to them, politely taking the food and drink she'd brought. Before he and his men had arrived, she had often sat to take her own meal with them after serving them, but there had seemed no place for her and Ellan at the crowded table after they had arrived—not to mention the fact that she didn't particularly want to sit with the Danes.

Yet he'd arranged for food for her this morning as if she were his equal. Or as if she were someone with whom he was attempting to court favour. Her throat went dry at that thought. What would he stand to gain from her favour? She might have the advantage of sharing Lady Gwendolyn's bloodline, but she didn't have a dowry to speak of, not one that a warrior such as Rolfe could command. He could take a wife who would bring an estate to the marriage, or at least a hefty amount of silver. Why would he want *her*? And why did the idea of him pursuing her in that way send pleasure spiralling through her?

It was too early to figure out those things, so she shook her head and looked for her shoes. He was a puzzle she wasn't quite able to work her way through just yet. She had slept in her clothes precisely so that she wouldn't have to dress this morning and risk exposing the jewel, so at least there was no need for her to dress. Shoes found, she ran a comb through her hair and quickly plaited the length of it in the near darkness. Grabbing her thickest cloak, she made her way downstairs.

The entire hall seemed to be asleep, so she

trod carefully lest she wake one of them. Now that it was colder at night, more of the warriors had begun to sleep inside so she wound her way around them as she walked to the front door. When she opened the door, Wyborn approached, tail wagging, to sniff her palm. She gave the fur on his head a quick pet and he walked back to stand beside his master. Rolfe held the reins of two great horses. Their hooves pawed the ground anxiously. Twin puffs of steam floated up from their nostrils to dissipate in the morning darkness.

'This is Sleipnir.' He stroked a hand down the neck of the stallion that he'd ridden into Alvey. His coat was a deep grey that darkened to midnight around his legs. 'You'll ride Gyllir. She's very gentle. I wasn't certain if you were an experienced rider.'

'I've ridden some.' Only while travelling occasionally to neighbouring villages or to Alvey. At home there was hardly a need for it.

The mare gave a soft whinny and Elswyth couldn't resist touching her velvet nose. Her coat was golden and seemed to glow in the pale moonlight of early morning. She rooted in Elswyth's hand for a treat, prompting a soft laugh from Rolfe. 'She's a greedy one.'

Despite the massive beauty of the horses,

it was Rolfe who held her in his thrall. Silver moonlight painted him in her generous light, touching his chiselled features with a soft hand so that she was struck anew by his masculine beauty. There was no room in her life for how her stomach fluttered in his presence or the way her gaze was reluctant to leave him. She refused to become what her mother had been.

'Come, I'll help you.' His low voice moved right down inside her to settle deep in her chest. When he moved around his horse to stand beside Gyllir, he held out his hand to her. She took in a deep, wavering breath as she touched his palm with hers. His long fingers closed around hers and he tugged slightly, bringing her to stand before him. There was no explanation for how protected he made her feel. In one easy movement he put his hands to her waist and lifted her to sit astride the horse. She tugged her tunic upward, leaving her leggings exposed from the knee down.

'I thought you might need this.' He tossed a thick fur up and around her shoulders before she could say anything. It smelled like him and she had to close her eyes for a moment to savour it. She should push it away and give it back to him, but it was deliciously warm in the morning's bitter cold. Her own cloak was no match for the frigid air without sun.

'Thank you,' she muttered, tying the thick folds closed around her body.

'You're welcome,' he said and pulled a small sack from Sleipnir's back, pulling out a honeyed cake. Her mouth watered at the sight. How had he known they were her favourite? Lady Gwendolyn always made certain that they were filled with the most deliciously gooey mixture of honey and walnuts. 'To break your fast.' He smiled as he held it up to her.

She took it, hardly able to find the words to thank him, but he didn't wait for her to say anything. He turned and pulled his powerful frame easily atop his horse, the perfect balance of power and grace.

He offered her a nod as he set his heels to the horse and led the way out of Alvey. She followed with Wyborn trotting along at her side and they rode in silence for a while as they both nibbled their honey cakes.

Finally they moved past the small city of tents and made their way into the forest. The silence was broken by the happy calls of the migrating thrushes beginning their day. Their songs were filled with a cheeriness that Elswyth was far from feeling. That blasted stone burned against her belly like an ember that only roused her guilt.

She needed to know something about him, something that would make her feel better about what she'd done. Something that would remind her that he was a ruthless Dane. Of course she wouldn't go back and not take the stone—Baldric needed to be saved from the Scots—but if Rolfe was really a ruthless warrior, then the knowledge would help to soothe her conscience.

'Why are you taking up so much time with me? Why teach me the sword and bring me honey cakes and be so nice to me?' That wasn't precisely what she'd meant to say when she'd opened her mouth, but that's what had come out and she couldn't take it back now.

The path was wider here, so when he looked over at her he slowed his pace to allow her horse to come abreast of his. He wasn't smiling, but his eyes were soft. 'Why shouldn't I do these things for you?'

Infuriating man. 'You know very well why. You are the commander of one of the most powerful armies in the north.' It nearly choked her to say those words, but they were true. 'I am the daughter of a farmer.'

He was quiet, so after a few moments passed she dared to glance over at him to see that he was studying her. His eyes were intense, but she couldn't begin to fathom what he was thinking. 'You sell yourself short, Elswyth. You are far more than that. Besides, your father's farm is the largest in Alvey. He produces enough food and wool to feed and clothe an army. Without that farm, Alvey is weak.'

She had never considered their farm that important to Alvey, but she knew that he was right in his assessment. She'd simply never viewed it in such mercenary terms before. It had always simply been her home. Slightly mollified, she said, 'Is that it, then? You want to align our farm and village more closely with Alvey?' It made sense. It was no secret that her father didn't care for the Danes.

'It's what Lord Vidar wants. He and Lady Gwendolyn both want to align all the villages with Alvey. They can see the potential risk in losing your farm.'

Her breath caught in her throat. 'You've spoken to Lord Vidar about me…about us?' They must have spoken of marriage. Had anything been decided? Did she even have a say in the matter? Her mind whirled with a hundred questions, only stopping when Rolfe reached over and touched her shoulder through the fur.

'Only for a moment. He plans for me to wed

this winter and he mentioned several names for consideration. Yours was merely one of many.'

One of many. Somehow she hated that even more than she hated the fact that they had spoken of her. Rolfe would wed this winter and it might not be her. She could only sit for a moment as that thought washed over her.

Unreasonably, that cold fist of jealousy tightened in her chest the same as it had the previous morning when the servant had left his room. Someone else could be the recipient of those breathtaking smiles very soon. Someone else could lie upon those warm furs in his bed alongside him, touching and…she couldn't let her thoughts go so far. But she did recall very vividly how he had looked when he'd stood from the tub. Nude, his skin golden in the candlelight. In her mind's eye, she imagined him walking towards his bed, only the woman waiting for him wasn't her and she hated it.

The bitterness with which she hated it surprised her. This was absolute madness. She would not allow herself to be seduced by a Dane, but somehow she was having these thoughts and they were far from pure.

Realising that it had been some time since she'd spoken, she forced herself to nod, not caring that it was a bit jerky and ungraceful. 'Did you plan to let me know that I was being considered?'

He shifted at her side, but she couldn't bring herself to look at him. 'I thought it best to allow you to get to know me before approaching the subject. If it turned out that you hated me—' the smile was evident in his voice as he said it, as if she couldn't possibly hate him '—then there would be no need to talk further about it.'

'I suppose I should feel grateful that you planned to consider my wishes.'

He laughed. 'The truth is that you had already lured me in before Lord Vidar mentioned your name.'

With wide eyes she looked over at him and he said, 'I noticed you on the wall the evening I returned. You looked so fierce and resolute, I took you for a lady warrior like Lady Gwendolyn. Then later when you came to my chamber you spoke to me so boldly as if you had no fear.'

'That's hardly—'

'Nay, it's true. This may seem insignificant to you, but hardly any woman has spoken so boldly to me since I was a boy.' The dimple shone in his cheek as he explained. 'I grew up the younger son of a farmer with no prospects.'

She had to stop her chin from dropping. If what he said was true, he'd grown up much like she had. He was a fierce and respected leader, and she had rather blindly assumed that he always had been.

'It took dedication and years of relentless training to become the leader I am today. I'm told that many find me intimidating. But not you. You're honest about your feelings, Elswyth, and I like that about you.'

But she wasn't honest. She wasn't honest at all. The bloodstone seemed to warm against her as if it had its own internal heat meant to remind her of her duplicity. 'Do you miss home?' she asked, because it was the only thing in that entire speech that she could latch on to without feeling even worse about what she had done. Baldric needed the stone, she had no qualms about saving him. Only she despised that she had to lie to Rolfe to do it.

'Aye, sometimes. I had a happy childhood... for a time, then I left to join with Jarl Hegard, Lord Vidar's father,' he supplied.

'Why did you leave home?' she asked, sensing he'd left something out.

'There was nothing for me there. My older brother was married with children of his own and he stayed to work the farm. There were six of us and my parents needed the silver I could send home to them. I craved adventure, anyway. Leaving suited me.' A thread of bitterness had entered his voice before he went quiet for a moment. Finally he added, 'For a while now I've found myself remembering my childhood and all the trouble I caused my parents. I once thought it was homesickness, but I have no particular desire to go home. I like Alvey. Now I realise that it's the desire for my own family that's calling to me.'

She was struck by two things. The first was that he was being more honest with her than she ever thought he would be. The second was that he was being so honest with her because he wanted her to share the life he had made for himself. She could hardly fathom that they were having this conversation when she hadn't even known him two days ago. He had been but a faceless warrior who would brutally end her people's struggle for independence. Now he was real and kind and not at all what she'd expected. She had to put a stop to what he was thinking before things went too far.

'I cannot wed a Dane.'

The words settled between them with a thud, making the silence seem louder and more obtrusive until he finally said, 'It's true, then, that you share your father's feelings about us?' His voice was low and even, making it impossible to tell his feelings. She couldn't bring herself to look at him again.

'Not precisely…' She realised that those words at least were true. She didn't hold the hatred for the Danes as she might have had she not spent months in Alvey. 'But neither do I welcome you here.'

He was quiet as he mulled that over. Finally the silence became too much and she had to look over to see what he was thinking. She was surprised that he didn't seem hurt, angry, or even confused by her words. There was a slight heat in his eyes, but it wasn't fury. 'Lord Vidar believes that our joining could bring peace. What do you think?'

Would it bring peace? 'Father would never agree to a marriage, so, nay, there could be no peace from our joining.'

Chapter Seven

Rolfe didn't respond to her, so they rode the rest of the way in silence. Elswyth had been chastising herself for turning him down with such finality, afraid that he would take them back to Alvey immediately. After all, if he was not attempting to win her favour, then what was the need to spend time with her? She was certain now that's what this sword practice was about, but when he made no move to turn around she kept quiet, afraid that to displease him further would mean she wouldn't be able to finish her task.

The sun began to crest the horizon, throwing the world into shades of grey as she followed him to the edge of the clearing where he stopped his horse and dismounted. Her gaze immediately took in the trees nearest them, looking for one large enough to hide behind so that she could rid herself of the bloodstone. A tall poplar stood about forty paces away. It was easily large enough to shield her and the evergreens crowded around it would help as well. Her palms were sweaty as she dismounted and made sure to lay his fur over the back of her horse. She missed its warmth already as a shiver ran through her.

Rolfe was busy lashing the reins to a tree so the horses wouldn't wander off to look at her. Thank goodness, because she could imagine how guilty she looked standing there, shifting from foot to foot, already breathless because her heart was pounding so hard. He must have noticed her stare, because he glanced over his shoulder at her. She said the only plausible thing she could think of to explain her fidgeting, 'I'm sorry. I wasn't able to use the… Do you mind if I take a moment before we start?' She glanced towards the tree.

He nodded, turning back to start unstrapping the wooden swords from his horse. She breathed a sigh of relief and hurried off in the direction of the poplar. It wasn't nearly far enough away to put her at ease, but her fear of discovery only made her move faster. Lifting her skirt once she was safely behind it, she reached beneath to untie the leather purse and breathed a sigh of relief when she pulled it free. At least now she could drop it beneath the limbs of a nearby tree if he came over. Just to make certain, she peered around the trunk of the tree, spying on him through the limbs of an evergreen to make sure he was still busy. He had finished untying the swords and was swinging one, she assumed to loosen his muscles, with his back to her.

Satisfied that she had a few more moments to herself, she brushed the leaves and needles aside with her foot and looked for a stick with which to dig a hole. If she came back with dirty fingers, she didn't know how she would explain that.

'Elswyth.' The harsh voice spoken so close behind her nearly made her scream in panic.

She turned with her arms raised to strike an attacker, but it was only Galan. 'Are you mad? He could see you,' she whispered.

Galan scowled in Rolfe's direction, but didn't leave her. 'Did you find it?'

'Aye. I think this is it.' She held out the purse and Galan took it, peering inside.

'It matches the description,' he confirmed. 'How did you get it?'

Her face burned as she answered him, 'I had to sneak into his chamber. It was hidden in a chest.'

Galan stared at her with a mixture of horror and anger shining from his eyes. 'Does he force you to share his bed?'

Somehow her blush deepened and spread to the rest of her body. She frowned, resenting the fact that Galan was questioning not only her methods, but her chastity as well. 'Nay. I was sent to tend his wound the first night. That's how I saw it. I sneaked back in last night after we spoke while he was below at the evening meal.' She glanced behind her, but couldn't see around the tree to tell what Rolfe was doing. 'What does it matter? You have to go.'

Galan glanced from her to the clearing where Rolfe was no doubt wondering what she was up to. He scowled and his eyes were fiercer than she'd ever seen them. 'Are you two alone?'

She nodded. 'But he won't try anything like what you're thinking. He's…he doesn't strike me as the sort to take advantage of a woman.' It was true. The Dane she had spent so much time fearing and even hating seemed to be honourable. She wouldn't have believed it herself had she not met him.

'Do not let yourself be fooled by a handsome face. I'm certain Mother thought the same thing and look where that got her. The Danes have no notion of honour. He wouldn't think twice about taking you here against your will.'

She flinched at the comparison. Would she spend her entire life proving to her family that she wasn't like her mother? 'He wouldn't do that,' she whispered vehemently, beginning to despair of ever finding peace between their people if everyone was like Galan and kept insisting on something that was plainly not true.

Galan didn't seem to be paying attention to her. He was staring between the evergreen needles, watching Rolfe. 'I could shoot the bastard right now if I had my bow.'

Despite herself, a wave of fear for Rolfe swept through her. 'You wouldn't kill an innocent man from behind.'

That made him look at her, his gaze seeming to see far more in her than she wanted to share. 'He's far from innocent, Elswyth. Don't ever forget that.' He looked back through the needles and his hand went to the handle of the axe strapped across his back. 'But you're right. I should kill him now, face to face, man to man.'

'Nay, Galan!' She gripped his arm to stay him, struggling to keep her voice low. 'You must go. Someone has to save Baldric. They could kill him if you don't return.'

He wavered, but finally lowered his arm

and turned to face her. 'You're right, Sister, as usual.' The moment of madness over, he gave her a brief smile and pulled her close. 'Take care of yourself. I vow to you that I will do all I can to save Baldric.' She didn't even have a chance to respond before he had disappeared into the depths of the forest.

Rolfe couldn't shake the feeling that something was wrong. There had been a wariness about Elswyth this morning that hadn't been present the day before. When he'd gently shaken her awake she'd looked upon him as if he'd come to do her harm. He could believe that was because it wasn't every morning a warrior came to pull you from your bed, except that her wariness had hardly changed as they rode to the clearing. Something had happened between their banter on the sparring field yesterday and this morning to put that caution in her eyes. Perhaps she had learned about what he had done in Banford.

He wanted to ask her. His nature was to be direct, but a subtle approach would work so much better, even though he despised ploys and artifice. If he could take them back to that place—the one they'd found the night of his bath before he'd known her identity—then he'd get further with her.

To do that, he'd have to forget who she was and he wasn't certain that was something he wanted to do. Something about her got under his skin so easily that she was dangerous to him. She could be a very big distraction. Wyborn picked his way around the trees, nosing through the dead leaves and foliage on the ground. A sound or movement that Rolfe wasn't aware of pricked his curiosity. The dog lowered his head towards the ground, his ears tilted forward as he faced the direction Elswyth had disappeared.

Something *was* wrong. Rolfe stared, unable to shake the feeling that someone was out there in the depths of the morning forest watching him. The hairs on the back of his neck raised in warning, so he dropped the wooden swords against the trunk of a tree and pulled his own sword from the sheath strapped on to his horse. Its familiar weight set heavy in his hand as he turned a slow circle, taking in the silence of the trees. Nothing moved. The weak rays of early sunlight that managed to penetrate the clouds and hazy fog showed him only grey.

For one tense moment he wasn't certain if Elswyth was in danger or if she was the one who had brought danger. Already his fascination with her was distracting him. Perhaps his instinct had been correct and she had found a way to bring her father and his men here to this clearing. He cursed himself for a fool for underestimating her as he listened for any sound to betray the danger. Just as he parted his lips to call to Elswyth, she stepped through the trees on her way back to him. He was struck motionless by the sight of her beauty. The dark smudges of her gracefully arched brows and long eyelashes stood out against the nearly ethereal glow of her face in the silver morning mist. Her eyes shimmered a depthless green in the grey light and the delicate curve of her cheekbones seemed emphasised beneath the smooth satin of her skin. Her mouth was a red swatch of colour that dropped open as she stared at him.

How had he only realised at just this moment how beautiful she was? He'd had a glimpse of it two nights ago in his chamber, but there she'd been turned golden and delectably human with the candlelight. Here the silver light made her look like a goddess stepping through the trees.

He swallowed thickly, shaken by the thought. She broke the spell when she looked over her shoulder to check the path behind her as she stepped into the clearing. Her gait had altered, not smooth and confident, but halting and worried. It was apparent that she was upset about something. Her eyes swung back around to settle on his sword, sliding along its length before coming up to meet his.

'Are you all right?' he asked into the growing silence. His thoughts turned to Hilde and how she had seemed gentle, all the while plotting behind his back. Was he doomed to only be attracted to women who would betray him?

She swallowed, her throat working before finding her voice. 'Aye.' She glanced back once more in the direction she'd come and he stepped closer. Wyborn hurried over to her, sniffing around the hem of her skirts as if he'd found new smells. She buried her fingers in his fur and knelt down to pet him, murmuring softly. From her place at his feet, she looked up at Rolfe. Her face seemed paler than was natural against the rich darkness of her hair.

'Are you ill?'

She shook her head and her gaze moved back to his sword. 'Are you planning to cure me with that if I am?' Her lips quirked upwards in a brief attempt at a smile as she rose to her full height, leaving Wyborn sniffing around her heels.

Appreciating the fact that the sword was menacing, especially to a Saxon woman who distrusted him, he slowly lowered it to his side. However, he didn't put it away, because he couldn't quite dismiss the feeling that something was wrong. Attempting a smile, he shook his head. 'It's more of a remedy than a cure.'

Her face went blank for a moment, but then she let out a burst of laughter as if she hadn't expected the humour. Colour rose in her cheeks and she wasn't quite so pallid any more. 'You're not what I expected, Dane.' Then as if the moment hadn't even happened, she stepped lightly around him to retrieve one of the wooden swords where they rested against a tree trunk. Turning towards him, she swung it out so that it was pointed right at him. With a nod towards the sword at his side, she said, 'I expect you'll have an unfair advantage if you're practising with the real thing.'

For the first time since she emerged from the forest, Rolfe found himself smiling genuinely and that feeling of unease drifted away in the face of her humour. 'Fortunately, I don't need a sword to hold the advantage. I already have it.' Stepping across the blanket of pine needles, he returned his sword to the sheath fastened to his saddle and retrieved a wooden sword.

'I'm surprised to hear such arrogance from a man who will be fighting with only one arm.' She nodded pointedly towards his left arm which was without its sling, though he still held it tucked against his side.

'It's much better.'

'But not healed. Perhaps we should postpone the sparring until you won't risk reopening the wound.' Her brow furrowed with concern and he found himself believing it to be genuine.

He swung the sword around with his right arm, loosening his wrist as he walked a slow circle around her. 'I apologise for my lack of a sling. My nurse was abed this morning and not able to help me.'

She smirked as she turned with him, her feet too close together and her posture far too rigid for proper combat. 'You're teasing me. You managed quite well yesterday morning without my help.'

Could that be jealousy flashing in her eyes? Probably not, but he couldn't help but goad her to make certain. 'Do you mean Claennis?' She was one of the girls brought from the villages to work at the great hall since the Danes had taken residence in Alvey. She'd dogged him relentlessly the previous winter and his absence had seemed to change nothing in regard to her intentions. The girl was free with her favours, but Rolfe was careful never to take his pleasure with a house servant. It led to bad feelings that close proximity didn't help when the girl eventually expected more than the occasional lay. Nevertheless, Claennis hadn't given up hope and had presented herself to him the morning after he'd returned home, before he'd even managed to pull himself from his bed. Instead of accepting her offer, he'd asked her to help him with the sling.

Elswyth raised her chin a notch. She probably didn't even realise that she had done it, but the movement revealed the long, smooth column of her throat and the soft, silken skin that disappeared beneath the high neck of her underdress. The urge to put his mouth there and taste her gripped him with a near-visceral force and refused to let him go. Across the sparse distance, he could see the flutter of her pulse and the way she swallowed hard. She *was* jealous. A flare of satisfaction moved through him, urging him to go to her. His boots scraped over the rough ground as he took a step away, not trusting himself in the grip of this sudden madness.

'Claennis does not share my bed.' He didn't know why the words came. One moment he was thinking of ways to prod her jealousy and in the next he'd admitted to the truth. 'She helped me with my sling.' He added that last as if it somehow erased the first.

Her full bottom lip dropped open the slightest bit, but enough to draw his gaze to settle on the lush curve. Fuller than its counterpart on top, it looked as soft as a flower's petal. He wanted to draw it into his mouth and scrape his teeth across it until she gasped in pleasure. Then he'd dip his tongue into her. She'd probably taste like honey from the cake. The knowledge sent a rush of blood to his groin.

He swallowed hard, bemused by his own thoughts. Elswyth was a challenge, a woman whom he was meant to seduce and here he was being seduced by her. And all she had done was hold a wooden sword on him and look at him as if he'd betrayed her in some way.

'I don't particularly care what you do with Claennis. It's no business of mine,' she lied. He could tell by the way her eyes dipped to the side as she spoke. He should be gratified that he had this hold on her—and a part of him relished it—but he found himself wanting to comfort her.

'I've brought the sling. Come help me with it?'

'Why didn't you say as much before now?' Her eyes flared with annoyance. 'You could have harmed yourself.'

He forced himself not to smile as he walked to his horse and retrieved the cloth from the sack tied to the saddle. She tossed the wooden sword to the side as she took it from him, drawing it out in lengths that she measured between her hands.

'Is Claennis the reason you left the poultice for me last night instead of seeing to my wound yourself?'

She hesitated. He probably wouldn't have noticed how her hands faltered in their manipulation of the linen if he hadn't been so intent on her every movement. The slender fingers paused, twisting the material, before picking up their previous rhythm and smoothing it out again. 'You seem far more concerned with Claennis than I,' she murmured. 'Last night I was tired and, anticipating the early morning, I went to bed rather than wait for you.'

She'd kept her eyes downcast so he couldn't tell if she was lying. When he opened his mouth to prod her further, she said, 'Lean down', and held the sling up so that she could put it over his head. He obliged and she set it against his right shoulder and held it down so that he could tuck his elbow into it. She made herself appear extraordinarily busy smoothing out the fabric and turning the edges so it sat just so against his chest.

'There, I only hope you haven't set yourself

back in healing time. The more you reopen the wound the longer it will take to mend.'

Her eyes were depthless pools of the deepest green when she looked up at him. An intoxicating mix of innocence and strength swirled within them. He could feel them tugging at him like a siren in a story he had heard once, tempting him to dive in and give himself over to her. At that moment he would have sworn that his instincts lied and she had no part in her father's crimes. It was proof that he lost his sense of right and wrong and duty when he was around her. Her hand had come to settle on his chest and the heat from her palm sank into him, seeping through the layers of his clothing.

The touch was so unexpected that he had to look down to make sure he hadn't imagined it. She jerked it away, curling her fingers towards her palm as if she hadn't realised what she'd done until he drew her attention to it, and he was sorry that he had moved at all. She looked stunned, her eyes wide and her lips parted.

'You don't have gloves?' he asked to break the strange awareness that had settled between the two of them. To bring attention to anything else except the way his heart pounded and his blood flowed thick and heavy through his veins.

She shook her head. 'Nay, I don't own a pair.'

He wasn't surprised. Leather gloves were expensive and, while not destitute, he was under the impression that despite being important to Alvey, either her farm didn't produce much wealth, or her father was a miserly sort.

As gently as if he were approaching a serpent, he took her wrist. She was fine boned so his fingers slipped around it effortlessly. She watched him without breathing, her chest still and her lips slightly parted. Bringing her hand to his, he placed their palms together. She had long graceful fingers, but he could still have closed the last joint of his fingers over the tip of hers. 'How did you ever make it through the winters?'

'My friend Osric made me a pair once, though they were more like wool sleeves that fit over the end of my fingers. They only lasted a couple of winters. Perhaps I'll request a new pair.' He released her as soon as she said the name and she gave him a hesitant smile as she took a step backwards, putting space between their awkwardness.

He didn't know why the name startled him. She was from Banford and it had been almost certain that she knew Osric, yet he hadn't expected such a personal connection between them. 'Osric?' he asked, because he couldn't let the name settle between them without comment.

She nodded and walked back to where she'd tossed her wooden sword. 'He works on my father's farm and is a good friend to me.'

Swallowing, he bent to pick up his own sparring sword while forcing himself to remember they were probably all traitors, including her. 'How good a friend is Osric?' he asked before he could stop himself.

She swung on him and would have hit him across his right shoulder had he not seen the movement from the corner of his eye and swung to block her. She seemed stunned, but ultimately impressed that she had been thwarted. A smile lightened her features. 'Not as good a friend as Claennis is to you,' she said with honeyed sweetness.

Osric had not bedded her. Rolfe knew that there were a hundred things he could have taken away from that statement, but somehow the most important was that they were not lovers. 'Claennis is not my friend.' The words came out as a grumble that made her laugh. The sound of her laughter unexpectedly tugged at some long-hidden knot within him, pulling at the tightly intertwined string until it loosened and he felt lighter than he had in a long time.

'He's only a few years older than I and he's worked on the farm as long as I can remember. He's like an older brother to me, only nicer, because Galan is frequently insufferable.' She kept her voice light and he didn't know if that was intentional or an indication of her affections for them both.

What would she think of him once she knew that Osric's brother was dead because of him? That he'd burned Osric's home? The significance of a battle that had been hardly more than a skirmish to him suddenly grew by a hundred. It settled like a weight on his chest, threatening to slowly squeeze the air from him.

'Loosen your stance. Your legs are too stiff and your knees too straight. One strong blow will knock you over.' His voice was coarse and harsh. Her eyes widened at the change, but she immediately tried to adjust her stance. He kept his voice more even as he explained, 'You must keep your limbs loose so that you can absorb the jolt of an impact.

'Good,' he praised when she complied. 'Hold the sword here.' He demonstrated with his own grip. 'Any lower and you can easily lose your grip. Higher and it will limit your range of motion.'

He made certain that there was no room for

idle talking for the rest of the lesson. The rules of his seduction had suddenly been changed and he didn't like it. He had known that she would despise him for his role in what had happened in Banford, but he had soothed himself with the knowledge that her anger would be rooted in misplaced pride. There was no wrong in his actions, no personal affront to her.

Only now he understood that she *would* take it personally. She would hate him for what he'd done.

Chapter Eight

'How was the sparring lesson this morning?' Lady Gwendolyn asked from her bath, giving Elswyth a sly smile as she ran a cloth over her shoulder.

Elswyth tried not to react, but she could feel her cheeks warm at the woman's tone. It was the same tone with which Ellan had asked her as soon as they'd returned that morning. Somehow she didn't think a hastily mumbled, 'It was fine', would suffice here. The range of emotions she'd experienced this morning had left her quite drained and unable to fully understand what she felt towards Rolfe. She'd gone from absolute terror that the warrior would find out about the stolen bloodstone, to jealousy about Claennis, to an awareness of him as a man that she hadn't been able to shake. The lesson with the sword had hardly signified after all of that.

She sat with baby Tova on the floor of the chamber Lady Gwendolyn shared with her husband, playing with the baby who crawled around her. She delighted in pulling a soft, thinly woven wool blanket over her head so that Elswyth could find her. 'Where is Tova? Wasn't she just here?' she said with a lilting voice. Tova pulled the blanket down to reveal herself, grinning widely to show several white milk teeth. Elswyth pretended to be surprised and the girl fell over with laughter. Her laugh never failed to make Elswyth laugh along with her.

But Lady Gwendolyn expected an answer. Though she smiled indulgently at Elswyth and her daughter, when the moment had passed, she looked at Elswyth with a raised eyebrow. 'It was fine.' A quick glance confirmed that the lady did indeed expect more in the way of an answer. 'I'm merely sceptical of how much I can learn in less than a fortnight.' She busied herself with folding up the blanket. Tova liked it better when she could unfold it before hiding under it.

Lady Gwendolyn went back to her washing, but the pregnant silence let her know that the conversation wasn't over.

'What do you think of Rolfe?' Lady Gwendolyn finally asked.

There was a question rife with difficulty. 'He's a fine teacher. Patient and not too demanding, especially when I do something wrong.' Much to her chagrin, the sword didn't seem to come to her as easily as the axe or the bow and arrow. Or perhaps she'd been too distracted by Rolfe to concentrate properly on her lesson.

'That's good to know.' There seemed to be a sliver of impatience in her voice, but Elswyth wasn't certain if she had only imagined it. 'Anything else?'

Elswyth shrugged as she set the blanket aside and watched Tova start to unravel it. 'He seems to be a great warrior. I've been impressed with the men under his command. They respect him and he respects them.' That was saying a lot actually. Her own father frequently became impatient with his men and was given to bouts of shouting at them. She had yet to see such behaviour from Rolfe. Of course his men were well trained and hardly needed the admonishment.

Lady Gwendolyn laughed. 'You know that's not what I'm asking you, Elswyth. What do you think of him…as a man?'

Not only were her cheeks flaming now, but the heat had spread to her neck and chest. Nevertheless, she made herself answer, because she knew that Lady Gwendolyn wouldn't be put off as easily as Ellan had been. She'd keep asking, because it was likely that she was in on this whole marriage idea. Besides, she liked Lady Gwendolyn. They'd developed an easy friendship in the time Elswyth had been here. 'He's powerful…and kind…and an impressive warrior. His men respect him—oh, fine.' She rolled her eyes at her lady's narrowed gaze. 'He's very handsome.'

The woman smiled knowingly. 'And you find favour with him?'

'Aye.' She was surprised to find her voice hoarse. A knot of guilt tightened in the pit of her stomach as she thought of her mother and what her attraction to a Dane had caused. Nothing good would come of this.

'That's good.' The relief in the woman's voice was so evident that it made Elswyth look away from the blanket-covered Tova to meet her gaze. 'I think he finds favour with you as well.'

'Why does that matter, my lady?' She swallowed against the tightness in her throat. She wanted to hear the woman give voice to the idea of their marriage, to confirm or deny the intention.

Tova peeked out at her from the blanket, so Elswyth went through the motions of trying to find her until the baby yanked the blanket off. The entire time her heart pounded as she wondered what this line of questioning meant. Was she being given to Rolfe? In some deep dark place inside her the thought appealed to her, which left her terrified.

'Come attend me, Elswyth.' Finished with her bath, Lady Gwendolyn stood and Elswyth walked over to wrap a light piece of sheeting around her. Tova was tired of her game by this time and crawled over to the edge of the rug to play with her wooden spinning figures on the hard floor.

After drying her body, Lady Gwendolyn secured the end of the sheet between her breasts and surprised Elswyth by taking her hand and leading her to the bed. She sat at the corner and indicated that Elswyth should take a seat next to her. 'I'd like to talk to you about marriage, Elswyth.'

With those words her heart began to beat in double its normal rhythm.

'Do you know how Lord Vidar and I have offered coin and gifts to Saxon and Dane couples who marry?' At Elswyth's nod, she continued, 'We've had some success with this, but we'd like even more success. For that reason, we've asked some of our best warriors—including

Rolfe—to take Saxon wives. We feel this is the best way to foster peace between our people.'

'I understand. I don't think I did until I came here, but I've seen how your own marriage has helped bring peace to Alvey. My father would have me believe that peace isn't possible and I confess that I once thought that was true, but you've opened my eyes to how well it can work in certain circumstances.'

Lady Gwendolyn smiled at that. 'It warms me to hear you say that. You've become a friend to me, Elswyth, and I couldn't bear it if you harboured ill feelings for me and my husband.'

Elswyth was shaking her head before she'd even finished speaking. 'Nay, my lady. I could never harbour those feelings for you. I admit that Lord Vidar, being a Dane, is a bit rough for me sometimes, but he treats you well and I can see the affection between you both.'

'Good.' She bit her lip in a rare moment of uncertainty, but then pushed on. 'I'd hoped to hear you say this, because it is my belief that Rolfe could be a good husband to you.'

Those were the words Elswyth had expected all along, but hearing them was far more potent than she'd imagined. In an instant she saw herself with him…sitting at the long table at his side, riding with him across the plains near the sea, walking hand in hand with him in the for-est…in every imagining he was smiling at her as he had that first night in his chamber. He was smiling because she knew that he would be kind and gentle with her as he had always been, not the monster that Galan and Father made him out to be. And just like that her imaginings dis-appeared, thoughts of her family chasing them away. She couldn't betray them. She wouldn't.

Thoughts of her mother, her father's meet-ings with the Scots and her own duplicity in taking the bloodstone swept through her. She sucked in a breath, but it moved in jerks and starts over the serrated edges of her regret. 'I believe that you're right. Rolfe would make a good husband…but not for me.'

The light in Lady Gwendolyn's eyes dimmed and her shoulders slumped as if Elswyth's re-jection had taken the air from her. 'But why ever not?'

'He…' The word had no sound, so she cleared her throat and tried again. 'He is a Dane, my lady. I could never marry a Dane.' Had this conversation taken place before she'd met Rolfe those words would have come out strong and high with the full force of Elswyth's conviction behind them. As it was, she was forced to say them now…after she had met Rolfe and knew how honourable he was. It didn't matter that she'd said the same thing to the man himself this morning. The words didn't come any easier.

'Because of your father?' Lady Gwendolyn prodded.

It would be so easy to say aye and end it there, but it wasn't the complete truth. She had worked too hard since Mother's abandonment to show everyone in Banford that she wasn't like her. Her mother might have been faithless and vain, but *she* was good and noble and would put her family first. She wasn't a silly girl to allow a handsome face to sway her. What would the people who had been her entire world since birth think of her if she turned her back on them now by marrying a Dane?

'Nay, my lady. You have chosen a Dane for a husband and I can respect your choice. I, however, cannot overlook what they've done. They are our enemy and I cannot marry one of them.'

A hand rose to Lady Gwendolyn's chest. She was clearly unprepared for the harsh declaration. 'I'm sorry, Elswyth. I had no idea that your feelings were so strong. Do you hate them, then? All Danes?'

Elswyth nodded.

'What of Tova?'

The question brought Elswyth head up

sharply. 'Nay, my lady. Never could I hate Tova.' Hearing her name, the baby made her way over to them with an adorable smile on her face.

'She has as much of her father's blood in her veins as she has mine. Many would say that makes her a Dane.'

'Nay. I didn't mean that. I do not hate Lord Vidar or even Rolfe.' It was true. She'd been genuinely afraid for Rolfe when Galan had threatened him. Tova reached for her skirt and pulled herself up, smiling proudly as she stood holding on to Elswyth's knees. Elswyth took the child up into her lap and hugged her close. The soft golden curls on top of the baby's head tickled her chin. 'I only meant that I despise their actions.'

'What do you despise?' Lady Gwendolyn kept her voice soft, but Elswyth knew that she had hurt her.

'That we are forced to do their bidding or face death.'

'I wouldn't say it with such dramatics, but we are all at the mercy of someone. Had I married a Saxon man to be lord here, the same rules would need to be followed.'

'But there's the crux, my lady. Forgive me,

but if you had married a Saxon man then he would be one of us. Not one of them.'

Lady Gwendolyn was silent for a moment, a myriad of emotions crossing her features. Elswyth wondered if she might have gone a step too far and ruined the friendship she had come to hold dear. Finally, Lady Gwendolyn said, 'They are not so different than us, Elswyth. Rolfe may be the leader of the warriors, but he's a gentle man. The choice is yours, but do not discount him as an option so quickly.'

'I fear that Elswyth isn't quite as amiable to a wedding as I had hoped,' said Lady Gwendolyn later that evening at the long table in the hall.

Rolfe tried to hide the smile tugging at the corners of his mouth, but he failed miserably. How anyone who knew Elswyth could assume that she would be agreeable to marrying a Dane was beyond him.

'We knew the girl held a dislike for us, love. It's no secret.' Vidar matched Rolfe's smile as he looked adoringly at his wife.

'Of course we knew, but she seemed so reasonable. I thought—naively, it seems—that she would agree to a marriage.'

'Has she told you nay?' Rolfe asked, curious about the details of their conversation. He wasn't surprised at her refusal, since she'd told him as much this morning, but he wondered what Lady Gwendolyn planned to do about it.

'In so many words.'

Vidar frowned, his glance moving to the newly constructed gallery above them where Rolfe's chamber was along with the alcoves. The woman in question had disappeared to the space she shared with her sister after the evening meal. The heavy curtain that hid their sleeping alcove was closed. 'What of Ellan? She seems agreeable to taking a Dane warrior as husband. I've seen her talking with quite a few of them.'

Lady Gwendolyn nodded. 'I've thought of that, but you remember when we approached Godric with the offer to bring them here. It was Elswyth who has his respect, as well as that of her people. Ellan is a charming girl, but the alliance wouldn't have as much consequence with her.'

Something inside him revolted at the idea of exchanging Elswyth for Ellan. Rolfe and Vidar shared a glance, their earlier conversation about forcing an alliance weighing heavily on Rolfe's mind. He liked Elswyth well enough. This morning had made him admit exactly how much he desired her. However, nothing had changed with respect to how he felt about marrying a spy.

'Have you mentioned an alliance with her father?' Rolfe asked. 'This whole discussion could be inconsequential if he opposes it.'

Vidar and Lady Gwendolyn exchanged a look that set Rolfe on edge. The look clearly said that they had been plotting. 'It's time for me to confess,' Lady Gwendolyn said. 'I had hoped to have Elswyth agree to the marriage without consulting her father. With her on our side, I assumed that the wedding was a certainty. She'd either get his agreement, or marry you anyway and damn the consequences. No one—aside from her father—in Banford would oppose the union if it's what she wanted.'

The table was silent for a moment. Many of the men had settled down to sleep on the benches at the perimeter of the room, but some still huddled around tables, playing dice games. After a while, Vidar said, 'We may have no choice but to force her.' It was stated with quiet conviction, but it made Lady Gwendolyn take in a sharp breath.

'I could not,' she said.

'Not even if it would save lives?' Vidar asked.

She looked uncomfortable, but she didn't say anything as her concerned gaze trailed off to the curtained alcove above them. Rolfe swallowed thickly as he renewed his commitment to his quest to prove or disprove her guilt. 'It's not a question we have to answer now,' he began. 'Give me a few days with her and we'll revisit the dilemma.'

He'd come to a grim conclusion. He'd bed her if that's what it took to get her to confess. If she confessed to being a spy, then the question of marriage was moot. If she was innocent, then bedding her would almost assure her cooperation in a marriage that would benefit everyone. He'd have an entirely new problem on his hands—how to take her as his wife while keeping his distance from her—but he'd deal with that when and if the time came.

Duty would always come first.

Chapter Nine

Rolfe stared down at the face that was quickly starting to take over his every spare thought. Thick, sooty lashes laid in a crescent over pale cheeks, drawing his attention to her near-perfect skin. It was smooth like the ivory handle of the knife he'd bought in Hedeby years ago. Only he knew that unlike the knife that was perpetually cool to the touch, her skin would be warm and soft. His fingertips ached to touch her, to feel the difference in the textures of the smooth skin covering the curve of her cheek and the silken heat of her lips. Her pink lips were parted as she took in deep, sleeping breaths. They looked soft and inviting, making him ache to cover them with his own and wake her with a kiss.

He shook himself from that fantasy before it could take root. He couldn't be seduced by her or any woman. Infatuation made him weak and he refused to allow the emotion to wreak havoc with his life again. He had so much more to lose this time. It was imperative that he kept control.

The woman slept like a child. He'd called her softly from outside of the curtained alcove to no effect. She and her sister both slumbered on, lost in dreams. He'd been forced to come inside as he had the previous morning and shake her awake, only she hadn't responded to his first attempt, which had given him ample time to become distracted by her.

'Saxon.' He raised his voice to slightly higher than a whisper and gave a gentle nudge to her shoulder.

She sighed and smiled in her sleep, turning on to her side to face him. Her warm breath feathered across his wrist, causing an uncomfortable stirring deep in his gut and a tightening farther down that made him crouch to hide any indication of what she had done to him. Surrendering to temptation, he allowed the tip of one finger to trace across her cheekbone. It was as warm and smooth as he'd expected. What he hadn't expected was how that warmth slid across his palm and up his arm in a low flame that burned hotter and faster than he'd ever experienced. He drew his hand back almost as if she'd burned him.

'Wake up, Saxon.' His voice was rather ineffectually hoarse and low, but she managed to hear him this time none the less.

'Rolfe,' she whispered in a voice husky with sleep. Her eyelids fluttered, but didn't open, lost as she was in that dream-filled place between wakefulness and sleep. The sound of his name in her mouth made him bite back a groan as it brought his body to full awareness of her. If they were in bed together, he'd have rolled her beneath him and found that sweet place between her thighs with his fingers, parting her to receive him. He'd kiss her awake as he nudged inside her.

As it was, he was nothing but a lecher, desiring a sleeping woman who had no idea he was here. He forced himself to swallow down his lust. There were better ways to use this unexpected gift of sleep, if only he could focus on his mission with her and stop behaving like a besotted fool. The way she affected him was nothing short of extraordinary. All his life he'd known control and discipline, but she brought something out in him that he'd rather forget existed. Hilde was the only other woman to do this to him.

As a simple farm boy turned warrior, he'd not been nearly good enough for the beautiful daughter of a jarl, but he'd wanted her anyway. In the two years he'd worked under her father as a warrior and oarsman, he'd kept every bit of coin he had earned in the hopes of having enough to be worthy of her. Rolfe had worked harder than any other man and in that short time had gained enough to earn the Jarl's grudging respect. Hilde had noticed him as well.

Eventually, she had begun to welcome his attentions, sneaking away to meet him when she could. Soon they had become lovers and she'd agreed to be his wife. Knowing that her father would never agree to their marriage, they planned to sneak away and come back in a month when her father would have no choice but to accept. Rolfe had no doubts that he would have, because Rolfe had proven himself and had double the required coin for her bride price.

But on the night they were to meet, she walked into the clearing cwith several of her father's men at her back, one of them a man named Bjorn who Rolfe had fought with before. She'd very calmly told him that she'd had another offer of marriage. Bjorn had smiled broadly as he stepped forward and put his arm around her, but it was her smile that had wounded Rolfe. She'd turned and left, leaving him to defend himself against Bjorn and the others. It was hardly a fair fight, eight against one, and they had beaten him until he'd blacked out.

Rolfe had awakened early the next morning with his coin and sword missing. Bloodied, bruised, and left with nothing, it had taken him several days to make the trip to his family's farm. On that long and agonising trip, he'd vowed to never let a woman deceive him again. As soon as he was able, he'd left to join with Jarl Hegard, and then Vidar, vowing to himself that he would become a warrior with whom to be reckoned. Now, years later, he commanded an army of warriors, yet one slip of a girl was on the verge of reducing him to the fool he had been.

Nay, he wouldn't allow it to happen, especially not with Elswyth, who was almost certainly a traitor. Pushing those useless thoughts from his mind, he forced himself to focus on the task at hand. 'Why are you here, Saxon?'

'Hmm…' was her completely useless reply. The sound of her voice whispered pleasantly over his skin.

Appreciating the fact that this was a very inept way to get information, he decided to try again as his usual methods of physical force and violence were unavailable to him. 'Are you here to obtain information?'

'Information,' she repeated, though the end of the word was rather garbled in her sleep.

'Aye, information about us.' He kept his voice gentle so it sounded coaxing rather than accusing. 'About the Danes... Lord Vidar...me...'

'Only you, Rolfe.' Her lips curved in another smile.

He frowned. Her father had probably wanted to know where they'd gone over the summer. It could be no secret that a large contingency of warriors had ridden out at the beginning of summer. Understanding that he would probably only get basic answers from her now with no detail, he decided to change subjects. 'Have you met with the Scots?'

'No Scots...just you.'

His frown deepened. What was he supposed to make of that? As he was trying to make sense of it, she surprised him by taking his hand in hers. It was the hand he'd touched her with and, instead of putting it away from her as he should have, he'd curled his fingers into the edge of her mattress where she'd found it. Scarcely daring to breathe, he tracked the movement as she set his hand to her cheek, settling his fingers there and covering them with her own. Despite his intentions, he allowed them to stay and even savoured the feel of her, warmth and velvet, beneath his fingertips.

'I would marry you, Rolfe.'

The words had been so distinct and clear, his gaze flew to her eyes, expecting to find her awake and watching him. However, she slept on, though she turned her face more fully into his hand until her mouth nearly brushed against the heel and her nose tickled his palm. She was stroking herself against him, he realised with a start, and an answering smoulder started deep in his belly. His breaths came heavy and harsh.

'You will marry me,' he repeated. He didn't know if the words were a promise or a hope as his thumb traced over the silky curve of her lips. She hadn't been talking about spying or information all this time. She'd been talking about him and this strange bond they seemed to have.

She smiled at the sensation of his touch and her hot breath caressed him when she whispered, 'Aye.'

Guilt that he had expected something far worse from her dropped into his stomach and settled there like a stone. A wave of fierce protection washed over him, as he saw her as the girl she was the night she had come to tend his wound. Nothing more. But he didn't know that for certain and the warrior in him couldn't let go of the idea that she could be a spy until he knew for certain.

Gently drawing his hand back, he called to her in a firmer voice, 'Elswyth, we must go.'

The sound of her name finally roused her. She sat up halfway, resting on her elbows. Her gaze wandered over the small alcove disoriented until she set her eyes on him. They widened slightly, but her face was still slack with sleep. 'Rolfe?'

He tried not to notice the way her breasts pressed against her linen nightdress, the only clothing she appeared to be wearing. Even in the deep shadows, he caught a glimpse of a pebbled nipple pushing against the fabric. 'You sleep like the dead.'

'What are you doing here?'

'Waking you so that we can continue your lessons.' When she looked at him with a question in her eyes, he clarified, 'The sword.'

The last remnants of sleep left her as her mouth dropped open in understanding. 'I didn't think you would want to continue…after yesterday.' After she'd told him in no uncertain terms that she didn't plan to marry a Dane, including him.

The blanket shifted as she sat up fully, falling farther into her lap. The laces of her night-dress were supposed to be tied at her throat but had come apart during the night so that it gaped open, revealing the soft swells of her breasts, but stopping just short of exposing her nipples. He sucked in a fierce breath and turned his head away from the sight as hot lust poured through him. He wanted to forget the lesson, take her in his arms and carry her back to his bed. Determining if she was a spy had very little to do with his desire.

'Meet me downstairs if you still want to learn. I have the horses waiting.' He left before he could make his thoughts a reality.

Elswyth hurried to get dressed, making Ellan grumble in protest as she turned her back and pulled the blanket over her head. She had assumed that Rolfe had only offered to teach her the sword because he'd hoped to soften her to him so that she would agree to marriage. The last thing she'd expected was for him to wake her this morning. As she'd stared at him beside her bed, she had realised exactly how pleased she was to see him and how much she wanted to learn from him. It was the only way she could explain how her heart had leapt to life in her chest at seeing him next to her bed. It wasn't fear of discovery as it had been the day before when she'd worried he'd found out his blood-stone was missing. It was excitement.

It had to be eagerness to continue her lesson. It could *not* have anything to do with how she had lain awake last night, tossing and turning as she had relived her conversation with Lady Gwendolyn in her head. Once, she had closed her eyes and allowed herself to imagine what it would be like to be his wife. Those thoughts had inevitably made her think of all the tender and good things about him. The dimple when he smiled…how often he seemed to smile at her…the gentle but firm way he instructed her with the sword. He was patient but command-ing in his instruction, which were attributes she greatly admired. A few times his hand had gone to her waist, or better yet, touched her hand to adjust her grip and his touch had been very nice, warm and firm, but gentle. Always gentle.

Her Viking warrior was the most gentle man she'd ever met.

If he were Saxon she was afraid that she'd have eagerly agreed to wed him. Even now the thought of that sent a thrill shooting through her belly, because it made her think of his nude body. She'd probably see much more of it if they were wed, perhaps even his front side. She giggled to herself, much to the annoyance of Ellan who mumbled from under the blanket.

Tying the end of her braid off with a piece of linen, she hurried out the curtain and down the steps to the front door. She felt as though she was floating and barely noticed the men sleeping in the hall. Rolfe was waiting for her as he'd been the day before with Gyllir and Sleipnir saddled and ready, and Wyborn in tow. As she stepped up to him, aware of the embarrassing way her face was glowing, he put the fur cloak around her shoulders. She went to mount, but he stopped her and pulled out a pair of leather gloves. The kid skin looked soft and supple. Without asking, he took her left hand as if he intended to place the glove on her hand.

So this was why he had held his palm up to hers yesterday. He'd been measuring her hand against his to size the gloves. 'Is that for me? I cannot accept such a gift.'

He seemed surprised when he glanced at her. 'Why not? It's cold and you'll need warm hands to grip the sword.'

'The expense…they're too fine.'

He shrugged and reached for her fingers again. 'It's nothing. I had the leather anyway. They're not that fine, they were made very fast.'

She knew that he spoke the truth because

she'd seen a few different bolts of leather when she'd searched his chamber. The guilt of accepting his gift after having stolen from him, combined with her suspicion of him, made her draw her fingers away from him again. 'Nay, I cannot accept.' His brow furrowed deeply in question. 'It's…it's been my experience that men only give gifts when they expect something in return,' she explained.

He met her gaze, those vivid blue eyes staring right into her as if to pull out all of her secrets. 'Did Osric expect something from you in return?'

Shocked that he would bring up her friend again, she paused to stare at him. His handsome features were solemn as he stared back. Some small part of her wanted to believe that she had heard jealousy in his tone, but she knew that couldn't be true. He had no reason to be jealous. They hardly knew one another. But then she'd had no reason to be jealous of Claennis, yet the fire of her jealousy had burned through her veins.

His gaze dropped to her mouth and she took in a ragged breath. When she'd awakened, she had felt the soft remains of a weight on her lips, as if he'd stroked over them. The remembered heat left behind from his imagined touch warmed her now, coming to life even though she knew that she had made it up.

'I believe that he also wants marriage,' she whispered.

His eyes jerked back to hers, this time with a fire burning in their depths. 'Are you promised to him?' The skin over his cheekbones tightened as he clenched his jaw.

'Nay. My father might wish it, but he's not the one I want.'

'Even though he's Saxon?' he surprised her by asking the impertinent question.

She might have taken offence had the sparkle of humour not returned to his eyes. Instead, she found herself shaking her head. 'It's not my only requirement for a husband.'

He raised an eyebrow in question and proceeded to help her put on the glove. This time she let him. 'But it is the most important one.'

She took in the breadth of his shoulders as she answered him. 'Nay, he must also be a fine warrior, strong and kind, generous and noble. Brave and patient.' It was only after she said those things that she understood she had described all the attributes she had come to associate with Rolfe.

'You find me lacking in those qualities?' He gently took hold of her other hand and helped her with the glove. Her palm tingled with warmth as his fingertips stroked over it. By the time he'd finished helping her put the gloves on, all traces of cold were gone.

'Nay, you're not lacking.' She honestly couldn't say that he lacked any one of those.

'Then it's only that I'm a Dane?'

He stood so closely that she should have felt dwarfed by him, or at least intimidated. He didn't make her feel either of those. She felt alive in a way she never had before and safe when he was near. 'You have to admit that it's a very large shortcoming.'

He laughed and the white puff of his breath brushed across her cheek. 'If I were Saxon... would you marry me?'

Even though she had known the question was coming, nothing could have prepared her for the way she felt when he asked it. The words asked too much, were too probing and personal, yet she could feel the truth begging to come out. It was as if she needed to compensate for the lies of omission she was forced to tell him by being completely honest with him in every other way. No other man had ever made her want to entertain marriage before. No other man had ever excited her in any way. Only Rolfe. Only the man most unsuitable for her.

'Aye.'

It was little more than a breath, but he heard, his vivid blue eyes widening slightly. His own breath sucked in sharply and his body seemed to vibrate with something he was trying desperately to contain. It felt right to say it and acknowledge what was between them. A weight lifted from her chest and she felt a moment of near euphoria as she allowed herself that brief instant to imagine, out in the open, how it could be with them.

'You understand that you've just issued me a challenge, Saxon?'

The slight hitch in her breath was only from the cold, she tried to assure herself. It had nothing to do with the excitement flooding her veins. His brows had narrowed, his gaze had gone intense with hunger and become slightly proprietary. For all that, she still felt safe, because there was a gentleness beneath it all. The way his gaze stroked her features was as tender as a caress. She might have stoked the beast inside him to life, but he'd never hurt her.

'Challenge?' She smiled, drawing strength from her certainty.

'To make you say aye, even though I will always be a Dane.'

'Have I?' Her smile widening, she shrugged and left him standing there as she went to mount the horse he had brought for her.

Chapter Ten

'Keep your weight centred here.' Rolfe's hands settled on Elswyth's hips and tightened as he moved her slowly from side to side. 'Your knees should stay loose so that you can move about freely, but your middle must stay solid.' One hand slipped around to her front to rest on her lower belly. Her muscles there instinctively tensed even more, drawing as taut as the string of a bow. Her grip on the hilt of the wooden sword tightened as pulses of awareness shot through her core. 'Now try again,' his deep voice wafted past her ear just before he stepped back to give her space.

She blinked furiously, trying to make herself focus on the grooves he had carved into the tree she was currently battering. Her task was to hit each one of them in a series of rapid whacks with the blunt wooden sword. Unfortunately, his touch had wrecked the little bit of concentration she'd been able to scrape together. After the question of marriage had been raised again, she'd had a difficult time thinking of anything else all morning.

'Better,' he praised her and walked around so that she could see him from the corner of her eyes. 'Try it with more force this time.'

She whacked, but the impact vibrated painfully up her arm.

'The trick is to move with the blow. Hit from your middle, not your arms. Keep them loose. It might help if you imagine the tree is a Dane.' The smile in his voice nearly made her smile as she swung again. This time she hit the marks with less effort and more force.

'Perfect.'

She couldn't hold back her smile and affected a mock bow. 'I'm glad to have met with my lord's approval.' Straightening, she added, 'Ah, I forgot, you're no lord.' He laughed when she teased him with his words from their first meeting. The deep sound suffused her with pleasure.

'Come and take a rest. You've earned it.' He walked to the nearby tree where he'd placed the packs which had contained their breakfast. A skein of water sat beside the pack, along with Wyborn who had grown bored with watching their antics and laid napping. He awoke when Rolfe retrieved the skein, unstoppered it and held it out for her. She drank gratefully as she watched Rolfe rub Wyborn's head in affection. Stray snowflakes had begun to fall as the morning had worn on and a few of them rested in the mongrel's dark coat.

Finished slaking her thirst, she handed it back to Rolfe and took a seat on the pine needles. Wyborn gave her hand a sniff so she held it still for him, only petting his head when he'd nosed her palm.

'He's warmed up to you quite fast,' Rolfe observed.

'I'm fond of dogs. We have a few at home. They help tell the sheep what's what.' She made the mistake of looking up into his eyes. Their colour never failed to strike her. To distract from the way he affected her, she asked, 'How old is he?'

'Almost three winters. I found him as a pup. We were south, outside York, driving the Saxons back and I came across a muddy lump of fur howling pitifully in a field. Sleipnir nearly trampled him. There were no litter mates around and no mother that I could find.'

'So you kept him.' She finished the thought for him. It was so easy to imagine this tender giant of a man showing kindness to such a piti-ful creature. 'It explains why he's so devoted to you. He follows you endlessly.'

The ghost of a smile shaped his mouth, draw-ing her gaze to the well-formed ridge of his top lip. The short bristle of gold hair there held her attention as she wondered if it would be hard or soft against her skin if they were to kiss.

'He refused to leave me even after he was old enough to be on his way.' Rolfe stroked the dog's thick coat in obvious affection. 'But I've found he can be quite useful at times. He's saved my hide more than once.'

'You were kind to take him in when you found him.'

He shook his head, meeting her gaze again. 'It wasn't kindness. There is nothing noble in leaving an innocent to suffer needlessly.'

He said it with such quiet conviction that she knew he spoke true. His sense of honour was one thing that had attracted her to him from the beginning. It wasn't kindness that had made him do it. It was duty. As much as she admired that about him, it was making it difficult to keep herself away from him. This would all be much easier if he was abhorrent and easy to hate. Honestly, it was becoming easier and easier to forget that he was a Dane. Perhaps if

Father met him, he would understand that Rolfe was nothing like the Danes they despised.

'What are you thinking?' he asked, his perceptive gaze picking up her unsettled thoughts.

Caught up in the relentless need to be as noble as he, she answered honestly. 'That I wish you weren't a Dane.' If he was a Saxon, she'd have never been put in the awful position of plotting against him. Would he look at her so gently if he knew she'd stolen from him? That she'd been sent to spy on him? Beneath it all was a deep-seated insecurity that had been present since her mother's abandonment: How could he want *her*? She was no one important.

He sensed there was more to her words and his gaze dropped down to her mouth before gliding back up to her eyes. 'Perhaps if you close your eyes you can pretend.' His voice held a dry edge of humour, but his eyes were fathomless and intense.

Somehow in the next instance, they were leaning over Wyborn, so close together that she could smell the sweet honey from the morning cake on his breath. She had no recollection of moving, but his mouth hovered over hers and she let her eyes fall closed. The butterflies in her stomach leapt for joy when his warm breath caressed her lips. In the next instance, his mouth pressed tenderly against hers. She'd never dreamed that his lips could feel so soft. They moved over hers in a gentle caress, searching and slow, but it wasn't enough for either of them. A sound she didn't recognise came from her throat and he moved to touch her neck, cupping the back of her head in his large hand and tilting her slightly.

His lips became searching, moving in gentle brushes along the rim of hers and taunting her with the promise of more. She'd never been kissed before and had only once or twice come upon Ellan kissing some boy, but she'd never thought that it could feel this way. It was lovely and gentle. The soft bristles of his short beard occasionally rasped against her smooth skin, but the sensation was pleasant, exciting even, scattering bolts of awareness that seemed to shoot all through her body with each touch. Even her fingertips and toes tingled with the pleasure.

This is why Ellan kisses boys. It was heavenly.

'Is it working?' he whispered against her lips.

She was so lost in the moment she barely knew what he meant, but a mumbled, 'Aye', tumbled past her lips none the less. Saxon or Dane, all that mattered was that Rolfe was kissing her. Before she could stop herself or think better of it, she chased him, her mouth finding his and searching for more. Much to her delight, he obliged her, pushing his hand up farther on her scalp so that he cupped the back of her head to hold her for his pleasure. An animal sound came from his throat, low and rough, but exciting her. It sent a pulse of excitement to some place deep between her thighs. She put a hand on his chest to steady herself and was pleased to feel his heart pounding as fast as her own.

Something wet and smooth touched her bottom lip. The feeling was so strange and unexpected that she jumped back slightly. His fingers tightened in her hair, pulling pleasurably as he brought her back to him. 'Shh...' he soothed, his lips brushing hers as he spoke. 'Open to me.' The harsh rasp of his voice was her undoing. The need and textured longing made her want to do anything to please him, so she complied with his request and parted her lips, though she had no idea why he'd want her to do such a thing.

The hot wetness stroked her again, sliding across her bottom lip before dipping inside, the contrast between the smooth and rough texture revealing to her that it was his tongue. His tongue! The first thought that went through her mind was that no Saxon would ever kiss this way. It was barbaric and it served her right for ever thinking for a moment that she could convince herself that he wasn't a Dane.

She should stop him…she meant to stop him. Only his tongue chose *that moment* to brush against her own. The slick glide was pure wickedness that left embers of heat crackling where he'd touched her. She made a sound of surprise, but he must have taken it as assent because it made him brush his tongue against hers again. This time he moved in a soft and silky rhythm, in and out, parrying with the tip of her tongue.

He might have been giving the bulk of his attention to her mouth, but her entire body throbbed to vibrant life. Every skilful thrust of his tongue caused a reaction some place else. Her breasts swelled and tightened, her stomach fluttered and farther down her body turned molten, slickening, aching for him in a way she'd never felt before.

Hesitant but somehow wanting more of the delicious torment, she touched him back, chasing his tongue with hers and delighting in the friction of their tongues sliding against each other. Shifting her weight to better reach him, she tightened her grip on his tunic and apparently displeased Wyborn, because he made a sound of discontent and shoved out from between them. They broke apart, her gaze falling to the dog who came to his feet and stretched, one paw sticking out behind him, before he trotted off to the opposite side of the clearing, sniffing the ground to look for a good spot to relieve himself.

Only when he'd sniffed his way around the trunk of an oak did she become aware of the rather large male next to her. His breaths came in deep, heaving pants that made his chest move up and down. His eyes were alive with a fierce hunger she'd never seen in him before. He'd always been so reserved and controlled with her. The pupils of his eyes had expanded, making the vivid blue appear darker. The way he looked at her made her feel like prey and he was the predator waiting to eat her up. By some perversity she couldn't begin to fathom, she liked that feeling, wanted to savour it. It made her think that she might enjoy being devoured by him.

As soon as the wicked thought crossed her mind, her face flamed with shame. This. This was the wicked temptation that had led her own mother astray. He was her enemy and for those few moments it hadn't mattered that he was a Dane. She'd have given him anything he wanted.

Was this how Mother had felt? Had this strange pleasure turned a once loving woman into someone who could turn her back on her entire family? With a clarity often born of experience, Elswyth understood that this was exactly what had happened. Her mother had traded her dreary life at home for the excitement of a Dane who had tempted her beyond her resistance. Worse... Elswyth could feel that same allure snaking itself around her, digging its roots into her and pulling her to the man at her side. She was just like her mother, maybe worse in some ways, because she had known of this temptation and had allowed it to happen anyway.

Shaking her head to deny it, she asked, 'How could you kiss me like that?' It was as sharp as an accusation.

The space between his brows became very small as he looked down at her. 'Like what?'

'Like...like a heathen. I am a Saxon and I won't be treated like a...a...'

'Dane?' He filled in the silence with the only obvious answer.

She shook her head, unable to reply.

The sardonic humour in his voice was unmistakable when he asked, 'Do you truly believe that a Saxon man wouldn't kiss that way?'

She had, but the way he asked the question had her wondering if she'd been wrong.

'Or is the problem really that you enjoyed it too much?' His voice was back to being soft and tender with the husky edge that she was coming to crave. 'And you were aware that I was a Dane the entire time.'

She closed her eyes as the truth of his accusation washed over her. That was exactly the problem. She very much feared that she was ready to allow him to do whatever he wanted with her and the fact that he was a Dane would matter very little.

The faint sound of a horn back at Alvey saved her from answering. It signalled the end of morning chores and was the call to the morning meal. It also meant the end of their sparring session. He rose and began to gather the wooden swords without another word.

'Ellan, what is kissing like?' That night after they had retired to their alcove for the evening, Elswyth finally got up the nerve to ask the question that had been burning through her all day. Ellan stopped with the comb halfway finished with its journey through a lock of her long hair. The lock shimmered with notes of honey and sunlight in the glow of several tallow candles set across the bench at the end of their shared bed.

'Have you never been kissed?' Ellan asked.

The air was heavy as even it seemed to await her answer. She'd already determined to not lie any more than she had to—the theft of the bloodstone and the fact that she was supposed to be spying on these people she was coming to respect sat heavy on her. She wouldn't compound her sins by becoming more of a liar. She couldn't look at Ellan's face, so she stared at the lock of hair as she answered, 'Not at the farm.'

Ellan took a moment to mull that over before her hands resumed working the comb through a small knot. 'You mean to say that Osric never...'

Elswyth shook her head, her brows furrowing as she finally met her sister's gaze. She was so tired of hearing about Osric. 'Nay! I told you that I had no plans to wed him.'

'Apologies,' Ellan said without any regret evident in her tone. 'He followed you around enough that I assumed he'd stolen one or two.'

'Well, he didn't.'

'That explains a lot actually about your lack of kissing. No other man could get close to you with the way he hovered.'

Elswyth held back a groan at the turn in the

conversation. She had known that asking the question to her sister wouldn't be straightforward, which is why she'd put it off for as long as she had. For a time she had even considered going to Lady Gwendolyn, but had put that thought aside as soon as she'd had it. She didn't want to explain to her what had happened with Rolfe. Not that she wanted to explain it to Ellan either, but she needed to talk to someone.

'But wait!' Ellan's exclamation made Elswyth startle, nearly dropping her own comb. 'You said not on the farm... Does that mean you've been kissed here? In Alvey?' Her eyes narrowed as her lips turned up in a shrewd smile.

Elswyth swallowed once...twice. It didn't help to moisten her dry mouth at all. 'Could you just answer the question, please?' she finally asked.

Ellan waited until Elswyth had almost decided she shouldn't have asked, before she said, 'I presume you know the general way it's done.' Her eyes softened along with her tone, and she moved across the bed to sit beside her sister, the comb forgotten. 'What is it precisely that you want to know?'

'Is it more than a touching of lips?'

Ellan's eyebrow rose slightly, but she didn't

seem to think the question completely foolish. 'It can often lead to more than kissing,' she answered with a smile.

'Nay, I mean the kissing itself. Is...?' Her cheeks burned with what she was about to ask, but she needed to know so she closed her eyes and forced out the words. 'Is the tongue involved?'

She had known it was a wicked deed, but Ellan's swift inhale of breath only confirmed it. 'Someone kissed you with his tongue? Who?' She gave a shriek that she quickly covered with her hands. 'It was Rolfe! Is that what you've been doing every morning?'

'Shh.' Elswyth was tempted to poke her head out to make certain no one had heard them, but decided it would only rouse suspicion. 'Aye, he kissed me this morning, but it's not what we've been doing *every* morning.' The muscles in her arms were sore from the sparring sessions over the past couple of days. They were making progress, despite getting diverted today.

'And he used his tongue?' Ellan prodded her.

If it was possible, she managed to blush harder. She could feel the heat all the way up to her ears. Why was she making her say it again? 'Aye. Is that...normal? Do Saxon men kiss like that?'

'Ah, I see.' Ellan nodded, assuming the look of a wise elder as she straightened her shoulders. 'In my experience, the Danes are much more…what's the word to use here? Knowledgeable.'

'In your experience? Ellan, how many of them have you kissed?'

'Only two. Don't look at me like that. How else am I to choose a husband?'

Elswyth scoffed, 'I didn't even realise kissing had anything to do with choosing a husband.'

'Oh, Elswyth.' She shook her head. 'Of course it has something to do with it. He must do it properly. If he doesn't it could go very badly when it comes to bed-play.'

Elswyth rose and put her hands to her flaming cheeks. 'I don't believe Father meant for this to happen when he allowed us to come here.'

'Nay, I'm certain he didn't. He wants us to be proper little puppets who will marry and produce babies as he chooses, but we are not puppets. I won't have just any husband and neither should you. Sit and let's finish our talk.' She reached up and gently took Elswyth's hand and tugged her back down. 'I'm sorry this is shocking to you. I think if you had spent more time with the women in the village and less time at home with the chores, this would all be much clearer. I should have realised that there are things you don't know. I apologise for not speaking with you sooner.'

Somewhat overcome by this whole trove of information she'd known nothing about, Elswyth gave a quick nod.

Ellan relaxed and set her comb aside. Taking both of Elswyth's hands in hers, she said, 'I didn't mean to imply that kissing was the only way to choose a husband, but it is very important. Men like to pretend that it doesn't matter, because it goes easier for them that way. If they don't have to try to make it good for the woman, then 'tis less for them to worry about. But I'm told that bed-play can be pleasant and not merely something a woman has to endure. How a man kisses can tell you a lot about how he goes about other things.'

'So what does it tell you when he uses his tongue?' Now that Elswyth had had the entire day to ponder that kiss and she was currently resolved to nothing but brutal honesty, she could admit to herself that it had been pleasant. Was that a sign that other things in bed with him would be pleasant? She wanted to ask, but it was too embarrassing.

Ellan gave her that sly, mischievous smile. 'It's very good, Elswyth. The boys at home were too sheltered to know to use it, but the men here know. It tells you that he's concerned for your pleasure.'

'Isn't it…wicked?'

'That depends on who you ask and who you kiss, I suppose. If it's only kissing and only for the purposes of finding a suitable husband, I think it's forgivable.'

'It seems…don't you think they kiss that way because they're barbarians?'

To her utter dismay, Ellan threw her head back and laughed and laughed. When she finally could stop herself from laughing enough to talk, tears were streaming from her eyes. 'Do you think a barbarian would care about your pleasure?'

Put that way… 'Nay, I suppose not.' It seemed silly that she had even been upset about it. Shame quickly overcame any lingering feelings of anger. He'd been attempting to please her and she had been cruel. Her words must have hurt his pride. The worst of it was that he was right. The true source of her anger had been because she was upset that she enjoyed it while being well aware that he was a Dane.

'Did you not enjoy it?' Ellan asked, her eyes solemn once more.

'I did, but I said some hurtful things.' Things that she would need to apologise for.

Ellan nodded, but seemed uncertain about Elswyth's mood. 'Did he…did he mention marriage or was he taking advantage of the fact that he had you alone? We can speak to Lady Gwendolyn and I'm certain—'

'It's not that. He does want marriage. Lady Gwendolyn mentioned that a marriage between us could be good for Alvey, but I refused.'

Understanding dawned across her sister's features. 'Because you won't have a Dane.'

Elswyth nodded. 'Ellan, you know as well as anyone the mark Mother left on our family when she left. The villagers all look at you and me as if they expect us to have the same weakness. Since she left I've done nothing but try to show them how proper and loyal I am. But this…the way he made me feel doesn't feel loyal at all—' She broke off to swallow past the lump that had formed in her throat. 'I feel as if I'm betraying Father and Galan. Am I wrong?' she asked, genuinely confused. Days ago her position was so clear, but now everything was muddled.

Ellan rubbed her shoulder in sympathy. 'Mother's betrayal is not your burden to bear.'

'But it is,' Elswyth insisted. She had never

understood how Ellan could brush off their mother's abandonment so easily, but it had never seemed to affect her as it had everyone else. Elswyth had always admired how easily Ellan could brush off the disapproving looks some of the elders had given them, the daughters of Godric's faithless wife.

Her sister shook her head. 'Mother's situation was different. She left her husband and children for a man we never even knew. You were always meant to marry and leave. It's only that the man is a Dane and not Saxon. It's not such a betrayal.'

'But you know how they feel about Danes. They'll see it as such.'

Ellan gave a shrug and said, 'You know my feelings on the matter. I think to fight the Danes is pointless. They're here. They're powerful. To survive, we must learn to live with them. The important thing is how do you feel about the Danes?'

'They do not belong here,' Elswyth couldn't stop herself from insisting.

'And yet they *are* here. Do you want peace or do you want to fight?'

The words were simple, but true. Sometimes Ellan had a way of making things seem not as complicated at Elswyth would make them. She did want peace. She wanted to go to bed every night knowing that the people she loved were safe. As that clarity came over her, she realised that she had amends to make with Rolfe.

'I need to go apologise for the harsh things I said.' Rolfe had been nothing but kind and had not deserved any of them.

Chapter Eleven

❦

Wyborn pushed up on to his front paws and cocked his head to the side a moment before a knock sounded at the chamber door. Rolfe sighed and tossed down the writing implement he'd been using. His head was beginning to ache from trying to translate the Latin scrolls in an attempt to teach himself the written language. He much preferred the simple lines of runes to the unnecessarily complicated curves and swirls of the letters of that language. A simple letter could appear in numerous variations of strokes depending on the handwriting of the author, making it nearly impossible to keep track of which symbol it was supposed to be.

The tight muscles at the back of his neck begged to be loosened, so he rubbed a hand over them as he rose and crossed the few steps to the door. A talk with one of his men would be a welcomed break. Elswyth was the last person he expected to see, but there she stood, looking up at him with a timid smile hovering around her lips when he opened the door. He hadn't seen her after their return until the evening meal, where she'd avoided looking at him and had disappeared soon after serving Vidar and Lady Gwendolyn. He'd half-expected to receive a dressing down from Lady Gwendolyn for kissing Elswyth that morning, but one hadn't been forthcoming. Since she hadn't behaved any differently towards him at all, he'd assumed that Elswyth hadn't told her what had transpired.

'Good evening,' he said when it was clear she wasn't going to offer a greeting.

Her eyes had gone wide as her gaze had taken in his bare torso. He probably should have pulled on his under-tunic—he wore only his trousers—but he'd expected the late visitor to be one of his men. Not a woman and certainly not Elswyth. In fact, he'd been entertaining the thought of abandoning their morning sparring sessions. There would be no point if she felt so disgusted and uncomfortable with him.

A faint pink tinged her cheeks when she finally brought her gaze back to his. Satisfaction rose in his chest that she apparently liked what she saw when she looked at him. 'I'm sorry to bother you so late, but could I have a moment to talk?' Wyborn pushed past him, nosing her hand for a petting, which she eagerly gave him behind his ears, before he went back to plop down on his spot next to the bed.

A moment to talk. That probably meant she intended to lay out all the reasons he should not have kissed her, even though she'd given him very clear signs that she had wanted the kiss. Closing her eyes, leaning into him, parting her lips so sweetly when he had asked her, making those soft sounds of pleasure in the back of her throat. She'd given every indication of having enjoyed it, except for the dressing down that had come afterwards. He wanted to tell her nay and close the door in her face, but the reasonable part of him recognised that as his own wounded pride. Best to let her have her say and be done with her. Stepping to the side, he allowed her to enter, though he took perverse pleasure in closing the door a touch too hard behind her, making it clear that she was very much in his domain now.

She didn't so much as flinch at the sound, so he crossed his arms in disappointment and took in the straight line of her back as she let her gaze sweep around his chamber. Her hair had been left to fall loose down to her waist and it shone from a recent brushing. The candlelight caught notes of chestnut and amber in its richness. Did she have any idea how inappropriate her presence was in his chamber?

Her gaze finally came to rest on the table with the tablet and scroll laid out. 'What is this?' Her voice was tinged with awe and wonder as she took the few steps necessary to reach the table. Her fingertips moved almost reverently over the wood frame of the tablet.

'It's a writing tablet. Have you never seen one?'

Despite his wish to harden himself to her, the look on her face was rather endearing when she shook her head and asked, 'Do you cipher?'

'I write runes,' he explained, walking over and pointing out the marks he had written in the hardened black wax on the tablet. 'Almost everyone can write or at least read them.' He meant Danes, of course. He'd learned that many of the Saxons he'd come across in smaller areas did not write. 'Have you seen the runes on the men's belongings?' They frequently carved their names into the items to mark the owner.

'Aye, I have seen them.' She didn't lift her

gaze from the tablet. She stared at it as if it was remarkable.

'It's a simple wooden frame.' He turned it over so that she could see all sides. 'Hot wax is poured in and when it hardens it's the perfect surface for writing.' Picking up the writing implement, he offered it to her. It was a slight iron rod set into a slender goat antler, but she turned it over in her fingers as if it were something truly amazing. 'Try it.' She shook her head, but a smile tugged at the corners of her mouth. 'Go on,' he encouraged her, momentarily forgetting his bruised pride.

A soft laugh escaped her and she took the tablet and made a line in the wax at the bottom with the iron end of the stick. Smiling at her handiwork, she tried again, this time copying the runes he'd already written there. 'What did I write?' She gazed up at him with a look of such joy on her face that he was mesmerised. Luckily, he didn't have to look down to know the word he had written before she'd disturbed him.

'Home.'

'Home,' she repeated, running a fingertip across the runes. 'These look different. What does it say?'

He was forced to tear his gaze away from her to see what she meant. She was pointing to the Latin word he'd written at the top of the board. He'd been working on coming up with a way to match the runes with the Roman letters. The work was giving him a horrible headache. The reminder made him squeeze the muscles at the back of his neck again to relieve the tension. Turning, he walked to his bed where he'd tossed his undershirt in frustration earlier and pulled it over his head.

She tried not to stare, but he could see her peeking out from beneath her lashes to watch him. The satisfaction he'd experienced earlier came back to burn within him. 'It's the same word in Latin. From the scroll.' He walked back to her and gestured to the partially unrolled parchment. 'I'm attempting to learn to read that language, but it's difficult.' He'd memorised the Latin passage written on the scroll and had thought to write the runes as a sort of translation.

Briefly, he considered donning his tunic, but rejected the thought. The under-tunic was the most he could offer her in the way of preserving her modesty. She'd seen more than this when she'd come to help him with his bath. He nearly smiled at the reminder, but didn't dare to dwell on that memory with her here. It was certain to awaken a part of him better left to sleep in her presence.

'How so?' she asked, a line forming between her eyebrows as she dragged her gaze from the portion of his chest and shoulders still exposed.

'For one thing, the letters are more complex. See this one?' He pointed and she nodded. 'It's a "G", but here it is again and it's written differently. There are too many curves in the language. It makes it difficult to follow when every writer makes the curves differently. Runes are simple with straight lines.'

He glanced at her only to see that she was staring at him in much the same way he must have been staring at her earlier. A little bit of awe and sadness tinged her expression. 'If only all the world were simple and straight,' she said with a miserable little smile.

The poignancy in her tone tugged at him. It nearly drew him right into touching her, sweeping the wealth of her hair back from her cheek and soothing her. He wouldn't do it, though. She had more than made it clear that any touching in that way from him wouldn't be welcome. Instead of comforting her, he stiffened his shoulders to block the impulse and took a step back. 'What do you need?' he asked, crossing his arms over his chest again.

As if she knew the moment of tenderness was over, she gave a slight nod of her head and set the tablet and utensil down on the table. Drawing in a deep breath, she turned to face him fully. Her expression took on an almost pained look and he knew that what she was about to say wasn't easy for her. He braced himself.

'I came to apologise for the way I behaved this morning.' His face must have revealed his surprise, because she elaborated, 'When you kissed me.'

'I'm aware of what you mean.' His voice came out gruffer than he intended so he cleared his throat and tried again. 'What part of that are you apologising for?'

'The way I behaved after. I called you a heathen and a barbarian—'

'You never said barbarian,' he pointed out drily.

She shrugged. 'In my head I'm afraid I did. The point is that I shouldn't have scolded you and, if I hurt you, I am deeply sorry. Ellan explained that by using your tongue you were only trying to make it better for me. I've never been kissed, you see? I thought it was…well, something other than what we did. Something that only involved lips and not— Oh, why are you laughing at me?'

The more she had talked, the pinker her cheeks had become, but her anger changed it completely. She was so red that it looked like she'd blistered from standing too long in the sun. Unfortunately, it only made him laugh harder.

With a huff of anger, she made to move past him towards the door, but he managed to pull himself together and cross the line he'd sworn never to cross again with her. He took her by the shoulders. She snatched away, so he held up his hands palms out and said, 'I apologise for laughing. It was terrible of me.' He even managed to stop the smile that threatened, though his lips still trembled from the urge.

'You don't look sorry.' She glared at him through narrowed eyes. The green slits glittered at him dangerously.

'I am. I wasn't laughing at your apology, only at the image of you getting your sister to explain kissing to you.' He could tell from the way she drew herself up taller that his explanation was hardly any better. 'Let's start over,' he said into the uncomfortable silence. 'I accept your apology. Do you want an apology for even daring to kiss you?' He didn't intend to offer one, but he wondered if that was what had prompted her own apology.

Much to his surprise her shoulders slumped and she looked down at the floor between them. 'Nay, that's not what I want. I gave you every indication that I wanted you to kiss me. I did want the kiss.'

He frowned. Certain that she was after something from him, he asked, 'Then an apology for using my tongue?'

She was shaking her head before he finished. 'Nay, I understand now why you did it. In fact, I should offer you another apology. I wouldn't have become so upset if you were Saxon. I was surprised and I used the fact that you are a Dane against you. It wasn't fair or right and I'm so confused.' With a groan of exasperation she turned away from him and sat down on the bench at the table.

For the first time he began to believe that her apology was sincere. Taking hold of the three-legged stool he sometimes used to prop his feet on, he drew it up to her and sat down. She had put her face in her hands, but she looked up at him when he was settled. He was surprised to see her eyes bright and miserable.

'I've been horrible to you. Both this morning and yesterday morning,' she said. A slight husk softened her voice and he was a little unsettled at the way it raked at something inside him, sending a flicker of awareness down low in his gut. 'How can you still look at me like that?'

'Like what?'

'As if you like what you see.'

He grinned. 'Because I do like what I see.' It was the undeniable truth. He was attracted to her. The comely length of her hair swung down around her hips, shining and glossy in the candlelight. He wanted to run his hands through it to see if would feel like spun silk. Her eyes always held a glimmer of mischievous daring, but somehow that seemed to be present in them more tonight. Or maybe it was that he was more focused on her now that she was in his chamber. Alone. Dangerously alone. He realised that he'd been leaning in and forced himself to sit back.

She took in a deep, wavering breath that made her lips tremble and she squared her shoulders. Obviously, she'd come to some unknown resolution and he was curious to find out what it was. 'I've decided that I have no choice but to be very honest with you.' Her fingers toyed with the horn end of the writing utensil on the table as if she was nervous.

He gave her a nod of encouragement.

'The absolute truth is that I admire everything about you. I have since you arrived. I look at you and I know that I should be afraid because you lead more warriors than I've ever seen assembled in one place in my life. I know that my father doesn't trust you and that I shouldn't trust you. That with one command from Lord Vidar, you could lead those warriors and completely decimate my village, my farm, my entire way of life, and it wouldn't even be that difficult of a task for you. I know all of that as plainly as I know my own name, but somehow it doesn't seem to matter. I'm not afraid. I look at you and I see the gentleness that you try to hide. I see how you care deeply for everyone under your command…everyone around you. I see you with Tova and I see a man who would care profoundly for his own children. I also suspect that same concern and tenderness would convey to a wife.' She swallowed, but rushed forward as if she were trying to get the words out before she lost her nerve. 'I cannot fear you. I cannot hate you as my father would have me hate you. I can only admire you, though it tears me apart.'

A tear had gathered at the corner of her eye as she spoke and it fell, landing on her soft cheek and sliding down to the corner of her mouth. He followed its path like a thirsting man, wanting to lap it up and taste the salt on his tongue. 'Elswyth—'

She held up her hand to stop him from speaking. 'I hope that isn't unfair to you, because I genuinely don't know where that leaves us. You see, you were right this morning. When you said that I was only angry about the kiss because I had enjoyed it and I had known you were a Dane the whole time…you were right. From the moment your lips touched mine, there was no pretending that you were anyone other than Rolfe. You are the only man I've ever wanted to kiss.'

Silence descended as he tried to take in all that she had revealed to him. He'd never expected this level of honesty from her. Even Hilde had never been so bold, preferring to hide her feelings and make him suss them out. Had he been wrong about his Saxon all this time? He had a difficult time believing that she could make herself so vulnerable to him while at the same time hiding the fact that she was a spy.

'Rolfe?' She said his name a moment before her warm hand touched his shoulder. The heat from her palm seeped through the soft linen and his skin prickled, reaching for more of her touch.

'It seems we are a matched pair.' His voice came out low. That line between her brows appeared as she tilted her head to the side in question. 'The first night you came here and tended to me, I had no idea who you were, but I liked you. You were tender and fierce, kind and spirited. I liked that about you. You challenged me in a way no woman has for a long time. Then I found out you were Godric's daughter. I, too, had my prejudices. I thought that Godric's bloodline was too bitter to hold any goodness, yet here you are.'

You are everything that I ever wanted in a wife.

The thought sent a shock like lightning through him. It pushed him to his feet where he paced unseeing to the door and back again. This couldn't be happening, not again. How did he always end up with the women who could hurt him the most? He had known that eventually duty would call him to marry. His wife was supposed to be passably pretty, dutiful and certainly kind, but she wasn't meant to inspire this mad longing inside him. She would give him strong children and in return he would keep her safe and in comfort. He was not meant to lose his heart to her.

In a moment of madness he imagined rushing down to tell Vidar that he would marry someone else, anyone else, but Elswyth. Only that would leave her free to take a Saxon as her husband, or worse—Aevir. He grimaced as soon as the thought crossed his mind. He'd rather die than see her with anyone else.

'Rolfe?' Her hand on his arm made him turn to see her standing before him. 'I would like to explain to you why my father is so bitter about the Danes.' Unable to do anything more, he gave her a nod. She dropped her hand and clasped them both together in front of her and explained to him what had happened with her mother, and how her father had handled the betrayal very badly. She ended with, 'It doesn't excuse his hatred, but I wanted you to understand. It's why I've fought my feelings for you so hard. I... I don't want to become her.'

He sucked in a breath, hardly able to speak past the tightness squeezing his chest. 'Your feelings for me?'

She nodded, looking shy, and a wave of tenderness came over him and he nearly swept her into his arms, but he managed to hold himself back. 'I feel affection for you, Dane. Except I...can't turn my back on my family.' Her eyes were pleading as she stared up at him.

'What if you're not turning your back on them? What if by our joining we can stop more bloodshed for all of the Saxons and Danes alike?' Why was he encouraging her, when to push her further away would end this madness inside him? 'What if our marriage could help foster peace?' His heart pounded hard against his ribs, almost as if it was trying to jump out of his chest. He didn't know why he was trying so hard to convince her to do something that terrified him. Marrying her would be one small step away from loving her. He saw it as clearly as he could see a storm approaching on the open sea from the bow of his longship and he was just as helpless to stop it.

The tender flesh of her throat worked as she swallowed. Her pulse was a soft beat at the hollow where it met her shoulder. He wanted to nuzzle that depression and lap at it with his tongue.

'Do you truly feel that's possible?' From her tone he could tell that she was moments away from telling him aye.

'I do.'

'Then I—I think that I could see myself as your wife and it wouldn't be so bad. Except...'

'Except what?'

'I'm afraid to feel more for you than what I already do. When my mother left...it hurt me deeply. I hesitate to open myself up to that pain again and I wonder why you would want me when there are so many other women who would have you.'

'That's only because you don't see yourself as I do.' A fierce need to possess her came over him. Her lips parted on a nearly inaudible gasp as he stepped closer, slowly walking towards her. With each step she moved back until she came up against the wall. 'You're a desirable woman, Saxon. Beautiful, kind, fierce when you need to be.' She blushed and glanced away. 'And you must know that if we were wed, I would never abandon you.'

Her gaze darted back to him, wide with an odd fear. 'I suppose I don't know that.'

He cupped her cheek in his palm. 'If you were mine, I would never let you go.'

'If...?'

He let out a soft laugh. 'I admit that I cannot let go of the doubt that you carry Godric's hatred for us within you.'

'I... I do not. I wanted to, but I can't.' She shook her head, and a tear fell. It landed on his wrist and they both looked down to see it shimmering there on his skin. Without even thinking, he brought it to his lips, letting the salt tingle on his tongue.

'Of course you can't. Hate is not in you, Elswyth, no matter how hard you try.' He wanted to leave it at that, but he had to know for certain. 'Have you given your father information about us?'

She didn't even hesitate in her reply. 'He sent me to spy, but I have not seen him since. When he comes I'll tell him the only logical conclusion from what I've seen: We must join with the Danes. To do anything else would be disastrous.'

None of that was a surprise, but relief lightened the weight on his chest none the less. 'Have you met with the Scots?' He sent up a silent prayer to all the gods he knew that she would tell him nay. As long as she had not betrayed them then he could have her. He still didn't know how he'd have her while keeping his heart away from her, but he'd manage it. He had no other choice.

'Nay…' She hesitated and looked away.

He touched her cheek again. 'But your family has?'

She gave him a slow nod.

'It's not a betrayal to tell me that.' He soothed her. 'We've long suspected their meetings.'

She swallowed hard and before he could say anything else, she pushed his hand from her cheek only to throw herself into him. Her arms wrapped around his waist and he pulled her against him, closing his arms around her. He buried his face in her hair and breathed in her sweet scent. She felt perfect against him, her softness filling in all the hard planes of his body.

'Why can't things be simple?' Her voice was muffled against his shoulder.

'They can be, Saxon.' They would be, he decided. She was no spy, not really, and one day she would find out about Banford and what he'd done there. One day soon, probably, but by then she would be his. He didn't fool himself that the knowledge would be inconsequential; only that in the end she would be happy things had turned out the way they had.

'How?' She looked up at him with shimmering eyes. Emeralds. They were like the deepest, darkest emeralds he'd ever seen. He determined then and there that if they wed he'd find her an emerald some day that matched her eyes.

'One choice at a time. Would you have me as your husband if your father bid it?'

She held his gaze without wavering as she said, 'Aye.'

'Then you have to decide if you'd have me if he tells you nay.'

She dropped her gaze to his chest and he could sense the panicked tension within her. 'I struggle with being disloyal to my family. After my mother left, well, I suppose I've spent my life trying to prove that I'm not like her. That I won't betray them. This feels like betrayal.'

Holding her closer, he lowered his voice. 'It's not betrayal to want peace.'

She took in a shuddering breath and closed her eyes.

'You don't have to decide now,' he whispered, running his palm down her back. 'Think about it, but know that if you have me I will protect you always and you will want for nothing.'

'And what of my family?'

He swallowed thickly, knowing that what he wanted was within his grasp and unwilling to say the wrong thing to have it taken away. But neither could he lie to her. 'Betrayers will not be tolerated, but I vow to you that I will treat them fairly.'

She gave him a wry grin. 'You would treat them fairly even if I did not become your wife.'

In that moment, he realised something profound about her. She would not take him to simply better her own life. She needed something more, something for her family to push her over the edge. It endeared her to him even more—however, he could not turn his back on traitors, even if they were her blood. 'What would you have from me?'

'Meet with my father and talk to him. Give him a chance to take your side.'

It was so simple. No jewels or gold required. She asked him for things that were so easy to provide her. Yet, a vain and undeniable part of him wanted her to want him without conditions, so he said, 'I vow to do that even if you tell me nay.'

She smiled and it was so blindingly beautiful that he could only stare at her, taking in her loveliness. 'Thank you, Dane.'

He couldn't help but smile at the word that had somehow become an endearment between them. 'Don't answer me now. I want you to think well before you tell me what you've decided, so we'll have no morning sessions for two days. On the third day, I'll come for your answer.' She nodded and, unable to resist, he bent his head to whisper into her ear, 'If you tell me aye, know that I will spend our nights together using my tongue on every part of your body,' he promised, alluding to the kiss that had brought her to his chamber tonight.

Her fingers clenched in his under-tunic and she let out a little breath of surprise, followed by a breathless laugh. The sound awakened the beast sleeping within him. He wanted to toss her on to his bed and show her what he meant. To spread her open beneath him and plunder the sweetness between her thighs.

'Kiss me again before I go,' she whispered.

Unable to deny that request, his lips brushed across her cheek on the way to her mouth. She turned to meet him, her soft lips pressing to his. He took them hard beneath his, the fierceness of his mood driving him to show her exactly what would be waiting for her if she told him aye. He'd try to be tender with her, but she stirred a longing in him that was too intense to be dampened. To his surprise, she didn't pull away. Instead, she parted her lips to accommodate him and made a sensual sound when he touched his tongue to hers. All it took was one tentative stroke of her tongue against his to bring him to full arousal. His hands tightened on her hips to pull her closer, practically grinding himself against her. It wasn't nearly enough and he was on the verge of taking her to his bed when he forced himself to pull away.

Panting as if she were as affected as he was, she smiled at him. It was the daring and mischievous smile he'd come to associate as being a part of the very fibre of who she was. She stretched up on her toes and gave him one last

kiss to his cheek before hurrying from the room,
leaving him there gasping for air and wanting
her with a madness he'd never felt before.

Not even with Hilde. Gods help him.

Chapter Twelve

By the end of the first day Elswyth had made her decision. By the end of the second day she had admitted that decision to herself. It hadn't come as a certainty, but as a creeping and crawling suspicion that choosing not to marry Rolfe was unthinkable. Both he and Ellan seemed to think things were simple, so she had resolved to follow the advice he'd given her. Make one decision at a time.

Her first decision would be to marry him. Her second one would be how to tell her father about it. He would disapprove. Nay, he would despise her choice. She knew it as well as she knew that Rolfe would do everything in his power to make her a happy wife. She hadn't been lying when she'd told him that she'd watched how he interacted with those he cared about. He might be a Dane, but he had a kind soul and he would make her a good husband.

If only her father would see it that way. She'd need help to tell him, which is what had brought her to Lady Gwendolyn's chamber. An afternoon snow had driven many people inside, and Lady Gwendolyn had disappeared to her chamber a little while ago with Tova. Elswyth could hear the baby squealing in delight from behind the door as she knocked.

'Come in,' Lady Gwendolyn's voice called out.

Elswyth stepped inside to see the lady seated at the table in the chamber, smoothing out a gown she was attempting to embroider for her daughter. Everyone knew that Lady Gwendolyn was the best archer in Alvey, but her skills with the needle were lacking. Elswyth found it admirable that it was a deficiency she was trying to rectify.

Lord Vidar had been lying on the large bed across the room, tossing his daughter into the air which was the source of her squeals of delight. He stopped when he noticed Elswyth and sat up with Tova in his arms. He held the infant with a tenderness that brought an ache to her heart.

She thought with a start that if she followed

through with her plan to marry Rolfe, she might have her own child by this time next year. Happiness warmed a spot in her chest and she knew that she was making the right decision in her choice of husband.

'Apologies for disturbing you, my lady, my lord, but I wondered if I might talk to you? Alone.' The last she directed at Lady Gwendolyn.

'You're not disturbing us.' Lady Gwendolyn smiled and seemed very happy to toss her embroidery to the side.

'Not at all,' Lord Vidar added as he rose. 'I suspect my wife is happy to be distracted from her needlework.'

Lady Gwendolyn laughed and said with mock tenacity, 'I'll conquer that needle if it's the last thing I do.'

Lord Vidar gave her an indulgent smile and held Tova against his chest as he bent over to press a kiss to his wife's forehead. 'Leave it. You don't have to learn embroidery if you don't want to.'

'But I do want to. It just won't co-operate.'

He laughed and shook his head as he left with the baby, closing the door behind him.

'Might I see, my lady?' Elswyth asked as she came to stand beside the table.

Lady Gwendolyn nodded and handed her the gown with the partially embroidered hem.

'It's much improved. I can see you've started taking note of the pacing we discussed.' The lines were straight, but the stitching itself was of irregular lengths, but it was better.

'Aye, it's coming along. I think the trouble is that I'm not accustomed to sitting still for this long. It takes patience that I'm afraid I don't have.'

'Nonsense, my lady. You have plenty of patience. Look how you taught me to shoot an arrow.'

Lady Gwendolyn inclined her head. 'I'm afraid that's an entirely different kind of patience. Besides, it's action. Working with thread is simply too tedious for me to enjoy, but I will conquer it before I set it aside. Now...' she took the gown back and set it along with the thread back into the basket she kept on the table 'sit down and tell me what you need.'

Elswyth took the bench on the opposite side of the small table. 'I've come to a decision.'

'Oh?'

'I'm going to marry Rolfe.'

The woman brought a hand to her mouth, but a smile lurked behind it. 'Truly?'

Elswyth nodded and gave her an abbreviated

version of the events leading up to her decision. 'The truth is that I can imagine no one else that I would want to be my husband. I think of returning home when my father comes and there is no one there that makes me feel the way Rolfe makes me feel. Perhaps it's unfair of me, but I don't want to be a simple farmer's wife.' Rolfe had seen so many things, been so many places, she wanted to spend the years of her life talking and learning about those places. But more than that, she wanted more of how he made her feel.

'I don't think it's unfair of you at all. You've found someone who is special to you. That is rare and I'm glad you've decided to try to hold on to him. I'm even happier that it will mean you will stay here. I've become quite fond of you while you've been here.'

Elswyth felt her cheeks turn pink. 'Thank you, my lady. I've come to like it here as well. However, I am concerned with how to proceed. I'm certain you're aware of the potential issue with my father. I can't imagine that he'll agree to this match.' Would he perhaps even turn his back on her? The very idea made her heart stutter. It wasn't out of the question, however, because her own mother had done just that. She didn't know if she could stand losing both of her parents, so she focused on the fact that she was doing this to further peace and save lives.

Lady Gwendolyn nodded in agreement. 'Aye, I expect him to put up quite a fuss. However, I know this is the right choice for you, and for Banford, though he'll be too stubborn to see it at first.'

'At first? Do you think he'll eventually come around? I don't want to lose him.'

'I do. It will take time and it won't happen overnight, but it will happen. Your father cares for you, Elswyth. I don't think you'll lose him.'

Elswyth smiled, the weight of her choice starting to slip from her shoulders for the first time. 'How do you think we should proceed? Tell him when he arrives and talk him into agreeing to the marriage?'

Lady Gwendolyn shook her head and for the first time her smile slipped. 'Nay, I'm afraid that won't work. I've given it some thought—oh, don't look at me that way,' she teased. 'You know how I hoped you'd say aye. I've been thinking of how to approach this ever since. I think the only way forward is for you to marry as soon as possible. That way, you won't have to go against your father's wishes to marry. He won't like it, but at least we avoid the situation where he tells you nay and you have to defy him.'

'I can see the wisdom of that, but what happens when he arrives and I am wed?'

'Lord Vidar and I will talk to him.' Reaching across the table, she patted Elswyth's hand. 'We can plan for that a little later, don't worry. Right now we must plan for your wedding. Have you spoken to Rolfe?'

Elswyth shook her head. 'He's given me a couple of days to think about it. The last time I saw him was two days ago.'

'Ah, that's why he hasn't been at the table the past two evenings. I thought you both had quarrelled.'

Elswyth could feel her face burning again as she thought of their last moments together. That kiss had been anything but a quarrel. She could hardly fathom what he had meant by using his tongue on her body, but she couldn't stop thinking about what he'd said.

'So we should have the wedding soon then?' Excitement leaped in her belly at the very thought.

'Aye, as soon as possible. Ordinarily, we'd plan something, but I'm afraid, with your father due soon, we can't wait. There's every chance that he could come early with the snow falling.'

The butterflies in her stomach took flight.

Rolfe could be hers sooner than she'd dreamed possible. 'As soon as possible then.'

Lady Gwendolyn smiled broadly and clapped. 'How exciting!'

Elswyth left Lady Gwendolyn's chamber a short while later. It was nearly time for the evening meal and she wanted to talk to Rolfe before then. Since her decision had been made, there was no point in waiting until the morning to tell him. Besides, from the open door in the hall she could see that the snow was beginning to stick. They might not even be able to have their practice as planned. She wanted to tell him now and, if she was honest, she wanted to see his face before Lady Gwendolyn or Lord Vidar mentioned it to him first.

He hadn't been in his chamber, so she walked through the great hall. Some of the men had started to congregate around the fire, drinking their ale, but he wasn't among them. Holding her cloak closed, she hurried out into the cold to find him. The wind was strong, promising more cold would be heaped upon them earlier than usual this winter. It had been snowing off and on for days.

Shivering, she hurried to look for him, finally finding his broad form as he spoke with the blacksmith. She was struck by how jovial their conversation was. Rolfe laughed at something the man had said and laid a hand on the man's thick shoulder. The blacksmith was a Saxon with bristles of white hair on his head and jaw who was nearing the age when he'd hang up his hammer. He could have hated the Danes like her father did, but here he was laughing with one of them in an easy manner. The sight reaffirmed that she was making the right choice. Saxons and Danes could co-exist peacefully in Alvey and she would do her part to make it so.

Pulling the folds of her cloak more firmly around her, she came to a stop at the edge of the wooden overhang shielding the forge. The blacksmith saw her first and his attention drew Rolfe's gaze. He straightened when he saw her, the smile dropping from his mouth as he searched her face for her answer. The blacksmith murmured a greeting, but Elswyth couldn't be bothered to pay attention to him. She was too drawn to her future husband. The fur he wore across his shoulders made him appear even more powerful than he was. He quite stole her breath away.

Rolfe's gaze narrowed in question, so she smiled. 'Aye,' she said with a nod.

A large smile curved his mouth and he left the blacksmith to come and stand before her. 'Aye?' he asked again, the flicker of uncertainty in his eyes only endearing him to her.

'Aye, I will be your wife.'

His smiled broadened, eventually becoming a laugh that was laced with nerves. 'You're certain? Even if your father—'

She cut him off, wanting to enjoy this moment of happiness without bringing dark thoughts between them. 'As soon as possible. I've talked to Lady Gwendolyn. She believes that it's best for us to marry before my father arrives. She and Lord Vidar will explain things to him.'

'As soon as possible. Tonight?' he teased.

She couldn't help but to give in to her nervous laughter. 'Nay, but as soon as things can be planned.'

'Tomorrow, then.' This he said with more certainty and her heart gave a little jump.

She could be married to him by this time tomorrow night. Her future was set on a course and for once, she didn't want to alter it. Her heart pounded and her stomach churned in a way that was far more fierce than the butterflies from earlier, but somehow it was a good feeling all the same. 'How do you feel?' she asked.

'Happy.' He gave her a tender smile and pulled her in close, though he stopped short of taking her in his arms as people rushed around them going about their evening. 'There is no one else I want as my wife.'

Though the words were tender, there was a hesitance in his eyes that she couldn't help but notice. If she was honest, there was some hesitance in her own heart as well, but it didn't stop the happiness she felt.

The wedding was two days later. Lady Gwendolyn had insisted on preparing a small feast while Elswyth and Ellan had hurried to make her bridal tunic, all of which took time. Although Lady Gwendolyn had offered to lend her something to wear, Elswyth thought that it was important to go to the wedding wearing only her own clothing. It wouldn't be right to pretend to be grander than she was—Rolfe needed to understand what he was getting: sadly only her and nothing else. So she and her sister had spent the past two days adding embroidery in fine blue and yellow thread to the bodice and hem of her best tunic, which was a pale green that she thought matched her eyes nicely.

They finished just in time for Lady Gwendolyn to help her to a steamy soak in the bathhouse. It was a new building in Alvey, built since Lord Vidar had been in residence, and was an entirely new experience for Elswyth. The only baths she'd had up until that point were hastily taken before the fire at home. This was luxurious. The entire chamber was filled with steam that left her feeling cleansed inside and out. That feeling was only enhanced by the way Lady Gwendolyn and Ellan scraped and polished every part of her body with a sea sponge. It left her skin pink and she felt as though she was glowing. Afterwards they rubbed a sweet-smelling oil into her skin that left her feeling soft and relaxed.

She tried not to think of why they were paying this much attention to her physical appearance, but it was impossible to keep her thoughts from the night ahead. As the warm water slid over her skin, she kept remembering Rolfe's kisses and his promise to use his tongue on her body. There was no telling what that meant and there was no way she could discuss it with Lady Gwendolyn or even Ellan, but every time she remembered his words and the husk in his voice as he'd said them, her stomach gave a little leap of anticipation. It hardly seemed real. He would be hers tonight. The old guilt that she was turning into her mother was still there, but now she was able to push it to the back of her mind, secure in the fact that she was helping her family. Rolfe had helped her see that and she was forever grateful to him for it.

'We have to hurry.' Lady Gwendolyn's eyes were bright in the shadowed light of the bathhouse. 'Rolfe will come soon to his own bath.'

Her face went hot at the thought of him preparing for the night ahead—for her—and both Lady Gwendolyn and Ellan laughed. They wrapped a soft woollen blanket around her and Lady Gwendolyn asked in a gentle voice, 'Do you know what to expect tonight, Elswyth?'

'I think I know enough. I *was* raised on a farm.' She tried to laugh as if she weren't nervous. However, the closer the time came the more worried she became. It couldn't possibly be exactly like she'd seen with the sheep, could it?

As if she sensed her unease, Lady Gwendolyn took her hand and brushed her wet hair back from her face. 'There can and should be pleasure for you in the act. Remember that. I believe that Rolfe will ensure that for you, but if he doesn't, then talk to him or, if you feel you can't, then come talk to me. Promise?'

Elswyth nodded and then hurried into her underdress and pulled her cloak tightly around her. There was no snow today, but the wind was biting as they hurried to the great hall and upstairs to the chamber Lady Gwendolyn shared with Lord Vidar. The rest of the time before the wedding was spent with Lady Gwendolyn telling them stories that kept them laughing from when she'd first met Lord Vidar while they combed Elswyth's hair dry and dressed.

Rolfe paced before the fire in the hall, anxious to see Elswyth and make her his wife. He hadn't wanted a feast and he couldn't have cared less what she wore to wed him, but Lady Gwendolyn had seemed to think both of those were important. He'd relented, because he'd had no choice, but as each day had passed it had only made him long for Elswyth more. He told himself that it was only the night ahead that he was anticipating and he almost believed it.

Night was beginning to fall when she finally made her way down the steps to the great hall with Lady Gwendolyn and Ellan trailing behind her. She looked lovely in a pale green tunic that only made her eyes appear deeper. The apples of her cheeks held a bit of colour as she stared at him, barely able to look away as she made her way to him. She was clearly nervous, her palms running anxiously down the side of the overdress. She and her sister had taken great pains with the stitching, but he could hardly notice it. His eyes were only for her face.

Aevir, who had returned from the north to attend the ceremony, said something about the night ahead from his place beside him. Rolfe was too intent on his wife to comprehend the words, but he knew they were crude by the way the other men snickered. Elswyth hesitated and Rolfe growled out, 'Shut up', which only made the men laugh harder.

'Enough!' Lady Gwendolyn scolded them in a harsh whisper when they were close enough. They quieted, but there were a few snorts among them.

Even though Elswyth's blush had deepened with obvious embarrassment, she didn't let that stop her from reaching out to take his hands. Pride swelled in his chest as she took in his form. He wore a well-fitted tunic of midnight blue, embroidered with gold-silk trim at the shoulders and hem. The material stretched tight across his chest in a way that he knew emphasised his broad shoulders. He knew that she liked what she saw by the way her eyes widened a fraction and she couldn't quite bring herself to meet his gaze.

'You're beautiful,' he whispered. And she

was. Her deep chestnut hair had been pulled back from her forehead in an intricate weave of plaits, but the heavy length had been left to fall around her waist. He couldn't wait to wind the silk of it around his wrists as he took her beneath him later. He was half-hard from watching her come across the room to him, knowing that she was his, knowing that nothing could stand in the way of his finally having her tonight. When he'd first seen her a primitive part of him had wanted to take her in his arms right then to let everyone know that she belonged to him.

'Thank you,' she whispered, drawing him away from the dark fantasy. She wore a wreath made of wheat and straw with rowan berries set around the crown of her head and she let one of his hands go to touch it as if she were ashamed of it. 'This is your last chance to make a run for freedom.'

'Why would I want to do that?'

'I...' She trailed off, but then seemed to resolve herself and she finally met his gaze. 'I'm sorry I can't come to you with more. I've heard some of the stories told around the hall at night. I know that you deserve a woman who can come to you with a crown made of gold.'

She meant the stories about great men and

their prize brides. He grinned and gave her a slow shake of his head as he recaptured her hand. 'Nay, I don't want that. I wouldn't miss all the Saxon vengeance you have in store for me.'

The bright smile she gave him settled inside him, warming some deep place he hadn't even known had needed her sunshine. In the back of his mind lurked the very real danger that their happiness might be short-lived, or that their happiness might blind him.

But right now she looked at him as if she could love him and he felt himself sliding towards that abyss and losing himself in her. He wanted to bathe in it, to drink it all in until he was drunk on that feeling.

Tomorrow would be soon enough to face the future. Tonight was only about him and his Saxon bride.

For the next few moments, the world kept moving around them, but he only saw Elswyth. Alvey's priest spoke, but she never broke Rolfe's stare, seeming to be as fascinated with him as he was with her. When it was time he spoke his vows in a clear and deep voice that he hoped conveyed to her how much he meant them. When her turn came, she made him proud by doing no less than he had, speaking in a strong, clear voice.

Finally, he broke the spell to look at Vidar who stood next to him. The man pressed a ring into his palm, the light from the candles glittering off the gold. Rolfe turned back to her and took her small, graceful fingers in his as he spoke the ceremonial words, 'With this ring, I take you as my wife. I give you my protection and my loyalty, and I pledge to you that I will give my life before allowing any harm to come to yours. We are one…from now until eternity.'

Her lips trembled as she took in a deep breath and her eyes reddened with unshed tears. Yet happiness shone out from her as she smiled at him and something around the vicinity of his heart threatened to break open. It didn't matter that the words were ceremonial. He meant them and her voice was steadfast when she said, 'I accept you as my husband.'

Gently, he nudged the band of gold down her finger until it settled into place, claiming her as his. He gave her hand a gentle squeeze before letting it go to turn to Aevir at his other side. Aevir held up the new sword wrapped carefully in linen. He unwrapped it carefully before handing it off to Rolfe. If they were back home, it would have been his family's sword, passed down from generation to generation. But they weren't home, so he'd had the blacksmith working for days—since before Elswyth had told him aye—to make a new one. The hilt was ornate with a scroll pattern on the guard.

Rolfe presented it to her on the flat of his palms. 'I am entrusting this into your care to be given to our first-born son. May we have many children.'

A nearly overwhelming feeling of pride swept through him as she took it from him and said, 'I accept.' Then with reverence—for the sword was symbolic of Rolfe entrusting her to further his bloodline and bear his children—she handed it to Lady Gwendolyn and took Rolfe's hands in hers. 'I will be proud to bear your sons and daughters.'

He squeezed her hands and pulled her close, brushing his lips against hers. A cheer went up through the great hall. As his arms slipped around her, he whispered against her ear, 'You are mine now, Saxon.'

They were officially man and wife.

Chapter Thirteen

The rest of the evening passed in a blur of activity. It was full of food, good wishes for their future, Elswyth pretending not to hear the many jests regarding their wedding night and drinking the special honeyed mead that had been prepared for them. Finally, although many people were still feasting around them, Rolfe put his arm around her and pulled her to his side to whisper, 'I can't wait any longer, Saxon. Are you ready for bed?'

She knew what he was really asking. The truth was plain in the way his eyes burned into her. At some point during the evening her nerves had given way to anticipation. Oh, the nervousness was still present, but excitement burned hotter. Admiring the comely bow of his lips, she said, 'Aye, I'm ready.'

Rolfe rose and pulled her to her feet, causing

another exasperating cheer to go up through the
hall, nearly shaking the rafters. She was confused when six men, including Lord Vidar and
Aevir, followed them to the stairs. There had
been no visible signal so she could only assume
that the six had been predetermined, but no
one had told her to expect this part. Squeezing
Rolfe's fingers tighter, she wrapped her other
hand around his upper arm. He gave her a smile
that she was sure was meant to reassure her, but
it was too wolfish to help.

The men followed them right up to Rolfe's
chamber, where he paused only to swing her
up into his arms and carry her over the threshold. Thank goodness he kicked the door behind
them, blocking everyone else out, even Wyborn.

As she slid down his body, Rolfe reached
back to secure the door, ensuring their privacy.
'Do you need time to prepare yourself, Wife?'
The way his arm kept tight around her waist
coupled with the look on his face told her that
he might give her time, but it wouldn't be much.
The blue of his eyes had deepened to almost the
same midnight hue of his tunic.

'Nay.' Her whisper was so low she couldn't
be certain that he'd heard her, so she gave a
quick shake of her head to make sure.

'You're so beautiful. All night I've only been

able to think how lucky I am.' He touched her cheek, her hair, his palm eventually moving down the long sleeve of her linen underdress. The heat from his touch nearly scorched her through the material.

'Will they stay at the door until…until…?' She couldn't bring herself to say it.

He nodded. 'The ceremony is useful, but we're not truly married until we drink the honeyed mead and I spend my seed inside you. Should the validity of the marriage ever be questioned, and there's a good chance it might, we need witnesses to stand up for us.'

God knew she didn't want to tempt fate and have them actually wait inside the chamber while the deed was done, but curiosity wouldn't allow the question to go unasked. 'But how will they know the deed is done?'

He grinned a grin that was full of sin and need. 'The walls are thin and there are sounds that…' Swallowing visibly, he said, 'I think things will become apparent as they happen.'

She nodded, satisfied with that for now. Having her curiosity sated only allowed her earlier misgivings to return. 'I'm sorry I have nothing for you.' Nerves coupled with the shame of coming to him in such a humble wedding ceremony made her start to babble. 'Lady Gwendolyn told me about the usual custom of gifting you with a sword. I don't even have a proper dowry.'

'I don't care about those things.' His voice was gentle and deep as his fingers came to rest on her jaw, slowly lifting her face so that she met his gaze. 'Jarl Vidar gave me the choice of any woman. I chose you because I want *you*, not because I want the things you can give me.'

'Are you saying that I should be grateful to have been chosen by you?' Seizing on his words, she attempted to bring levity to the moment and gave a curtsy. 'Thank you, oh, Lord Dane, for choosing such a humble wife.'

He chuckled and tickled her waist to make her straighten. It worked and she laughed as he hauled her back into his arms. 'Why do I think I might long for the missed opportunity to have chosen a biddable wife?'

'You won't. You'd get bored with biddable.'

'I would,' he agreed, his eyes already losing the humour that sparkled within them. 'Kiss me,' he said.

His mouth was only a breath from hers so it was no trouble to lean forward and close the gap. He quickly took control of the kiss, covering her mouth with his and gently scraping her bottom lip with the edge of his teeth. She

gasped at the sensation and he took advantage,
thrusting the tip of his tongue against hers. The
sensual stroke made her body come alive as
his earlier kisses had, only this time her reaction was more intense because she knew there
would be no stopping. Heat raced through her
core, throbbing deep down inside her.

His hand moved from her waist, up her ribcage, to mould itself against her breast. Her
flesh filled his palm briefly before he cupped
the weight, allowing his thumb to stroke over
the tip. Her nipple pebbled in response, her
entire breast seeming to swell as it ached for
more of his attention. But he kept his touch slow
and leisurely, continuing his tender assault of
her mouth while his thumb moved in a teasing
circle around the tip of her breast. When she
arched against him, silently pleading for more
of his touch, he moved his attention to her other
breast, teasing that nipple until it, too, ached for
more of his touch.

'More, Rolfe.' Without meaning to, her hips
pushed against him and she grasped at the back
of his tunic, wanting to get beneath it and feel
the heat from his skin against her own.

He drew back to look at her and the admiration shining down at her was enough to take
her breath away. He moved slowly and deliber-

ately, as if he was afraid he would frighten her, to work the brooches at her shoulders, unfastening one and then the other until her overdress dropped to the floor with a swishing sound. She stepped out of the slippers she wore and kicked the dress away, watching as his long and graceful fingers went to remove his own tunic. He tossed it towards the trunk at the end of his bed and moved to sit down on the edge of the bed, working at the fastenings of his boots. His fingers shook a little.

'I'll help you.' She moved to kneel before him and together they worked to rid him of his boots. When they'd both been set aside, her hands went to the hem of his under-tunic and she lifted it over his head. She tossed it over her shoulder, but had no idea where it landed. All she knew was that he was perfect and she allowed herself a moment to appreciate his singular male beauty.

His chest was lightly furred with dark blond hair and his skin had a golden sheen that she assumed he'd acquired from going without an under-tunic and tunic over the summer. She'd itched to touch it ever since she'd attended him in his bath. The two candles that were lit caressed him in equal parts shadow and light, revealing the strong lines and sculpted curves of his muscled torso.

'You can touch me.' He was grinning at her, drawing her into the space between his knees.

She moved reverently, almost afraid to claim that which was now hers. His skin was warm and supple beneath her palm when she finally made contact. Slowly, she allowed her hand to move down over his solid chest, his hard nipples and down farther to the ridged planes of his stomach. She would have gone even lower, but when her fingertips touched the waist of his trousers he stopped her by grabbing her wrists. She looked at him in question and he shook his head. 'Not yet. By the gods, if you touch me there I won't trust myself.' He kept his smile, but the fierce need in his eyes made her gulp. It wasn't fear as much as anticipation that coursed through her heated blood.

'Take off your dress.' He stared down at her body as if willing himself to be able to see through the material.

Setting back on her knees, she wrestled with the hem of the billowy dress and slowly pulled it up. There was a brief moment when fear kept her still, but she wanted to go further and she even wanted him to look upon her as she had looked upon him. Hoping it would increase his pleasure, she pulled it over her head and tossed it behind her, leaving her in only her winter leggings.

'So beautiful,' he whispered, bringing his hand up between them to touch her as he had earlier when she'd been clothed. Only this time there was nothing between his fingers and her breast, so the pleasure was more intense. His fingertips and palms were hardened from years of sword work and battle, but the coarse touch only seemed to please her. His fingers rasped against her tender skin, making her ache as he plucked at her nipples.

A soft groan escaped her, prompting him to say, 'Come.' His hand went to the small of her back, lifting her up on to her knees and pulling her towards him as he dipped his head down. Before she fully realised his intent, he took her nipple deep into his mouth, the rough and silky stroke of his tongue laving her. So this is what he meant when he'd said he'd use his tongue in other places. A dart of pleasure shot straight to her core, making that place between her legs throb. She wanted something there, but she didn't know how to say it or even what to ask him for. Instead she tangled her fingers into the dark blond hair at the back of his head and held him close, unwilling to relinquish the pleasure he was giving her for the unknown.

As he continued to suckle her, his hand moved down past the small of her back to fill itself with the generous curve of her bottom. She moaned a little in the back of her throat as the rhythmic squeezing of his palm combined with his mouth at her breast made the ache inside her seem nearly unbearable. She shifted, rubbing her thighs together to alleviate the throbbing between them, but nothing seemed to help.

His mouth finally released her and his hands moved to the fastenings of her leggings, pushing them down over her hips before helping her to stand so that she could step out of them. In but a moment she was nude and standing before him.

His admiring gaze stole over her, finally making its way up to her face where it settled on her eyes. 'You've done me a great honour in becoming my wife,' he said.

She wanted to tell him that she was the one who was honoured, but she couldn't speak past a throat that was swollen nearly closed with emotion.

'Lie down for me?' His voice was textured with emotion and longing.

She nodded and moved on to the thick furs piled on the mattress. His bed was a hundred times more comfortable than the one she shared with Ellan, she thought as she settled on to her back on a fur, sinking into its warmth. He made to turn and join her, but she didn't want to be deprived of the sight of him. 'Can I see you first?' When he raised a brow in question, she nodded towards his trousers, biting her lip in mild embarrassment at how forward she was being, but it was her wedding night and he made her feel like she could say anything to him.

He grinned at her and rose to stand beside the bed. Powerful and beautiful, he looked down at her as he unfastened his trousers and pushed them down his muscled thighs. Once free from the confines of the fabric, his manhood sprang upward, nearly reaching his navel. Her lips parted on a silent gasp as she stared at him. Somehow she'd never thought that part of him would be quite so large or quite so domineering. It stood there as proud as a conquering... well, as proud as a conquering Dane. She nearly laughed at her own jest, until she realised that *that* part of him would have to somehow work its way inside her to spend. To say that it was as thick as her wrist might be a slight exaggeration, but not by much.

He released the ties that held the bed curtains back and they closed around him, sending their world into shadowed darkness as he joined her on the bed. She pushed up on to her elbows at the same time he lowered to his knees above her. 'Rolfe, I don't—' His mouth took hers in a deep and searching kiss, leaving her breathless when he pulled back to trail hot, open-mouthed kisses across her jaw and down her neck. Her skin prickled in absolute adulation to be the recipient of his attention, but she couldn't put the sight of *him* from her mind.

'I don't think…' Her voice trailed off. How did one properly address this? No one had told her he'd be so large. Maybe everyone had known but her.

'Hush…' he whispered, coming back up to take her mouth. 'Don't think about it yet. Lie here and let me love you. I'll tell you when it's time to think about that.'

'Do you vow it?'

His easy smile against her lips somehow reassured her. 'Aye, you have my word.' With a gentle hand on her shoulder, he pushed her lightly until she relented and laid back. Then his hand trailed from her shoulder to her breast and down farther to ease over her belly. His mouth followed, trailing hot kisses over her skin. When he stopped to lavish each of her nipples with attention, she closed her eyes and sank her fingers into the silk of his hair. With his mouth working over her, it was easy to forget the coming invasion and even the men waiting outside their door to listen as the deed was done. In the dark cocoon of their bed, there was only the pleasure he was giving her.

Much to her surprise, his mouth moved even lower, past her breasts, scaling over her stomach as his arm skilfully moved under her thigh, sending it farther across the bed so that he could slip between her legs. She stiffened, but he didn't take his mouth from her, moving down to her hip and then her thigh, shifting lower so that he could kiss the inside of her knee. Rotating her slightly, he let his tongue dip into the sensitive crevice behind her knee. She relaxed immediately as the slick pleasure of the caress. It wasn't until he was pushing her thighs farther apart that she realised he'd worked his way upwards, settling his shoulders between her thighs.

He placed a kiss on the dark curls guarding the mound of her womanhood. 'Rolfe!' He did it again, this time letting his tongue dip out to touch her. 'That's wicked.' Remembering his comment about the thin walls, she was sure to keep her voice very low.

'It's not. I'm your husband. Nothing we do together in this bed is wicked.'

She couldn't think of an immediate response and he'd spoken so loudly she was certain the men had heard. She'd never be able to face anyone tomorrow if they guessed what he was doing to her now.

'How does that feel?' he asked. When he repeated the action, he pressed deeper, his tongue penetrating the folds to the tender and throbbing flesh beneath. How did one answer that? There were no words to convey how the slick and rough slide of his tongue against an area so intimate she didn't even have a name for it felt. Instead of answering with words, she settled for an incomprehensible sound that she hoped he took for aye. He couldn't possibly mistake how her thighs fell open to welcome him.

With a soft laugh, he renewed his attack on her body. His fingers held her open, so that his tongue could swipe out in slow and lazy glides against her aching flesh. She didn't mean to, but she bucked beneath him in response, somehow needing more of that delicious stroke. Her thighs fell open even wider and her fingers curled in his hair to hold him against her.

His attack became less lazy and more focused.
His tongue swirled around the aching nub, giving her just the right amount of pressure, but
somehow not enough all at the same time. She
needed more...*of something.*

Then his finger stroked her as he continued
to lick her, the coarse pad moving through her
wetness and pressing inside. She moaned when
he filled her with it and retreated, only to press
inside again. The rhythm was mesmerising and
she moved with it, seeking even more. Much to
her delight, another finger quickly joined the
first, stretching her, leaving her feeling deliciously full of him.

He growled against her flesh as he pleasured
her. 'Come apart for me, Saxon. I want to taste
your pleasure.' That harsh and raspy command
was her undoing. Combined with the steady
rhythm of his fingers and tongue against that
swollen nub, she felt a tidal wave of pleasure
cresting over her. It took her over completely,
making her body tighten and pulse, trembling
around his fingers where they pressed so deeply
inside her.

Delicious tremors were still pounding
through her as he moved smoothly up her body
to hold himself just over her with his weight on
his right arm. His hips settled into the cradle of

hers and she felt the broad tip of his manhood pressing against her.

'Now,' he whispered against her lips and she tasted pleasure on him. 'Now I must come inside you.'

She nodded, but she wasn't as afraid as she might have been without the pleasure still coursing through her and weighting her limbs. Her arms went around his shoulders to hold him close and fit herself against him. Distantly, she heard his gasp as he pushed inside her a little. The fit was tight and it burned a bit as he stretched her, but at the same time she wanted more of him, wanted to be as close to him as she could get. She could feel her channel grasping at him and he must have, too, because he groaned in the back of his throat and pressed forward. Pulling back a little, he thrust forward again. In the little bit of light that seeped in around the curtain she could tell his face looked pained.

'Only a little further,' he whispered.

She wasn't certain what he meant until he retreated, only to thrust until he was fully seated within her. She couldn't help the little cry she gave and he immediately tried to soothe her, his lips brushing across her temple and whispering tender words. A hand came to her breast, his thumb strumming over the nipple.

She felt completely full of him, but after a moment of his careful attention, a tug of longing began where they were joined, an echo of the pleasure he'd given her. She shifted, testing the tight fit.

'I can't wait any more.' His voice sounded pained.

She realised that he was asking for permission to continue. 'Aye,' she whispered, wanting to give him the same pleasure he had given her. The pain had receded to discomfort, aided by the tremors that still occasionally shook her.

He moved his hips and she was surprised at the pleasant sensation. It wasn't nearly as intense as that he'd given her before, but it made her want more. She lifted her hips to meet his motion and he made a harsh sound, his hand moving to her hip to stay her.

'Don't move or I'll spend now. I want to make it good for you again,' he whispered as he rocked his hips against hers.

Spending now didn't seem like a bad thing to her. The entire point of this was to get him to spend, but his strong hand on her hip kept her in place. So instead of moving her hips, she clenched her inner muscles, tightening around his thick manhood where it was buried deep inside her, testing her ability to give him pleasure.

'Ah, Saxon!' He made a low, groaning sound deep in his chest and said something harsh in his language that she didn't understand. As if he had no control, his hips bucked against her and he took her with an intensity that stole her breath away. Aching to get even closer to him, she tightened her arms around him and wrapped her legs around his thighs. With his face buried in her hair, he gave a deep guttural cry as he found his release, pumping his hips in a few last desperate thrusts as he spilled his seed. His voice was so loud and deep, so unmistakably filled with male satisfaction, that she knew that's what the men outside had been waiting for.

She kept holding him when he fell over her, in awe of the power she had over him and the wonderful thing that had happened between them. She'd never dreamed that such pleasure was possible. It seemed like sorcery. As his body shook with leftover tremors, much like her own had, she buried her face against his chest and stroked the hair at the back of his neck. Fate had given her a gift in the form of Rolfe and she never wanted to let him go.

Chapter Fourteen

Sounds of feasting filtered into the chamber from below, but here in their warm, dark bed, there were only the sounds of Elswyth breathing and the echoes of her cries of pleasure ringing in Rolfe's ears. For as long as he lived he would never forget the sweet sound of his wife—his Saxon—coming apart in his arms. The soft and desperate cry had urged him to lead her to an end whose existence she probably hadn't even been aware of, yet she'd trusted him to take her there anyway. Brushing a palm along the length of her lithe body, he squeezed her hip and placed a kiss to her temple as his heart swelled with tenderness for her. He was dangerously close to losing himself to her. He could feel it, but he had no way of stopping it from happening, save walking away from her and that was something he couldn't do.

Easing from the bed so as not to wake her, he pushed back one of the curtains to allow in some candlelight. It swept across her breasts, giving him a view of the lush mounds of flesh with their pink tips. By the gods, she was beautiful. His manhood tightened and swelled, so he forced himself to look away. She'd be too sore for any more bed sport tonight.

Some thoughtful servant had left a pot of water along with a pitcher of mead on the table before they had retired for the evening. It had grown lukewarm, but he still used it to clean himself and then picked up a square of linen and wet it for Elswyth. She roused when he sat on the bed, smiling up at him with a flush on her cheeks. He eased her knee upwards and with gentle strokes washed away the evidence of their joining before tossing the square away. To his surprise she hadn't resisted, only lain there watching him with joy and contentment shining in her eyes.

'How do you feel? Was I too rough with you?' He couldn't resist dragging a fingertip down the sweet, intimate flesh that was still open to him. She smiled and he ran his hand down her soft inner thigh, unable to stop touching her.

She shook her head. 'I'm a little sore, but

that's to be expected. You were actually quite gentle for a barbarian, Dane.'

Chuckling, he grabbed her hips to hold her in place as he moved quickly to lie on top of her. She giggled and swatted at his shoulders, but he grabbed her wrists and held her arms to the furs at her back. 'Is this more of what you had in mind, Saxon?'

'Aye, I knew the tenderness wouldn't last.'

She didn't sound as if she minded, turning her head and offering more of her neck to him as he kissed her. He was awed and surprised when she curled her legs around his waist to hold him in place. After the way she'd reacted to their first kiss, he hadn't known what to expect from her in their bed. His fear had been that she wouldn't allow herself to enjoy the things he could show her, but she seemed to have put her initial reservations behind her.

Unfortunately, this position wasn't conducive to his resolution to allow her sufficient time to recover before he took her again. He'd already swelled to his full length against her and was aching to be inside her again. Instead, he let her go and pushed away to sit back on his knees. 'The rough bed sport starts tomorrow. Every bride deserves one tender night.'

She pushed up on an elbow, shocking him

even further when she looked directly at his
engorged shaft with curiosity. 'You're...' She
paused as if searching for a way to describe
him. 'Hard again?'

'Aye, it's possible to spend more than once
a night.' It was also possible that he'd pass the
rest of his life in this particular state with her
as his wife.

She glanced up at him as if she'd never considered that possibility, before staring back
down at his length. 'May I touch you?'

He nearly groaned, knowing it would only
make him desperate for her, but wanting her
to be comfortable with him, so he nodded, not
trusting his voice to speak. Her initial touch was
tentative and soft, but she soon grew bolder and
took him in hand. He could tell that she grew
aroused by touching him; her breathing came
faster and her eyes darkened. Finally, she whispered, 'I won't mind if you want to...put yourself inside me again.'

A deep groan of frustration escaped him before he could stop it and he moved away from
her touch. 'I would love nothing more, wife, but
you must heal.' If he was honest with himself,
there was a healthy dose of self-preservation
in his refusal as well. Bedding her had broken
down the meagre barrier he'd been able to erect

against her. He needed some time to put the pieces back together before taking her again.

Picking up a fur, he wrapped it around his waist to hide his desire from her. Not that hiding it did anything to make it go away. Deep pulsations of need continued to pound through him, so he moved to the table in his chamber and poured himself some mead before taking a long swallow.

'Is something the matter?'

He turned to see her sitting up in bed, holding a fur to her breasts, but her soft shoulders and the curve of one hip was still exposed. Emotion squeezed his lungs so tight that he couldn't breathe as he took her in. How could she tell? How was it possible this slip of a girl could break him down so easily? He gave a shake of his head in answer.

'You don't still suspect me of treason?' Her mouth smiled in jest, but her eyes were wide and serious.

The question was nearly his undoing. 'I know how difficult of a choice it was to marry me.' As he spoke, he set his cup on the table and crossed to her. 'You chose peace and I believe that peace is in your heart.'

Her face brightened and she took his hand and brought it to her chest. The steady rhythm of her heart beat beneath his palm. 'Once I thought of losing you, it wasn't that difficult a choice.'

Fighting the urge to crush her against him and never let her go, he closed his eyes. Every fibre in his body told him that this was dangerous. It was too soon. He hadn't even known this woman a month ago, yet she called to something deeper within him. It reached for her, needed her, longed to drink up her every touch.

'Then it must be something else,' she whispered.

'What do you mean?'

Taking his face in her hand, she said, 'Ever since I told you aye there's been something... you've been holding yourself back from me. There's been a distance.'

He let out a breath on a laugh because he knew she was right. 'There wasn't any distance between us earlier tonight.'

She blushed, but she didn't back down. By the gods, she was fierce and he was doomed. 'Not that.' Her lips curved in another smile and she continued gently, as if afraid to scare him off. 'Perhaps wariness is a better description. If it's not me and my family, then why are you wary of me? Did... Is it something that's happened to you?'

Her eyes were so open and honest when she stared up at him that he couldn't stop himself from putting his arms around her and holding her against him. This woman had more courage than he. The notion struck him with a certainty that he couldn't deny and he felt shamed and proud at the same time.

When he couldn't speak of his fears, she had come to him with hers and spoken of them openly. She'd sought his comfort as she'd told him of her mother's betrayal and her family's hatred. It had quite literally cost her the life that she had known to come to him as his wife and he'd had to give up nothing in return. The least he could do was be honest with her and let her know that there were certain boundaries he couldn't cross. Perhaps he'd been selfish not to tell her before they had wed, but it wasn't something he'd rectify even if given the chance.

She was his.

Pulling back enough to look down at her without letting her go, he said, 'The truth is that there was once another woman. I thought that I loved her, but I realise now that I was merely infatuated.' He'd never felt this bone-deep pull with Hilde. There had been excitement and affection, but not whatever was happening with Elswyth. He held her close as he told her everything, even how it had driven him to become a warrior. She watched him with a mixture of sadness and understanding.

When he finished, she said, 'Hilde was a fool, but I can't say that I'm sorry for it. Had she not been, I wouldn't have you now.' Taking his face between her hands, she rose to her knees to meet him at eye level and the tip of her nose touched his as she spoke. 'And you have me. I won't betray you, Rolfe. I give you my word.'

'I know that you won't.' It was all he could manage against the swell of tenderness he felt for her. The barrier had crumbled with her words and he was tumbling headlong into the abyss with only her to catch him. It didn't matter if he trusted her to catch him or not. He was already lost.

She kissed him with all the passion smouldering between them. A groan tore from his lips when her hand came between them, tightening around his semi-hard length and bringing him to full arousal again. 'Saxon,' he murmured, though he didn't know if it was a warning or a welcome.

'Is it possible to pleasure you without you being inside me?' she whispered.

He nodded, somewhat amazed that in her

innocence she was able to conceive of such a thing. 'Aye.'

'Show me.' Her hand tightened slightly, pulling the breath from his lungs.

So he showed her how to use her hands to bring him pleasure, then he spent the rest of the night making good on his vow to use his tongue on every part of her body.

Rolfe left her the next morning to go meet with his men, but when Elswyth had moved to rise with him he'd pressed her to stay in bed. Exhausted from their activities the night before, she'd slept a fair amount of the morning only waking up when someone knocked on the door. She had barely donned her underdress when the knock came again.

'Elswyth?' Ellan called, her voice insistent.

Rolling her eyes at her impatience, Elswyth opened the door, barely getting out of the way before her sister barrelled in holding a tray of breakfast. 'You are awake,' she said as she set the food on the table.

'I am now. Thank you for bringing breakfast.'

Ellan shrugged off the thanks and walked over, looking her up and down as if she expected her to be different somehow. Elswyth laughed at the expectant look on her face. The truth was that she did feel different, but she was certain she still looked the same from the outside.

'How was it?' Ellan asked. Subtlety had never been her strong suit.

'What do you mean?' Elswyth smiled, intentionally baiting her sister, as she walked over to take a seat at the table.

'Elswyth,' Ellan groaned and sat down on the bench beside her. 'Was he…gentle? Did you enjoy it?'

Taking pity on her, Elswyth nodded. 'Aye to both. It was perfect and I went to sleep knowing that I am a lucky woman to have him as my husband. This morning I can still scarcely believe it.' If not for the fact that she had awakened in Rolfe's chamber and her body bore a slight tenderness from the night before, she might think she had dreamed it. Never had she expected marriage to be like this.

'If I had to guess, I would say he feels the same.'

'Did you see him?'

Ellan's smile widened. 'I did at the morning meal. He seemed happier than I've ever seen him. The men were teasing him, but he didn't get angry once and smiled the entire time.'

Elswyth felt her cheeks burn hot. 'I suppose everyone knew what we did.'

Ellan laughed and rubbed her shoulder with affection. 'Well, it was your wedding night.'

She was embarrassed, but she couldn't find it within her to regret the night or their lack of privacy. There was no room for regret in her happiness. Turning her attention to the bowl of pottage, they spoke for a while about the wedding. When Ellan turned the conversation back to the wedding night, obviously desperate for specifics, Elswyth shook her head, laughing. 'You'll find out soon enough for yourself. How goes your hunt for a husband? Any prospects?'

Ellan shook her head and looked away. The change in her mood from borderline rude curiosity to meekness immediately made Elswyth suspicious. 'You've met someone.'

'Nay.' Ellan shook her head again, but the look on her face had turned serious. 'We've not met. Not really.'

'But there is someone who's caught your eye?'

Nodding, Ellan rose to her feet as if the strength of her thoughts couldn't be contained to merely sitting. 'It's too soon to think of marriage. He's unmarried, but I don't know if he's promised to someone. I don't think he is.' She wrung her hands and paced, a faraway expression in her eyes. 'He's tall, handsome and quiet. He doesn't say very much, but when he does the men listen and his eyes... Elswyth, his eyes say so much. He watches me sometimes and I swear to you that the feeling is more powerful than the flattery of any man.' A pretty blush tinged her sister's cheeks and she smiled like a woman in love.

'Such emotion for a man you've never met.'

Ellan grinned and nodded her agreement. 'I know you won't believe this, but I can't seem to find my voice when he's near.'

'Who is it?' When Ellan shook her head, Elswyth rose and took her hands. 'You must tell me.'

'It's Aevir.'

An image of the powerful warrior came to mind. There was a quiet intensity about him that might have drawn her interest as well if she hadn't been so consumed with Rolfe. He was handsome, but where Rolfe was gentle, there was a hint of something dark in Aevir. Not cruelty, exactly, but something complicated. 'Does he return your interest?'

Ellan ducked her head. 'Aye, I believe he does. I see him watching me and once...'

'Once what?'

'Before he left for Banford we found ourselves alone one night and I think if we hadn't been interrupted he might have…well, it hardly matters. We were interrupted.'

'You kissed him?' Elswyth's voice rose in surprise.

'It was an accident really, but, aye.'

'Do you want me to talk to Rolfe? Find out more about him?'

Ellan shook her head. 'Nay, please don't mention anything. I'd rather wait for Aevir to return and see if there is even anything to consider first.'

Elswyth assured her that she wouldn't ask about Aevir, but she couldn't help but worry at her sister's choice. Aevir was respected among the warriors and he treated them well, but there was something about his quiet intensity that unnerved her. His eyes sometimes seemed almost haunted, making her unsure if he would be a good match for her often playful sister.

On the first morning after their wedding, Rolfe knew that he was enamoured of his wife. He had wrongly assumed that he could go about his duties and his life would stay much the same as it had been before. The only difference would be that his wife's lush and lithe body would be waiting for his pleasure in bed every night. But she'd invaded his thoughts as well as his bed.

She was always there. While on the sparring field, he'd try to catch glimpses of her with her bow and arrow and secretly long to be with her instead of his men. While in the bathhouse, he tried to think of ways he could get the place to himself so that he could bring her there and take her while their bodies were slick with sweat and steam. In the evenings while listening to the stories told by the skald, he would seek her out to hold her against him, savouring how well she fit with him. At night, long after their bodies were sated, he enjoyed talking with her about his childhood home and learning how she had spent her days before him. It was this that frightened him more than his physical attraction to her; it was this intimacy that was far more potent than anything he'd known with Hilde.

By the time several days had passed, he knew that enamoured wasn't a strong enough word to describe his feelings for her. Obsessed would more closely name the feeling. Or, if he were a bitter sort, he could claim that she had bewitched him. Only he knew that women held no such power and that she herself was as lost in him as he was in her. Any fool could see how her eyes lit up when she saw him. When they spoke, even at the table eating their evening meal with everyone around them, the world fell away and it was just the two of them.

But even their obsession with each other couldn't keep the world at bay for long. Her father would arrive soon, which meant that news of what had happened in Banford would finally reach her. As each day had passed, the lump of dread in his stomach had become more noticeable. He knew that it would be best if she heard the news from him, rather than some other source, yet he couldn't bring himself to disturb the bliss they'd found.

Each morning when he awoke, he told himself that he had to tell her today. Except she'd awaken next to him, warm and soft and eager, and he'd lose himself in her for a time. Afterwards, as the day wore on, he'd find himself beguiled by her happiness and he couldn't bring himself to say anything that would change that for her. Then he would make a deal with himself to let them have today and he would tell her in the morning, only to have the whole cycle start again.

Finally he ran out of time. Men had come in late that morning to alert them that Scots had been seen on Alvey land to the north, just outside Banford. Rolfe would have to ride out immediately to see to the problem. Hurrying inside, he found his wife seated near the fire with Lady Gwendolyn and Ellan, helping the former with her embroidery skills. Tova sat next to them on a pallet on the floor near Elswyth's skirts, playing with a woollen doll. Wyborn lay near the group, far enough away to discourage the baby's curiosity, but close enough to keep a watchful eye on Elswyth. He'd become her protector, as if he knew that she belonged to him and Rolfe now.

The group laughed at a particularly crooked line Lady Gwendolyn had sewn and Rolfe felt a tug near his heart as he stared at Elswyth's happy face. He didn't want to rob her of her happiness, but he had no choice. She would probably hate him for what he'd done in Banford before they had wed and what he was about to do would guarantee it. There was little doubt that the Scots had been seen because they had met or had planned to meet with Godric.

'Elswyth.' She glanced up and the ready smile fell from her face as she took in his grave expression. His heart twisted as she stood, the blood leaving her face as she approached him.

'What's happened?' she asked, taking his arm.

He drew her to the side of the room for a bit

of privacy. 'The Scots have been sighted on Alvey land.'

'Where?' But it was as if she already knew. Her brow creased and a pain came into her eyes.

He nodded. 'Near Banford. We have no proof, but we suspect they are here to meet with your father.'

Shaking her head, she said, 'But they've never come this far south before.'

'I know. It's a bad sign that they've grown bolder.' He rubbed her shoulders in a steady motion to soothe her. 'I have to go.'

'Let me come with you. I can talk to my father.'

The idea was so abhorrent he immediately shook his head. 'Nay. I won't have you in danger.' He was certain there would be a fight. If they caught the Scots crossing the Alvey border, there would be a battle.

'As far as Banford, then.'

'We can't be assured the Scots won't attack Banford. I won't take the chance. You must stay here behind Alvey's walls.'

She opened her mouth to argue, but he tightened his hold slightly on her shoulders. 'I have to go, Saxon. We can't argue about this.'

Throwing her arms around him, she squeezed him as if she never wanted to let him go, but the hall was abuzz with action now as the word had spread and they had no choice but to part. 'I'll help you pack your things,' she whispered, a husk in her voice as she blinked back tears.

He let out a groan and pressed a kiss to her forehead. 'I will come back.'

She nodded, but her fists tightened in his tunic. 'Soon.'

Chapter Fifteen

❧

It took Rolfe and his men two days to hunt the Scots down. The longships took them north, but the Scots knew enough to stay away from the waterways, forcing the warriors to travel on foot across the frozen earth for much of the journey. Cnut brought men from Banford to join him, bringing their count to nearly eighty strong. Finally, when the sky was still dark and the moon covered with low-hanging clouds, Rolfe and his men approached their encampment.

They crept silently, but the scream as the first battle axe found its mark quickly alerted the men to their presence. A surge of vigour drove Rolfe forward—suddenly the battle wasn't about taking land or maintaining territory, it was about protecting his home. An image of Elswyth as she slept flashed before his mind's eye. More than anything else this battle was about protecting her and ensuring that she could continue to sleep and live in peace. A guttural battle cry fell from his lips and his warriors followed suit as they attacked.

The Scots rose, but many of them met their deaths before fully coming to their feet. The ones towards the middle of camp stood the best chance. They stood in a circle three rows deep, facing their attackers on all sides, but Rolfe's men were too fast, too ready and prepared to be held off for long. Rolfe's sword took men down faster than he could see their expressions and soon there was a gap in their defence as a group ran off towards the wood instead of fighting. The grey light of morning spread over the camp, illuminating their path.

'After them!' he yelled to the man on his right. 'Keep as many of them alive for questioning as you can.' The warrior took the group of men under his command, running after them, and Cnut quickly took his place so that Rolfe would not be left undefended.

The clang of steel on steel sounded close, drawing Rolfe's attention away from the fleeing men to the action before him. As if his face had been culled from the depths of Rolfe's deepest nightmare, Osric loomed before him and time itself seemed to grind to a halt. The pale skin of the Saxon's cheeks was burnished with exertion as he hacked at an attacker. The Dane warrior deflected, surging to his left to meet yet another Scot, leaving Osric free to skewer his unguarded ribs if he so chose. But something caught Osric's attention and he turned towards Rolfe, meeting his gaze.

Fury transformed his features, his teeth shining white as he bared them and trudged forward. Rolfe stared, hardly able to breathe as he heard Elswyth's voice near his ear as she laughed about the time Osric, then a boy, had helped her convince her father that one of the sheep could talk. She had told Rolfe that story one night as they'd lain abed. Her throaty laughter had filled the cocoon of their curtained bed as she remembered how her father's bewildered disbelief had turned to grudging acceptance when he'd been unable to find the source of the voice and then anger when he'd found out he'd been duped.

This boy—now a man—was important to her.

Rolfe's muscles froze, unable to carry out his natural instinct to protect himself as Osric came closer. His grip tightened on his sword, but his arm stayed up, caught in that moment of slackness before attacking. 'Osric! Don't!' His words fell on deaf ears as the Saxon lunged, swinging his blade.

Cnut yelled, plunging before Rolfe to intercept his would-be attacker. Before Rolfe could even call out, Osric fell to the ground, blood pouring from a deep wound across his torso. It was a death blow. The light had faded from Osric's eyes before his shoulders landed with a dull thud.

The horrible moment was over as quickly as it had begun. Rolfe was forced to step over him and continue the battle until it was finally over. Whether Osric had been there as a messenger or had joined the Scots, Rolfe didn't know. Despite the order to take prisoners, no men had been left alive. They had defended themselves too fiercely, clearly determined to die fighting.

With Osric's death, the glimmer of hope Rolfe had carried that he and Elswyth might be able to find their way to happiness had died. She would never be able to forgive him for the killing her friend. But even if she could, Osric's presence only furthered the theory that Banford was ripe with treachery. Godric had to be behind it and Rolfe had no choice but to try to prove that theory.

Elswyth would hate him. It was a certainty, but if only that had stood between them, he might have found some reason to hope. As it was, his standoff with Osric had proven that which Rolfe most feared. Elswyth had made him lose his focus. Because of his growing infatuation with her, he'd allowed himself to shirk his duty, to feint when he should not have hesitated in meeting Osric with his sword. He might be dead now if not for Cnut. Or worse. Had Osric posed an immediate threat to one of Rolfe's men, could Rolfe have saved him? Would he still have hesitated? That hesitation was an unforgivable crime as far as Rolfe was concerned.

Darkness settled over him as he made his way through the next hours. Men were sent with Cnut to Banford with the news of Osric's treachery. Aevir was to be called in and Godric was to be brought to Alvey for questioning. Rolfe went home to his wife with a heavy heart.

They arrived near midnight and Rolfe stayed downstairs long enough to relay what had happened to Vidar and to wash the stench of battle from himself in the bathhouse. Only then was he able to take himself to his wife. Silently pushing open the door to their chamber, he lit a single candle and pulled the bed curtain back to watch her sleep. He was exhausted, but his body still stirred at the sight of her. In fact, he'd left Wyborn downstairs by the fire, because he wanted one more night with her before seeing the hatred on her face. Before he had to put necessary distance between them. Tomorrow he would have to somehow figure out a way to remove her from his heart.

Stripping off his clothes, he crawled into bed with her and pulled her soft, warm body against him. She sighed, instinctively curving herself into him.

'Saxon,' he whispered against her neck as her familiar scent washed over him.

'Dane,' she answered back, but her voice was still thick with sleep and dreams. The woman could sleep through an invading army.

His palms moved over her body through her nightdress, remembering the planes and curves, filling themselves with her softness. His mouth found hers, drinking her sweetness, as one of his hands found its way beneath the linen to her bottom. It was the touch of his bare skin on hers that finally broke her sleep.

'Rolfe,' she whispered against his lips, then repeated his name with more urgency as she pulled away, turning in his arms, to see him. 'You're home!' Her arms went around him and she kissed every part of his face as if checking for damage. 'Are you injured?'

'There was a fight, but I'm not injured.' He hoped she didn't ask him for details, because he couldn't talk about it now. He only asked for one more night with her. Tomorrow would be soon enough to push her away.

'Thank God.' She said it like she meant it, repeating it as if she'd spent the hours of his absence praying for his return. Perhaps she had. Perhaps she had missed him as much as he'd missed her. Her hands travelled over his naked chest and farther down as if she couldn't quite believe he was unharmed.

Rolling her on to her back, he rose above her, taking in her precious face as she stared up at him.

'What's wrong?' Her brow furrowed and she touched his cheek even as she widened her thighs so that he could settle between them. 'Something's happened.'

He shook his head, too overcome with her to talk. Instead of asking again, she only smiled and pulled him down to kiss him. He closed his eyes and put all of his regret and, aye, even love into that kiss. Her hands worked between them, pulling her clothing out of the way to make way for him. Finally, her fingers wrapped around his length and she guided him to her. He gasped as his rigid length slipped into her moist heat. She arched beneath him, beckoning him for more and sighing against his lips when he gave it to her.

He took her slowly, knowing that tonight might have to last him a lifetime.

When Elswyth awoke the next morning, Rolfe had gone. Downstairs the men had already sequestered themselves at a table in the corner, discussing the battle, she assumed. Lady Gwendolyn hadn't been very forthcoming with information, only saying that aye, the men had battled the Scots and that her family had not been involved, before keeping her busy all day in her chamber with mending and embroidery. It had been enough for a time, but as the day had become night and she'd only been able to share quick glances with Rolfe, Elswyth was losing her patience. It was as if everyone had made a concerted effort to keep her from her husband.

Aevir had arrived during the evening meal, and when she thought that meant the men might break for the night, it only sent them into another round of discussion. Elswyth had finally taken up a stool by the fire where she played a dice game with Ellan, determined to wait them out and approach her husband as soon as he rose.

Something was wrong. She didn't know what it was, but something had happened in the time Rolfe was gone and it had changed him. It was in his face. She had seen it last night and cursed herself a fool for letting him distract her before finding out the truth. Whatever it was, it scared her and she wouldn't rest tonight until she got to the bottom of it. There was a distance between them that frightened her.

The door came open and a man rushed in. She recognised him as one of the men who stood guard on the wall. His eyes were wide and determined as he walked to Lord Vidar. The dice slipped from her hands and she rose to her feet, knowing instinctively that something had happened.

'Godric is here,' he said a bit too loudly.

'What are you doing?' Ellan asked, coming to her feet when Elswyth turned to go get her cloak.

'I'm going to see Father. Something has happened and, if Rolfe won't tell me, I'll ask him.' There was also the small issue of delivering the news of her wedding to him, but somehow that seemed secondary now.

She hurried upstairs and came back down just in time to see Rolfe heading out the door. Determined to find out what was going on, she hurried through the hall before anyone could stop her. Lady Gwendolyn called to her, but she pretended not to hear and kept moving forward. When she stepped outside, it was easy to see where to go. A group of men had gathered beneath the light of the torches inside the wall.

'I asked for my daughters.' She heard her father's deep voice through the crowd as she pushed her way through.

'And we have come instead.' The iron in Lord Vidar's voice was unmistakable.

'You would deny me my own daughters?' Godric's voice rose a fraction.

'Nay, but I would know what you're about first. My man tells me you left Banford days ago,' Lord Vidar answered.

She neared the front to see Father grin, revealing well-kept teeth, though a few were missing. 'Went hunting. No harm done. I've come to take my daughters home and I'd like to leave in the morning.'

'Won't you stay and take a meal with us tomorrow?' Lord Vidar asked.

He shook his head and at his side Galan

crossed his arms over his chest. 'No time for feasting.'

'Elswyth won't be returning with you,' Rolfe answered, drawing the man's astute gaze. 'She's my wife.'

Elswyth winced at the words. She had a speech prepared, one in which she would have gently let her father know what had happened. Instead of the anger she had expected, her father only looked pensive. Galan was the one who grew angry. His arms dropped to his sides and his fists clenched as he took a step towards Rolfe. 'Did you force her?'

'Nay, I didn't force her. She was very happy to become my wife.'

'What did you do to her, you bastard? She would never marry a Dane willingly.' Galan's voice rose a notch on that last part.

Elswyth winced when confronted with the bald hatred she had known to expect from them. They would think she had betrayed them when they learned the truth of Rolfe's words. Part of her wanted to go back inside before one of them saw her.

Rolfe's voice interrupted that thought. 'She did marry me and she did so willingly. The marriage is valid with witnesses and the endorsement of your lord.' She couldn't see his face, but his voice was hard, nothing like the man who had come to her last night 'We regret that it had to be done in haste and without your agreement, but I'm prepared to reimburse you for the omission and to give you a fair bride price. I'd like to offer you twenty-five pounds of silver.' It was more than double the typical amount.

Father scoffed. 'Do you think silver is all it will take to buy my acceptance of this farce?'

'It's no farce.' Rolfe's voice had gentled, but only slightly. 'The deed has been consummated and she is content as my wife. I have vowed to give her my protection and keep her safe.'

A flicker of uncertainty appeared on Father's face and for the first time something very close to pain displaced the hatred. She longed to reach out to him and tell him that she was happy. It was time to reveal herself.

Father's next words brought her up short.

'Safe,' the older man said. 'Does that include her home? Her family? Did you tell her about your actions in Banford before or after the wedding? Have you told her about Osric?'

She had expected Rolfe to scoff, to deny any knowledge of the wrongdoing her father's tone implied, but that didn't happen. A damning silence fell over the men. A sick feeling formed in the pit of her stomach and she knew that this was why Rolfe had appeared so hollow. Something had indeed happened.

'Rolfe?'

He turned, eyes wide with guilt as if he were stricken to see her. The crowd made room for her and she stepped into the clearing in the middle of the circle they created. When Rolfe didn't speak, she turned to her father. 'Father, what happened in Banford?'

'Go back inside.' Rolfe's voice was hard, leaving no room for argument as he pressed his hand to her waist. It wasn't the sort of touch she associated with him. It was cold, almost impersonal, as if she were an object and not the woman he'd held with such tenderness in the past. A shiver worked its way down her spine.

Elswyth stared up at her husband, having been aware that this side of him existed—the forbidding commander of warriors—but she'd almost forgotten it. Nor had she expected to see it directed at her. It only reinforced the distance she had felt growing between them since his return. Telling herself that she was mistaken, she pressed a hand to the one at her waist and gave him an uncertain smile. 'I want to stay. What is he talking about?'

'We'll talk about this later. Inside,' came his

immediate and unyielding reply. There was
something in his face lurking behind the command, something that she dimly recognised
as fear, and it frightened her. She'd never seen
Rolfe afraid. It told her that whatever they were
talking about was important and it concerned
her. She wasn't going anywhere.

Turning to her father and Galan, she stepped
away from Rolfe's hand on her waist and asked,
'What happened in Banford and what is this
about Osric?'

Her father opened his mouth to speak, but
before a sound came out Lord Vidar said, 'Do
not, Godric.' His voice was deep and strong
with authority.

She stared at his hard face, taken aback that
the men she thought she had come to know so
well were behaving in this way. A threatening
wave of premonition came over her, and she
looked to Rolfe. He appeared angry, but the fear
was still there, twisting his handsome features
with pain. 'Elswyth.' His voice had gentled a
bit. 'Come, let me tell you in our chamber.'
There was a subtle question in his voice as he
held out his hand to her.

Her gaze fixated on that hand, wavering. She
so wanted to disappear with him, hiding away
in their chamber from whatever horrible thing

was about to happen. She wanted it more than she'd ever wanted anything. She might have actually taken his hand. Her palm tingled, already anticipating his familiar warmth and comfort, but Galan spoke. 'He killed Osric.'

'Lie!' Rolfe yelled, staring at her brother as if he could strike him down with one look.

Elswyth reeled from those words. She thought of Osric's boyish smile and the way his hair always had the one curl that would flop over his forehead. The way he would tease her about getting too attached to the baby lambs who lost their mothers, but he would stay up late right beside her the entire time helping her care for them. His heart had been just as soft as hers when it came to them. And now that kindness was gone, stripped from the world as if it had never existed.

'He can't be gone,' she whispered to herself, but Rolfe was there behind her and he heard her, confirming her worst fears.

'I'm sorry, Elswyth.' His voice was soft, but it was cold and distant. The man she knew would have called her Saxon and his voice would have ached with the admission as he touched her. This man was not the husband who had left her.

She whirled to face her husband. 'You killed

him?' She couldn't even conceive of a scenario where that event was likely.

'Nay.' His voice hardened and he glanced at her brother in annoyance, before looking back to her. 'Come inside with me. I vow I'll tell you everything that happened.'

'You'll lie to her, you mean,' Galan said before she could answer. 'Your men killed him because he was talking to the Scots. Because you're so arrogant a man must be cut down for even talking to someone you dislike.'

'Damn you! Shut up and let me speak to my wife!' Rolfe shouted.

'You've had plenty of time to talk to her,' her father cut in. 'You came back last night, didn't you? That's plenty of time.'

'Last night?' She stared up at her husband and she knew he was remembering just as she was how they had passed the night in bed. He'd known this horrible thing and he hadn't come to her once today to tell her. The guilt was shining from his eyes, proving that her father spoke the truth.

'You've had even longer than that to confess the destruction you wrought in Banford.' Father's voice cut between them.

'What did you do in Banford?' she asked,

feeling very much as if the man before her were a stranger.

Rolfe swallowed and proceeded in a precise voice as if he were explaining something complicated to someone slow, or trying to distance a deranged person away from the knife in their hand. She wasn't certain which scenario applied to her at the moment. It seemed that everyone knew everything except for her and she very much felt as if she could strike out at someone if she wasn't let in on the secret soon. 'Osric was with the Scots we found,' he said. 'He fought alongside them when we attacked. Our plan was to take prisoners, but it was clear from the beginning that they only wanted victory or death.'

A lump welled in her throat and her lip trembled with the force it took to ask, 'He's gone?'

Rolfe gave a curt nod and her vision blurred with tears.

'Even before that they burned Osric's home and Durwin's, too,' Father said. 'Claimed they found Durwin across the border in Alba where they killed him.'

Her hands were shaking when she brought them to her face, needing a moment to take in what had happened without everyone staring at her. But it didn't help. She could feel their eyes on her. A spasm of pain tore through her body as she imagined Osric cut down by Rolfe's order. The sight of his dear face wouldn't leave her. She'd never see his smile again, or his kind brown eyes as he brought her a pudding from his mother. And poor Durwin. He'd been married with a child on the way. Why had he been with the Scots?

Then a thought came to her. If she had married Osric, none of this would have happened. He'd still be alive and smiling at her. Father had wanted her to marry him. He'd not made a secret of it, not really. She'd pretended surprise when Ellan brought it up, but only because it wasn't something she had wanted to entertain. Osric had been like her brother, or maybe she'd been too stupid to understand how to pick a proper husband. He would have been kind to her and she had no doubt that she could have talked him out of joining her father's cause. Had she married him, he would have been home and not out with the Scots. He would be safe and alive. Guilt nearly made her drop to her knees.

As she'd had her crisis the conversation and shouting had continued around her, but the words, 'grounds for divorce', spoken by her father brought her back to what was happening.

'There will be no divorce,' Rolfe was saying. They spoke as if she wasn't there. As if deciding her future wasn't a conversation worth including her in. But then that should come as no surprise, because no one had bothered to tell her any of this before the issue had been forced. She barely managed to stifle a sob as she pushed her way through the crowd, needing to isolate herself from the madness around her.

Chapter Sixteen

No one approached Elswyth as she ran back to the chamber she shared with Rolfe. Behind her the men's voices rose in anger, but she couldn't be bothered with them any more. She had too much to sort out. The only problem was that once she was alone with the door latched behind her, there was no feeling of sanctuary, no clarity. Only more confusion.

Osric was dead and her husband had caused it. Rolfe might not have held the weapon, but he had ordered it when he had ordered the attack. She couldn't wrap her thoughts around that and she didn't know how to accept it. Where did this leave her? Them? Father would never come to see the logic in her marriage to a Dane now. Even if her earlier argument would have convinced him, Osric's death would weigh too heavy on his heart. He'd loved Osric like a son.

In the silence of the chamber, there was only one conclusion that became clear in the madness. If she did not turn her back on Rolfe tonight, she would lose her family. Father and Galan would shun her, casting her from their lives as her own mother had been cast out. If she chose to be with her family, then Rolfe would be lost to her.

That thought brought her to her knees. They fell out from under her and she crumpled into a heap next to the bed. If today and tonight had been any indication—a terrible shudder tore through her as she remembered his cold touch, his hollow voice—then he might already be lost to her. Guilt or something more powerful was driving him to keep his distance from her.

The knock on the door drew her from her thoughts. There was no one she wanted to talk to, so she asked, 'Who is it?' without rising.

'It's me,' Ellan answered. 'Please open the door.' Her voice was as distinct as if she stood inside the chamber. Elswyth found herself thinking no wonder the men had had no need for further confirmation of the wedding-night consummation. They had heard it all.

Torn with the need to be alone and to find comfort from the only person she knew who still accepted her as she was, Elswyth ultimately rose to her feet and unlatched the door. Ellan came into the room and took her into her arms. Much to Elswyth's shame, she started to sob. Ellan crooned softly, 'I'm so sorry', and led her to the bed where she sat beside her on the furs, gently rubbing her back. Once the tears came, it was a long time until they stopped and, once they had, she felt drained. But she knew what she had to do.

'What are you doing?' Ellan asked as she jerked away to get to her feet.

Elswyth was already at the door before her sister's voice stopped her. 'I have to talk to Father. I want him to know why I married Rolfe.' She needed to hear his reaction, to know for certain if he would truly reject her.

Ellan nodded and stood. 'I'll come with you as far as the gates. I can't chance him making me return.'

Not for the first time, Elswyth wondered how choices could be so simple for Ellan. She always seemed to know how to get what she wanted. Elswyth always struggled, because what she wanted seemed to be at odds with something else she wanted.

The pair were able to move through the great hall undetected as excitement was still high and the house was in general chaos as the men drank. It wasn't until they were outside that Elswyth saw Rolfe's broad shoulders as he stood talking to Lord Vidar and Aevir. She hoped to make it past their group unnoticed, but Aevir saw her and spoke to Rolfe, who turned to regard her. She sucked in a deep breath as he walked over.

'Where are you going?' he asked, his eyes sharp as she pulled the fur cloak tighter around her as if that could shield her from his coolness.

'I'm going to spend the night with my family. I wasn't able to speak to my father alone.'

Rolfe immediately shook his head, but she couldn't tell what he was thinking. His eyes were closed to her. 'Nay. It's late. You can speak to him in the morning if you must.'

'If I must? Rolfe, he is my father. I wed knowing that he would not approve. I must speak with him.'

His mouth pressed into a grim line as he stared at her. Part of her wanted to throw herself into his arms and seek the comfort that she knew he was capable of giving her, but he seemed so far away from her.

'He's camped outside the gate. You can stay tonight, but you'll come back in the morning.' He spoke as if she were no one important to him and her heart broke a little bit more, if that was possible. It wouldn't be possible to break her heart if she didn't love him so much. The realisation of how quickly she had fallen under his spell was enough to make her nod. Words failed her.

Turning quickly, she hurried to the gates. Once there, she glanced back to see that Rolfe had moved back to the men. Ellan took her in a quick hug. 'Please remember that you are not our mother,' her sister whispered against her ear. 'No matter what Father or Galan say, you married Rolfe because you chose peace.'

A lump of gratitude towards Ellan formed in her throat and she nodded, afraid that to speak would bring more tears and she needed to be strong now. Giving Ellan a squeeze, she turned and walked through the gates.

Her father had made his camp near the village of tents set up by the Dane warriors outside the walls. He was squarely outside of Dane territory, though not so far as the forest.

'Elswyth!' Galan called to her as soon as he saw her and ran to take her in his arms. 'He let you go?'

Father stood by the fire, holding his hand out to her. She nearly sobbed as she moved from Galan's arms to take her father's hand. 'How is Baldric? Were you able to get him back?' In her pain and confusion, she'd forgotten to ask about her younger brother earlier. That guilt was heaped on to the other that was weighing her down.

Her father's brow furrowed and he shot a glance at Galan. Galan cleared his throat and said, 'Aye, Sister. We were able to get him back. He's at home.'

Relief swept through her. At least taking the bloodstone hadn't been for naught. She'd helped to save her brother. Father put his thick arms around her and her shoulders started to shake. Sobs threatened again, but she managed to hold them back.

'Did he hurt you, girl?'

'Nay.' She shook her head. 'He'd never hurt me. I married him because I thought it would bring peace to Banford. Osric wasn't supposed to die. Why was he there, Father? Why was he with the Scots?' Her fists clenched in his tunic, but his expression was impassive as he stared down at her.

''Tis true then? He didn't force the marriage?'

A lump lodged in her throat. 'I wanted to.' She wanted to claim that it had only been for peace, but she wouldn't deny that she loved Rolfe. 'I cared for him deeply.'

Pain lashed across his face and it was quickly followed by white-hot fury. 'How could you care for one of them?'

Taken aback at the abrupt change in him, she let her hands drop and stood rigid. He looked at her the same way he'd looked upon their mother that night Elswyth had heard them arguing. It was exactly what she had feared would happen, yet she had somehow made herself believe that she could make him see things differently. 'He's not a monster. Rolfe is a good man.'

'A good man who killed Osric.'

She winced at the accusation, because it was true enough and she couldn't deny it. 'That's not all he is. He wants to help us. He believes that if we work together then we can make Banford even more prosperous. The Scots only seek to enslave us, but the Danes could—' Father's hand came up as if to strike her. She broke off and cringed, waiting for the blow, but Galan stepped forward.

'Father!'

The harshly spoken word was enough to stay his heavy hand. He lowered it with a look of pure disdain. 'Will you stay with him or leave with us?'

The ultimatum wasn't unexpected. It was

her worst fear realised, and yet still she asked, 'Wh-what do you mean?'

'You've disappointed me deeply, girl. If it were Ellan, I could understand. She always was most like your mother. Faithless and silly. But you... I expected more from you than to lay yourself down for the first Dane who showed interest.'

Blood whooshed in her ears as every cruel word hit her with the force of a blow. 'That's not what happened. He loves me.' Loved her. As soon as the words left her mouth, she realised that he didn't any more. Perhaps he'd realised how impossible their love was in the face of battle.

'Your mother said the same thing, even when she came to me with the Dane's bastard in her belly.'

Elswyth gasped. Mother had been with child. 'Is that the night you argued?'

His brow furrowed, surprised that she'd heard them, but then he nodded. 'She sobbed and claimed to be torn. She loved the Dane, but loved you children, too, so I did her a kindness and took her choice away.'

'You made her leave.' The accusation shot out of her like an arrow aimed true to its target.

'I wouldn't have a wife who had sullied herself with one of *them*.'

'And what of a daughter?' She held her breath, very much afraid to hear the answer. Despite his faults, he was her father and she cared deeply for him.

He stared her down and she sensed Galan at her side, holding his breath as he awaited their father's judgement. 'You can choose. You either stay here or you come with us.'

Lose her family or lose Rolfe for good. 'Back to Banford?'

He shook his head. 'The time has come to act. Killing Osric was a step too far.' He lowered his voice as if realising that the enemy might overhear him. 'We'll get revenge now.' His words implied that the Scots would help in that.

'Father, nay, you cannot mean that you will join them?'

He nodded and she felt the press of Galan's fingers on her back. 'We will.' Galan's smooth voice confirmed her worst fear. 'I believe Father is too hasty in forcing you to choose,' Galan said, drawing her gaze to him. He stood tall and as proud and defiant as the leader of a rebellion should look. Her heart ached, because she couldn't help but to imagine that he could be dead soon.

'I am not,' said Father with a bite in his voice.

Galan narrowed his eyes at the older man before looking at her again. 'With you as Rolfe's wife, you'll have more insight into their battle plans. You can tell us everything we need to know.' The world started swimming around her and her heart sank. Her father's face blurred only to be replaced by Galan's smiling features. 'I'd be proud of you if you had planned this,' he teased. 'You'll be the perfect spy.'

Her knees went weak and she would've fallen had Galan not grabbed her. Her brother expected her to spy on her husband and her father was forcing her to make an awful choice. Her entire world seemed to be caving in on her.

'Nay, Galan. There will be none of that. It's too late. Either she leaves with us in the morning or she stays here to lie in the bed she made.' Father levelled her with a glare and said, 'If you stay, you will no longer be my daughter.'

She brought a hand to her mouth to stifle the sob that wanted to escape. Father didn't know it, but Rolfe had already withdrawn his love. There was no reason for her to stay here. But neither could she meekly go with him. She wasn't that dutiful daughter any more, hoping that if she didn't make a misstep that she would earn his love with her loyalty. She had to get away from all of them. She'd go to Banford. Perhaps she'd find some clarity there, away from this madness. If not, at least she could go to Baldric and keep him safe.

Chapter Seventeen

'Where is my wife?'

The sun had not yet crested the horizon, but Rolfe hadn't been able to wait any longer to take Elswyth back. He'd spent a fitful night in their bed, barely able to find any sleep because every time he drifted off he'd reach for her and become aware of her absence all over again.

It was only a slight exaggeration to say that he felt as if he'd been waiting for her all his life. In the short time he'd been with her he knew what would make her laugh and what would make her only smile, and somehow he knew just what to say to make her eyes go very fierce before her temper flared. He could hardly credit the thought, and he'd never give voice to it, but it was as if the gods had meant for her to be his. She *was* his and he would do everything in his power to keep her with him, even if he was forced to keep his distance from her.

If only he knew where she was. As he stared down at the empty place near the embers of the fire where she should have been, Godric and Galan roused in their blankets.

'She won't be your wife for long,' Galan muttered as he sat up.

The anger that coursed through Rolfe's body was so spontaneous and fierce that he was on top of Galan before he could think better of it. 'What have you done with her?'

'Nothing.' He didn't miss the way Galan looked towards the place where she should have been.

'She's gone, you fool.' Rolfe stared into the distance, hoping she'd merely walked away for a bit of privacy, but genuine panic was started to rise within him. The warrior tents were back towards Alvey's wall, but there was no sign of her wandering among them. He briefly wondered if one of them had taken her inside for his pleasure, but none of them would be so stupid. She was his and everyone knew that. He twisted towards the forest, but her form wasn't visible through the dim light of the waning moon. He told himself that she'd merely gone into the forest to relieve herself, or to walk and think things over, but he knew—*he knew*—that she was gone. There was a great void inside him that said she was already far away from him.

'She's gone.' Godric's voice, still harsh with sleep, broke the silence. 'She chose her family over you and she left to go home.'

Pain as sharp as a knife's blade slashed through his chest. The man couldn't have found better words with which to wound him. 'You lie.'

Galan sneered, standing next to his father, 'We have no need of lies when you've made certain she hates you. She found out who you really are and she left.'

Anger surged through Rolfe, so hot and furious that it propelled him across the glowing embers of the nearly dead fire. He swung his fist and knocked Galan to the ground. 'What sort of brother are you to tell her about her friend in that way?' he shouted. She should have been told in soft, gentle words that would take into account her deep grief.

Wiping the blood from his mouth, Galan smirked from where he'd fallen to the ground. 'What sort of husband are you to have killed him?'

The words were meant to wound and they did. They hurt deeply, nearly bringing Rolfe to his knees with the agony. Stifling a groan of anguish, he ran back to the safety of Alvey's walls hoping that he would find her there, but one quick search of the stables proved that Gyllir was not among the other horses.

Elswyth was gone.

He couldn't move for a moment as that horrible reality pulsed through him. She must have really left for Banford. There was nowhere else she could go. She had chosen her family over him. The devastating pain of that was enough to make him stumble, his hand grasping for the wall.

'Grim!' Rolfe shouted for the boy who guarded the horses at night.

He poked his head over the railing of the loft, straw in his hair as he rubbed his eyes. 'Aye, Rolfe?'

'Have you seen my wife? Gyllir is missing.'

The boy's eyes grew round and when he shook his head, Rolfe's heart sank. He didn't bother to berate the boy for not watching as well as he should have. There was no time. He had to get to Elswyth. Whether she had chosen her family or not, he needed to talk to her, to hear her tell him herself. By the gods, he might just bring her back anyway.

The blow of the horn sent another shard of

terror through him. A blow this early meant something was gravely wrong. 'Ready my horse,' he ordered Grim and ran to the gates to figure out what was happening.

The Saxon Aldred stood heaving for breath, his horse beside him lathered in sweat. The men on watch had gathered around them, listening.

'What's happened?' Rolfe asked, and they relayed the story to him. There were Scots in the north. Aldred had come upon them during his routine ride through his assigned territory. The area Aldred described wasn't directly on the path that Elswyth would take, but it was close enough to make Rolfe fear they might find her. Turning to the men of the night guard, he asked, 'Did any of you see my wife leave on Gyllir?'

'Aye,' one of them said. 'Around midnight she came and took the mare out.'

He stared at them, incredulous. 'Not one of you stopped her?'

They looked at each other in discomfort before one said, 'Should we have stopped her? Is she a prisoner?'

'Nay, but she was alone at night. Did you not suspect anything? You could have sent for me.'

They shuffled in discomfort again. 'She said that she was staying with her family tonight. We didn't know that you had forbidden her to leave.'

He hadn't forbidden her to leave, but neither should she have gone. He wanted to yell at the helplessness he felt. 'Send for Jarl Vidar and Aevir. Tell them we leave within the hour.'

That hour seemed endless. If Rolfe could have gone, he would have, but he couldn't simply ride out with the threat of the Scots lingering. They needed to assemble the warriors and prepare for battle. Finally, Rolfe had gathered his men and took Aevir, leaving before the allotted hour. He'd leave Vidar to take the other warriors in boats up the river. They'd make faster time and come from the west.

Rolfe set a brutal pace, the horses of more than forty warriors tearing up the ground in his fervour to find Elswyth. The Scots would have to come second to that. He'd never felt such an obsession in his life as he did now, needing to know that she was safe more than he needed his next breath. His only goal was to find her and take her in his arms. She could hate him for ever, but he was never letting her out of his sight again.

They had ridden hard for over an hour— the sides of his horse were already lathered in foam and he heaved in deep breaths—when they broke through the edge of the trees to see a single horse on the path ahead. The gathering sunlight glinted off its golden coat as it grazed on the grasses of the valley floor. Even from this distance, Rolfe could tell that it was Gyllir. His heart gave a leap in his chest as he urged Sleipnir even faster.

As soon as he approached, he vaulted down before his horse had even stopped, landing hard on his feet. He ran past Gyllir, expecting to see Elswyth resting in the tall grasses, but she wasn't there. A quick survey of the small valley found that it was empty.

'Elswyth!' He yelled her name over and over, but there was no response.

'Rolfe!' Aevir's hand on his shoulder finally got his attention, but Rolfe could tell from his expression that it wasn't the first time Aevir had called his name.

'She has to be here,' Rolfe said.

Aevir shook his head, then said very carefully, 'She's not here, Brother.' He led Rolfe back to Gyllir where it was obvious she was wounded as she favoured a foreleg. Dried mud caked one side of her as if she had fallen. She must have thrown Elswyth as she fell. An image of his wife, hurt and broken on the ground, came to mind.

With more than a day's travel to Banford ahead of them, there was no chance she'd reached the village and sent the horse back on its own. Something had happened to her. Either the horse had spooked and thrown her or she had come across the Scots.

Fighting nausea and a bone-deep fear he'd never felt before, Rolfe gave the order to keep riding.

They had been forced to a slower pace, so it was a few hours later when they reached the area where she'd been taken.

It was obvious a skirmish had occurred. Horse hooves had made deep prints in the mud left from the snow earlier in the week. There were at least a score of horses, maybe more, it was difficult to tell. One horse had taken a tumble, probably hers given the mud on Gyllir's side and her injury. The disturbance in the mud where the horse had lost its footing and slid on to its side was unmistakable. It appeared that Elswyth had been ambushed or had run right into the unaware Scots. Either way, they had her. He couldn't think too deeply about what that might mean. He only knew that he had to find her.

* * *

Elswyth had been lucky. Her arm had been scraped when Gyllir had fallen, tearing the sleeve of her underdress, but she'd managed to jump free to avoid the horse landing on her leg. It had been small consolation, because she'd had no chance to gain her footing before the Scots had captured her. It had happened so fast that she'd not even had a chance to pull her axe. One moment she'd been racing through the trees and in the next she'd come upon them. Her impression had been that they had been just as surprised as she had, but it hadn't changed the fact that they had taken her.

They had stuffed a cloth into her mouth to keep her silent. She hadn't made it easy, fighting until one of them had boxed her ear, sending her into a world of pain and stars. When she'd regained her senses, her arms had been tied to a horse and a Scot rode behind her. Struggling only sapped her strength and bruised her body, so she'd resolved to wait until they stopped. Turned out that struggling with the Scot behind her had hurt her worse than falling from the horse.

She had counted a group of seventeen. All men. All warriors. She didn't know what they were doing this far south. Were they scouting?

Had they become lost? Surely they hadn't come for battle with so few men? After they had taken her they'd travelled fast, as if they were afraid of pursuit, but after a few hours it had become apparent that they'd succeeded in their crime so they'd relaxed. A few of them had even given eerie calls of victory that had made her blood run cold.

If she had to guess, she would say this was no sanctioned jaunt to the south. They had probably escaped their leaders, hoping to return home with a Dane prize. They reminded her of adolescent mongrels testing their boundaries with the way they jested and spoke to one another, and they all seemed fairly young. The oldest and apparent leader was probably only a few years older than her. He was clean and well dressed, making her think he was someone of power. It was only later in the day when someone had spoken his name that she realised he was Domnall, the King's son. Though the most frightening thing about him was that he wore the bloodstone she had stolen from Rolfe on his cloak. She recognised its size and the gold filigree, though it was missing its chain.

She had debated if it would be better to tell them her identity or to keep quiet. Not that there was much time for talking. It appeared they were trying to make it back to their own territory with all possible haste. They had stopped only briefly a couple of times to water the horses and eat a little bread. Night had long since fallen and they'd shown no signs of stopping to camp, which was a relief. She feared what would happen to her if they made camp. But she was also starting to fear what would happen if they didn't. Snow had begun to fall the farther north they travelled and as day had become night a layer of it had accumulated on the ground. Somewhere during the struggle she'd lost her fur so her limbs were numb from the cold and the Scot at her back showed no signs of taking pity on her.

Light of a new dawn was just beginning to crest on the horizon when a shout from behind them drew the attention of Domnall. He pulled up short and all the other men stopped to watch as he doubled back. A figure rode out of the darkness and she recognised him as one of the group who had dropped off some time back. Apparently he'd been left behind to watch for Danes. She'd been so tired that she'd drifted in and out of sleep on the horse, so she wasn't entirely certain where they were. She'd guess they were north of Banford, perhaps already in the Scots territory.

Domnall shouted back to his men and she cursed herself for not being able to understand his words. There was no mistaking the change in momentum that ran through the group, a potent mix of anticipation and bloodlust, but all of it was tinged with fear. The fear was in how the men darted glances from one to the other as if attempting to draw strength from their own arrogance. A battle was coming. Her heart pounded and she knew the man had brought news of the Danes coming. It was Rolfe.

Domnall rode back, dismounted and walked straight towards her. She tried to keep her fear in check, but she couldn't control the shaking of her limbs as he cut the bonds attaching her to the horse from her arms and dragged her off. He set her on her feet, but they were numb from the cold and the hard ride, so she sank down before she could find her strength. He left her there and walked back to his horse. Her heart leapt as she thought that maybe he'd decided to leave her. Perhaps he thought she wasn't worth the risk and if he left her here the Danes would halt their pursuit. Her hopes fell when he walked back to her holding another set of rope and she realised he meant to tie her up again.

By this time she was able to get to her feet and she tore the cloth from her mouth. 'Let me go and I'll make sure you are not followed.'

He grinned and spoke in her language. 'How will you ensure that?'

'I am Elswyth. My father is Godric from Banford and I am the wife of Rolfe from the Danes of Alvey.'

He paused in his approach, but his smile only widened. 'Godric's daughter.' Then he tapped the bloodstone affixed to his cloak. 'I've you to thank for this. Those Danes killed my brother and took this from his dead body. Your brother, Galan, says that you retrieved it from them. He did not say that you had married one of them.'

She hesitated, uncertain how much glory she wanted to accept for an act that she despised. 'Aye, I took it,' she finally said. 'But only because you had Baldric. I did it to save him, not to help your cause.' The last thing she wanted now was to help the Scots. All she wanted was peace.

He watched her curiously, his head tilting to the side. 'Baldric? The boy?'

She nodded and a feeling of unease came over her as she remembered her father and the peculiar look on his face the previous night when she'd asked about Baldric.

'We never had Baldric,' the man said easily. 'Godric secured the bloodstone as a gesture of his loyalty.'

Her knees nearly went out from under her again as the pain of her family's betrayal tore through her. Baldric had never been in danger. They had told her that to make her steal from Rolfe. She'd betrayed Rolfe's trust for nothing. For a foolish test of loyalty to a king she had no love for.

'Your father lied to you,' he concluded, taking a menacing step closer to her.

Despite the fact that she knew she would get no help from his men, she looked for it anyway, only to see that they were all busy scurrying in every direction. They were planning to hide and lie in wait for whoever was coming.

'Tell me, Elswyth, to whom do you give your allegiance? Your father or your husband? You cannot serve both of them.'

She flinched from the question. Dear God, was it meant to follow her always? But what else had she expected? She was a Saxon who had married a Dane. Tangled loyalty and distrust would haunt her for ever.

Her family needed her and Rolfe...even thinking his name brought physical pain. He'd spent hours worshipping her body, but that alone wasn't enough to earn her devotion. Nay, he'd earned that with his noble strength, his sense of honour and gentle teasing. He'd earned that with the way he had always made her feel safe and protected. The memory of the way he had looked at her as he'd spoken the words that would make him her husband came back to her, as if she were the only woman he wanted, as if he had truly meant every one of them.

It was all those tiny moments added up to create a bond that she had known would only grow stronger in the days to come. Until it had all come crashing down around her.

'What does it matter to you?' she asked him coldly.

'It doesn't, but we're about to find out whether it matters to your husband.'

His eyes gleamed cruelly as he came for her. She screamed, hoping that the sound would warn Rolfe and the others, but it was cut off short by his open palm against the side of her head. It hadn't been terribly hard, but the strength hadn't yet returned to her legs so the blow knocked her to the ground. Her knees landed with a heavy thud on the hard ground, followed by the nearly dead weight of her exhausted body. The cold wet snow seeped through the fabric of her tunic and leggings. He tore the cloth from her hand, intending to tie her mouth again, but she refused to make it easy.

Drawing on the last of her reserved strength, she lashed out, catching him in the groin. He groaned in pain and fell to his knees, but he was only momentarily slowed, enough to allow her to rise, but not escape him. He grabbed her arm and with his greater strength was able to pull her beneath him so that he could tie the cloth behind her mouth and then wrench her arms in front of her to tie them. She fought him mercilessly so that by the time he'd finished, galloping horses could be heard coming up the slight hillside.

Her heart gave a leap of joy the moment she saw Rolfe's beloved face in the pale sliver of the coming dawn. His hair had come loose from the usual way he wore it pulled back from his face to swing in a wild mass around his shoulders. His eyes widened with visible relief when he saw her. In that moment everything became clear to her. She hated what he'd done and she despised the coldness with which he'd treated her, but she should have stayed and talked with him. Anything to keep him from danger. The rest of the Scots were out there hiding. One of them might even now be waiting to jump him.

Chapter Eighteen

Rolfe drew his mount up short the moment he saw Elswyth with Domnall, heir to the Scots King. Her eyes were round with terror. The sleeve of her dress was torn and much of her hair had fallen from her usually tidy braid, but otherwise she looked whole and unharmed. Domnall stood behind her with a dagger at her throat. It was only one of the many reasons Rolfe wanted to see him dead.

'You've taken my wife, Domnall. You will die for the crime.'

Domnall's laugh sent a chill through Rolfe's body. It was said the man was touched in the head and, looking at him now, Rolfe could believe it. His eyes were those of a man unconcerned with his current situation, which was an unbelievable show of arrogance in one so young and undermanned. Rolfe knew that he had at most twenty men. Aevir had split off a while back and had managed to pick off a few, but the rest were probably spread out in the shadowed dawn, watching them. Rolfe had ten men at his back, the rest silently closing in from the other sides. Domnall had to know Rolfe would come with more than ten men.

'If I die, then so does she.' Domnall pressed the tip of the blade closer to her tender neck, drawing a bead of blood. However, Elswyth didn't flinch, she stared at Rolfe as if attempting to warn him with her eyes.

Rolfe wanted nothing more than to attack and pull her away from Domnall. He'd take her in his arms and thank the gods she was safe while vowing to never let her out of his protection again. But he couldn't think of that now. First, he had to get her away from the madman.

'Why were you on Alvey lands? It's an act of war,' Rolfe said, attempting to distract the man while showing no sign of the rage that pounded through him at the sight of his wife's blood.

'We're already at war, Dane. You know that. The truth is that I didn't come with the intention of taking such a prize, but I'm glad to have found her.' He ran his hand over her torso, from her breast to her hip. Elswyth's wrists were tied in front of her but she still managed to send a sharp elbow into Domnall's side.

Domnall grunted and tightened his arm around her in what looked to be a merciless grip.

'I doubt you could handle her.' Rolfe forced an unconcerned grin.

'It seems that you couldn't handle her either. What was your wife doing wandering the forest on her own in the night? Did she get away from you or was she going on a spy's mission to report to her family?'

'She's no spy and it's none of your concern what she was doing unaccompanied. Hand her over and I *might* let you live.'

Domnall laughed again. 'Your words are very compelling, but I'll keep her. I quite like her. Had I known Godric's spy was such a beauty, I'd have demanded he give her to me as a sign of his loyalty rather than the bloodstone.'

The words were so odd, that Rolfe had to ask. 'What bloodstone?' From across the distance he met Elswyth's gaze and the guilt shining out at him nearly stole his breath. He didn't want to believe it was his bloodstone, but there was no denying the pained way she looked at him, as if her heart was breaking this very moment.

Domnall shifted her slightly to the side, revealing the stone fastened to his cloak. A surge of blinding anger tore through Rolfe. It was the same stone he'd brought home, set in the same gold-filigree design. It was supposed to be in the chest beneath his bed.

The guilt stamped into her features told him that Elswyth had taken it. When? Had she delivered it tonight? Was that the true reason for her mad dash in the middle of the night?

If he'd had any doubt about her guilt, he only had to look back to his wife to see the way her face scrunched with pain—or perhaps it was anger that her game had been found out—and the way she would not meet his gaze. It was clear that she had used him and chosen her family in the end. He had allowed his feelings for her to blind him to her true character. First Hilde and now his wife. He let out a bitter laugh.

He didn't want it to make sense, but it all came together perfectly. Her family had wanted her to wed him, probably in an attempt to eventually control him, or at the very least to gain insight to his plans. It was the perfect plan, because she was so unlike any seductress he'd ever come across. Instead of using pretty words and her body, she had used her innocence to seduce him.

The breath wheezed out of him in a hiss. The lies she'd fed him hurt far worse than the theft. Hilde had left him broken, but Elswyth's betrayal cut far deeper. Down to his core where it mangled him.

'Do you recognise it?' Domnall's voice had turned bitter. 'You took it from my bastard brother after you ran him through with your sword.'

The anger was followed by a very real and a very hated surge of fear that the man would kill her before Rolfe could save her. Rolfe shouldn't care any more. He didn't want to care, but he couldn't stop himself. Not yet. Perhaps soon he would be able to wrest control of the flicker of tenderness that still lingered for her and extinguish it like the hated spark that it was, but for now it was there and he could no more put it out than he could allow it to live.

Despite her crimes, she didn't deserve to die for them. He could devise a far better punishment than death. Besides, like it or not she was his wife and he'd vowed to protect her, to give his life for hers if need be. He'd honour that commitment.

'Aye, I recognise it.' He did not, however, recognise his own voice. It had gone soft and

menacing with a raw thread he'd never heard
in it before.

'Shall I cut off her cloth?' Domnall ran his
dagger up her neck and over her jaw, coming
to a stop on the cloth that had been put between
her lips and pulled cruelly around to the back
of her head and tied so tight that it bit into the
tender flesh of her cheeks. 'She can tell us how
she came to have it and how she delivered it.
Perhaps she could also tell you how we came
to know where your sentries were so that we
could avoid them.'

She finally deigned to meet his gaze again
and Rolfe held it, refusing to allow her to hide
from him. He'd get answers from her, but it
wouldn't be with Domnall watching. It would
be when they were alone and he would get the
truth from her whether she wanted to tell him
or not.

Elswyth could hardly bear the stone-hard hatred she saw in Rolfe's face. This was the commander she knew lingered beneath the surface
of the man she had come to love. This was the
enemy warrior capable of violence. It was not
the man who had smiled at her so tenderly, nor
the man who had whispered deliciously wicked
things in her ear as he'd come inside her. This

man was as cold and beautiful as the moors in winter, with hard plains and jagged edges that were as beautiful as they were inhospitable.

As the coldness of his gaze crawled inside her, making her shiver even harder, she had to wonder if he would even try to get her back from Domnall. He looked as if he could turn and leave without even giving her a second thought. And why wouldn't he? They were very possibly in Alba. Domnall had won. Any attempt to get her back now would be an act of aggression that would likely bring retaliation to Alvey. He knew she had stolen from him and she couldn't use her voice to tell him that Domnall lied about her supplying the Scots with information. Why would he want her? If she wasn't so exhausted and heartsore, she might have cried again.

'Nay,' Rolfe finally said, answering the question she had nearly forgotten hung in the air. 'I do not care to hear from her. Tell me what you want to give her back to me.'

She would have tumbled to the ground with relief had Domnall's grip on her waist not have been so tight she could barely breathe. It was a short-lived relief, however. She barely wanted to face Rolfe any more than she wanted to go with Domnall at the moment.

'You still want her, knowing she's a traitor?'

Despite herself, Elswyth stiffened, bracing herself for the answer.

'I want her because she's my wife. You will pay for taking her, Scot.'

It shouldn't have hurt, but it did. Rolfe wanted her back because the slight of taking a wife could not go unseen. It had nothing to do with her. He probably hated her. If the coldness in his eyes was an indication, he did hate her. She wanted to go back to the day before her father had come, when everything had been good between them and she'd been falling in love with her husband. She was afraid that now they could never go back. Nothing could change what either of them had done. She had lost both her family and her husband.

'Have you harmed her?' Rolfe asked.

'You mean have I taken her?' Domnall replied. 'Not yet.'

From somewhere in the deep shadows of the nearby trees a piercing cry broke through the silence that had fallen. Rolfe didn't react, but Domnall stiffened behind her. She didn't know how he knew, but it appeared they all assumed it was a Scot calling out as he lost his life. It was followed by another one on the opposite side. Rolfe's men had them surrounded. Domnall began to subtly tremble behind her while Rolfe looked on.

'Let her go and I'll give you a head start,' Rolfe said.

The sharp tip of the dagger pressed harder into her neck. A warm trickle of blood oozed out of the tiny puncture to slide down her neck. Before she knew what was happening, Domnall was pulling her backwards. Her feet stumbled over the uneven ground and she slipped a bit, but tried to hold her neck away from the blade's point. Rolfe and his men didn't move. They stayed vigilant.

Finally Domnall made it to where his horse was waiting. He mounted, half-pulling her up with him, so that she draped over the side of the horse facing Rolfe. 'Dismount!' the Scot yelled.

Rolfe and his men slowly moved to comply, but as soon as they did Domnall pushed her away and took off. His horse went flying off into the grey morning. Elswyth landed with a painful crash, her head throbbing and her limbs shaking as she rested on her hands and knees.

Strong hands grabbed her shoulders and pulled her to her feet. She knew without looking that it was Rolfe, she would know his touch anywhere. Though his face and eyes were still hard, he did keep his touch gentle as he cut the binding around her head. Hooves thundered past them on either side as his men set off after Domnall, but Rolfe stayed calm as he looked her over. 'Did he hurt you?'

She shook her head. 'Nothing that won't heal quickly.' Her tongue felt swollen and slow from having the cloth shoved in her mouth.

Rolfe turned back to Sleipnir and pulled a skein of water off his back, pressing it to her lips. She drank greedily, some of the water trickling down her chin to moisten the front of her dress. When she'd had her fill, he took it away to replace the stopper and she brought her bound hands up to wipe the water away.

'How did you know they had me?'

'We got word of the Scots being sighted as I was planning to ride out after I discovered you missing. We followed your path towards Banford and came across Gyllir.'

'Is she hurt?' Elswyth had been so worried for the gentle horse, not having seen what had happened to her after being taken.

'She has a slight limp, but it looked to be minor. We found where you had come across the Scots and it was a simple matter to follow them here.' He spoke without emotion. She could have been anyone he had saved in keeping with his duty.

'Thank you, Rolfe. I… I wasn't certain that you'd want to have me back.'

He paused briefly in tying the skein to his saddle, but then he finished the task and looked back at her. She could not tell what he was thinking or feeling. Perhaps saving her hadn't meant he'd wanted to have her back at all.

'Would you untie me?' She held up her wrists to remind him, but he merely looked at them. His face was impassive and her stomach sank. 'Am…am I a prisoner?'

'Did you steal the bloodstone from me?'

She swallowed, hating the answer that she had to give. She hated that she had taken it. If she had to do it all over again… She closed her eyes and put that useless thought away. Nothing could change the past. 'Rolfe, I—'

His hard voice cut off her words. 'Tell me "aye" or "nay".' His tone brooked no argument, drawing her gaze to his impassive face.

'Aye,' she said, her voice a little more than a whisper.

'Then you're a prisoner.' His words were flat as he turned to pull a fur that had been wrapped up behind his saddle. He shook it out and wrapped it around her shoulders, his movements as impersonal as if she were a stranger. Though his hands moved up and down her arms to help warm her faster and get her blood flowing, there was nothing to hint at the tenderness or the passion they had shared.

'What will you do with me?' she managed to ask as he boosted her on to his horse.

He didn't say a word as he mounted behind her and turned Sleipnir around, heading south towards Alvey's border. His left arm hooked around her waist to keep her stable. Her body felt so tired and she trembled from the cold that had seeped deep into the marrow of her bones that she wasn't certain she'd be able to stay up without his assistance.

'Rolfe, you must know that I only took it because—'

'Enough! I can't talk to you now.' The bitterness in his voice was the only outward sign of the deep anger burning inside him.

Rolfe despised how good she felt in his arms. After a day and nearly two sleepless nights without her, he'd longed only to have her in his arms again, to hold her against him and know that she was safe and his. It didn't seem to matter that he had learned she had used him ruthlessly for her own purposes. He knew that and his anger burned so hot that he could scarcely contain it, but his heart and his body hadn't yet caught up to his mind. They craved her with the intensity of an animal too long separated from its mate. So he allowed himself this time to hold her. They should reach Banford by afternoon and then that would be the end. He'd turn her over to Vidar and she would have to answer for her crimes just like anyone else.

At first she'd tried to hold herself stiffly against him, but soon the motion of the horse became too much for her exhaustion and she slumped forward. That was to be expected. More concerning was the fact that she had yet to stop trembling. The sound of her teeth chattering along with the occasional sounds of Sleipnir's huffs of breath was the only thing that broke through the stillness of the morning.

'Elswyth?' He hoped to rouse her, thinking that even though they were in a hurry, he should make her walk a bit to get her blood flowing again. She didn't stir, so he repeated her name a bit louder and with more authority. When she still didn't rouse, a flicker of fear moved through him.

A few years ago he'd been to the Great North with a group hunting the great white bears that lived there. They'd been besieged by a snow storm and had sought shelter, but it hadn't stopped a few of them from being overtaken with the cold. They'd shivered uncontrollably even after they'd found the warmth of the fire. Two of them had fallen asleep and never revived. It had been much colder then, but those men had been stout and large-boned. Elswyth was smaller framed and more delicate and she'd been without a fur for at least a day and a night with steady snow. A twinge of guilt tightened his chest uncomfortably. Her clothing was the same as that she had come to him with, barely adequate for winter, much less the extended exposure she'd endured. They hadn't had time to commission new clothing for her in heavier fabrics. Or perhaps there had been time, he simply hadn't seen clothing her as a priority when he'd wanted her without her clothes as much as possible.

Allowing Sleipnir his head, he pulled the knife from his boot and cut the bindings at her wrists. Then he turned her in his arms to see her pale face and the faint blue shadows around her lips and beneath her eyes. 'Saxon,' he called.

She shifted and the relief he felt nearly sent him falling to the ground.

'Saxon, talk to me,' he said, unable to stop himself from cupping her cheek. It was nearly as cold as the snow.

'Dane.' It was the softest whisper, but it

brought a smile to his face none the less. He found the pulse in her neck and breathed another sigh of relief when it was strong and steady beneath his fingers. 'So tired and cold,' she mumbled, seeking the heat of his body and turning into him. 'Please can I sleep?'

'Aye, Saxon. I'll keep you safe.' He held her against his chest and pulled away her fur, tucking her against him so that only their clothes were between them. She needed as much heat from his body as she could get. Then he wrapped his fur around them both and tucked hers around her so that she was doubly protected. The new position hindered their speed, but they were still able to make slow and steady progress. He checked her often to make certain she wasn't slipping into a deeper sleep. Each time the strong beat of her pulse reassured him.

Chapter Nineteen

Rolfe had not seen Elswyth in three days. She'd been sleeping—very nearly unconscious—when they had finally made Banford around nightfall. He'd meant to take her to one of the huts Cnut had built for his warriors, a small, thatched-roof structure that was little more than a place to sleep overnight. Instead, he'd taken one look at the inviting trail of smoke coming from the opening in the roof of her family's farmhouse and had taken her home.

An elderly woman—he'd later come to learn she was their housemaid—had been tending the fire when he'd kicked the door open with his booted foot. She jumped up and grabbed a cooking knife, but settled when she recognised him. Her wide eyes had gone to the fur-wrapped bundle in his arms as he'd ordered her to bring a straw mattress to set beside the hearth. That's where he'd laid Elswyth. The old woman had immediately began to cluck over her like a concerned hen. Rolfe had stayed until he was certain his wife would recover and then he'd left, commanding a Dane warrior to guard the front door. None of the Saxons in Banford could be trusted until he had questioned them all.

Aevir had returned at the end of the first day with Rolfe's warriors. Only a few of the Scots who had taken Elswyth had managed to escape, but Domnall was regrettably one of them. It was a fight Rolfe was more than prepared to fight another day. With Aevir's help, they were able to speak with every person in the village over the course of the next two days. All of them claimed innocence when it came to joining with the Scots and to his surprise he was inclined to believe them.

Godric, both of Elswyth's brothers, ten single men and four men along with their wives hadn't been seen for days. The popular opinion was that they had gone north to join with the Scots once it had become apparent that taking Banford would come to naught. In fact, many of the villagers seemed to breathe a collective sigh of relief when he spoke to them. Most of those left behind were families and the elderly who seemed more than willing to trade their anger for peace with the Danes.

Something told him that his wife not one of them. She had demanded his presence to every Dane he had stationed at her door, arguing when they wouldn't allow her to leave the home, and was once driven to physical violence so that he'd had to order every blade in the house confiscated. He told Aevir and even himself that he was content to await Vidar's arrival—after all, it was up to the Jarl to mete out justice for a crime done within his own walls. But even Rolfe couldn't hide from the truth late at night when he sought the meagre comforts of his bed.

The truth was that he was afraid of what he might do when he saw her again. Anger at her treason and lies had nearly burned him alive from the inside, but he couldn't deny the swell of tenderness he felt when he thought of her. As much as he tried to turn it to hate, he couldn't. She had betrayed him just as Hilde had—in some ways even worse—but some part of him would not let him forget how she had relaxed into him every night after giving him her body. How her elegant fingers would curl his hair around them absently as she stroked his shoulders and chest, whispering that she had never been happier. Most of all he couldn't forget how he'd thought they'd have the rest of their lives together and how happy that had made him.

Her mind was keen and eager to learn so he'd planned to keep teaching her the sword and even how to read and write the runes in which she'd shown interest. They were supposed to have had many long winter nights ahead when he'd tell her about his travels and his family. Perhaps he'd even take her back home to meet them one summer. And their children… His throat inevitably closed when he thought of those imagined, yet already beloved creatures with their loving mother. He'd already had their entire life in his head, but it was gone now.

Their future was gone and he couldn't decide between anger and heartache, so they both ate at him with vicious teeth until he was snarling at everyone and everything that crossed his path. He didn't *think* he would harm her when he saw her—he had sworn to protect her and he would abide by that until she was no longer his—but he couldn't chance what he might do. So he stayed away from her and he avoided his straw mattress—a sorry excuse for a bed if he'd ever seen one—for as long as he could until he could fall into it each night and have exhaustion overtake him. Unfortunately, he was a man of action and, while they waited for Vidar to reach them and for some sign of the missing Banford citizens, he only had to wait.

The evening of the third night found him sitting at the hearth in Cnut's longhouse with Aevir at his side. He had long ago finished his mead, but he held the tankard in his hands as he stared at the fire.

'Go to your wife, Brother,' Aevir said, giving him an infuriating smile before he threw back the remainder of his own mead.

'Don't call her that,' Rolfe said, his voice husky from disuse.

'It's what she is, isn't she?'

Rolfe shook his head. 'Not for long.' He'd already decided that divorce was the best option. Vidar would grant it given the circumstances.

'You'll have to talk to her for the divorce.' Aevir's easy voice was grating on his nerves.

'Then I'll talk to her at that time.'

Aevir sighed and then said the words that could have been his last had Rolfe not known him so well. 'I've never known you to be a coward.'

Rolfe threw his tankard to the floor where it landed with a loud thwack and dented the wooden plank. He was on Aevir before the man could defend himself, knocking the bench he sat on backwards, taking Aevir and the two men who sat next to him to the floor with it. 'Words of a dying man,' Rolfe growled, drawing back his fist to blight out the infuriating smirk Aevir still wore.

Aevir managed to dodge the blow and struggled upwards, reversing their positions so that he had the upper hand. Grabbing Rolfe's tunic, he said, 'I know the look of an infatuated man when I see it. Go talk to her and put us all out of our misery.'

Rolfe managed to knock him in the stomach, taking the air out of him and startling him enough so that Rolfe could flip their positions yet again. This time when he had Aevir beneath him he swung and managed to clip his chin with the edge of his knuckles before Aevir dodged away completely. 'You know nothing about what I'm feeling.'

Aevir twisted and managed to get a foot under Rolfe's knee, knocking him off balance. Aevir used the momentum of his fall to get behind him, locking his arms around Rolfe's torso to confine him while his heavy thighs worked to contain Rolfe's struggles. The men were evenly matched in strength so it was anyone's guess who would come out on top, though Rolfe could hear several men calling out wagers.

'I know what it is to love, you fool, and I know what it is to lose that love,' Aevir growled in his ear as they struggled. 'I would give anything to have her back for even one day, to say all the things I didn't have time for. *You* have time now, don't waste any more of it than you already have.'

'It's not the same,' Rolfe hissed, knowing that no one else would hear him over the cacophony of noise the men were making as they cheered them on. 'She lied to me. She stole from me. I cannot forgive that.' Everyone knew how Rolfe's own wife had betrayed him.

'Then go and tell her you're divorcing her now. Go talk to her before you get yourself killed.'

Rolfe hated Aevir's interference, but deep down he knew that his friend was right. He needed this resolved so that he could stop being consumed by Elswyth—if such a thing were even possible. He'd lost his focus and it would go badly for him and his men were they needed for battle while he was like this. Resentment fuelling his struggles, he twisted free enough to drive a powerful elbow into Aevir's side which made his friend huff out a breath of air and loosened his grip so that Rolfe could escape. Coming to his feet, he shoved Aevir away and strode for the door, but not before Aevir's mocking voice called out, 'I hope you know that by "talk" I meant—' The slamming door muffled the vulgarity and the roar of laughter from the men inside that followed it.

Blinded by his rage, Rolfe kept walking across the moonlit field, not caring that the cold turned his breath to frosty puffs, or that he'd forgotten his cloak inside. The cold couldn't touch him. Nothing could touch him and that was the problem. Only one name pounded inside him, driving him forward until he approached the farmhouse door. He hadn't even been aware of his destination until the warrior who was her sentry came to his feet, then stepped aside quickly when Rolfe showed no intention of stopping.

The door opened easily and Rolfe stepped over the threshold, slamming it behind him and setting the latch with a perverse satisfaction. She had come to her feet the moment she'd seen him and there was no mistaking the momentary flare of joy that had crossed her features. It made her cheeks flush with health and her emerald eyes brighten. He'd not seen her since he'd left her here and the rush of relief he felt at

seeing her whole and thriving staggered him.
It had the effect of cold water thrown on hot
metal and cracked through the anger harden-
ing around his heart.

'You look well,' he said rather lamely.

'I am well…thanks to you.' Her voice was
like a balm to his ravaged heart and the way
she looked at him…

That balm came with a warmth that threatened to further assuage his anger. Desperate
to keep stoking the flames so that he wouldn't
have to face her without them, he said, 'Why are
you mending clothing?' The pile had dropped
to the floor when she'd stood, but she still held
the needle with the thread attached, binding it
to the clothing at her feet. 'Where is your servant?' The woman could have been standing
right next to her and Rolfe wouldn't have seen
her. His entire awareness was consumed with
Elswyth.

A flicker of unease marred her joyful features. 'She spends her evenings elsewhere.'

'What? Why?' He'd thought Elswyth would
have someone with her at night. He hadn't
meant for her to be confined alone.

'We…argued.' She dropped her gaze and he
finally took in the state of the small house. Several stools had been overturned and their legs

broken, a pitcher—nay, several pitchers—had been shattered, their pieces swept neatly into a pile in a corner. It seemed that only a few basic items had been spared her wrath.

'You did this?' he asked.

Her eyes met his and her chin raised a notch higher than was necessary. 'I wanted to leave and your warriors wouldn't let me. I tried to overpower them and she said I was deranged and she wouldn't stay here at night alone with me.' Drawing in a deep breath as he stared at her in shock, she asked, 'Is there something you want?'

'You asked for me.'

'Days ago.' Accusation burned in her eyes.

'I'm here now.' He shrugged and her eyes burned bright with fresh anger. Good. He wanted her anger.

'I want to leave.'

'You're a prisoner.'

The words hurt her and though that hurt brought him a small measure of satisfaction, it brought him far more pain. And this was why he had avoided her, he realised. To hurt her was to hurt himself.

'Then at least let me see Baldric, my brother.'

'He's not here. We suspect he's already with the Scots to the north and awaiting your father.'

She took a moment to digest that and he would have sworn her surprise was genuine. Drawing herself together, she said, 'The reason I left Alvey was so that I could come here. I wished to see Baldric and visit Osric's mother. I'd like to see his grave, if that's possible.'

He clenched his molars so hard he was surprised they didn't crack under the strain. 'You're a prisoner,' he repeated.

'Then I would like the chance to answer for my crimes. Surely I deserve that?'

'Aye, and you will have that. Jarl Vidar will hear your pleas and decide on a punishment.' Silence descended between them, so Rolfe gave her a brief nod and turned towards the door, quietly cursing Aevir. Nothing had come of this talk with her. He'd been foolish to allow Aevir to goad him into it.

'Rolfe, wait!' Leaving her mending behind, she hurried across the distance, stopping just short of reaching him. 'My crimes were against you, not Lord Vidar. Let me explain to you.'

He was already shaking his head before she'd finished. 'You were a spy, so your crimes were against Alvey. Vidar will hear you, I don't care to hear more of your lies.'

She drew back as if he had struck her and the pain reflected on her face hit him twofold, so that it was momentarily difficult to breathe. 'Damn you and your stubbornness, Dane. I never spied.' As she started to explain, he stepped towards her, but she only stepped back out of his reach. 'Aye, my father sent me to spy, but I never gave them information. I told you all of that already. The only contact I had with anyone in my family aside from Ellan was the night after you returned and Galan came to me.'

'Nay, I don't want to hear more!' He raised his voice to drown hers out and leaped for her, but she easily sidestepped him.

'Why don't you want to hear?' she yelled back as she moved to the other side of the open hearth to avoid him. 'Are you afraid that the truth will make you realise how cruel you've been keeping me locked up here?'

'Because I cannot believe anything you say.' He stepped around the hearth which was in the centre of the house, leaving her with half as much space to run from him.

'Can't you identify the truth when you hear it?' She steadily backed away from him as she spoke.

'Not when one is as skilled at lying as you.' It seemed he was blind when it came to women.

Her mouth dropped open. 'I stole the blood-stone because Galan told me the Scots had Baldric and were demanding it back in exchange for his life. I barely knew you then. It wasn't personal when I took it from you.' She had come to the back wall of the house when she finished. She made to dart around him, but he grabbed her around the waist and pulled her back against him. Her familiar scent washed over him, stealing his breath, so that they stayed a moment like that until he could speak.

'Even if what you say is true, you made it personal when you married me without confessing. You took me as your husband, you drank the mead and took me into your body, all while knowing what you had done. Perhaps I could forgive your reasons had I known them earlier, but I cannot forgive your lying to me.' Or her betrayal. He'd didn't know if the pain of that would ever go away.

Her breath hitched, but when he thought she'd lost her fight, she stomped on his booted foot and pulled away. She slipped from his grasp, and he prepared to chase her, except she didn't run. She stood with her back pressed to the wall and glared at him. 'You know all about lying by omission, don't you? You didn't tell me of Osric, or the destruction you wrought in Banford. You never gave me the chance to choose to forgive you and yet you expect me to do what you couldn't.' Her voice might have been bitter, but the tears on her lashes ruined the effect.

'Damn you, Saxon.' Her tears were his undoing, just like the night she'd come to him in his chamber. The fight left him, leaving only pain, aching and bleeding, in its wake. He brought his hand to her cheek and his voice was raw when he spoke. 'I knew you would hate me for what I had done, so I wanted to wait to tell you until after you loved me.' It was perhaps the most honest thing he'd ever said in his entire life.

A sob stuck in her throat. With a groan he slid his hand around her nape and pulled her close. His mouth covered hers and she opened to him, eagerly, greedy even. The tip of her tongue touched his and he growled at the fierce need for her sweeping through him. It was like adding kindling to low burning fire. He went up in flames.

Chapter Twenty

The need to take her…own her…*possess* her tore through him with a savageness that left room for nothing else. He needed her once more. She was his mate and he'd not touched her for days and days. The want was primitive and tinged with a deep-seated urge to make her come apart in his arms. He wanted to feel her trembling beneath him with want and hunger, knowing that he was the only one who could assuage her desire.

The soft heat of her mouth pulled at him as he kissed her. She opened beneath him and invited him inside. He wanted her hard and fast and panting with desire. Pulling away from the touch of her eager tongue, he caught a glimpse of her heavy-lidded gaze as he tore at her night-dress. The linen came apart with a loud rending sound that seemed to echo in the small house.

She gasped and that sound only spurred him onwards.

Turning her so that her breasts pressed to the wall, he tore the back to match the front until the linen fell from her shoulders. The smooth skin of her back called to him and he couldn't resist touching it in a slow caress as he pushed the dress to a puddle at her feet. She arched into his touch and he couldn't bring himself to stop until he reached her bottom and filled both of his palms with her. She moaned deep in her throat when he squeezed and kneaded, shifting and pushing back against him in a silent plea for more.

Possession was what he wanted. Simple and crude. He wanted to bury himself deep between her thighs and own her as she writhed, begging him. The image of that made him swell to aching.

Elswyth turned abruptly against the wall to face him. She was nude, her beautiful body flushed with pleasure and desire as she pulled him against her, her mouth seeking his as she fitted herself against him. Her leg came up to hook around his thigh and he couldn't resist taking her mouth savagely and pressing her back to the wall. His arm went under her knee, opening her to him so that he could grind his hardness against her willing body. She gasped into his mouth and writhed. His fingers found her slick with arousal and he was surprised to find her as ready as he was.

Abruptly he pushed away from her, letting her settle against the wall as he backed away. 'Get on the bed,' he growled out in response to the question on her face, his hands going to his trousers.

Her gaze fastened on that movement as she hurried around him to comply, rushing to the straw-filled mattress near the fire. Almost immediately, his hands were on her waist, shifting her around so that her hips pressed back against him. The absolute need to dominate and reclaim her coursed through him. They belonged to each other no matter what might happen and always would. She complied so sweetly, as if she needed the reaffirmation, eager and ready to be his again.

His. The mere thought made blood surge into his groin, pounding through him as it urged him to take her.

He nudged her thigh and she opened to him, spreading herself so that he could settle on his knees between them. His trousers around his knees, he guided his manhood to her. There was something wild and primitive about having her nude before him, ready to receive him while he was clothed. It made him mad with excitement. As he pushed the swollen head of his manhood into her, she made a low sound of pleasure in the back of her throat and pressed back, seeking more of him. A rush of triumph burst through his chest.

Aye, beg me.

Gritting his teeth, he was determined to fight the surge of need that bid him to simply take her. So he played with her to draw out her pleasure, withdrawing, moving in a maddening rhythm along her crease, only giving her a taste of what she wanted. He paused at the drenched entrance to her body again, teasing her with his plump head, when she suddenly lurched back in an attempt to fill herself with him. A hoarse groan escaped him and he was helpless to do anything except jolt forward, joining their bodies in a hard thrust that rooted him deep within her. Spots of white light played behind his eyelids as he fell over her, keeping the bulk of his weight off of her on a straight arm while his other wrapped around her hips, holding her tight against him.

'Please, Rolfe.' Her voice was barely coherent, but the desperate rhythm of her hips was unmistakable as she moved beneath him, begging for more.

There was only her beloved softness beneath him, squeezing him in her tight grip as he moved. She sighed in a sound of unmistakable appreciation as he pulled out nearly all the way and slid hard back into her. She angled her body so that he could sink even deeper and he was lost. His hips began a hard tempo, pumping in and out of her in a desperate rhythm of possession. No longer able to keep himself away, he buried his face in the back of her neck so that her scent filled him. His name fell like a mantra from her lips as she clawed at him, her hand coming around to hold his thigh as if she was afraid he might leave her.

Soon she cried out in a hoarse sound as her sweet body clenched at him, convulsing around his shaft in delicious shock waves that drained him of his release. But even then he couldn't stop. He kept pumping until every last bit of his seed had been wrung from him and his tremors had subsided. He fell against her heavily, his heart threatening to pound out of his chest as he struggled to catch his breath.

He couldn't believe how consumed he'd been by her. For those few brief moments nothing else in the world had existed. Only her. Tenderness for her welled in his chest and his hands clenched at her, already wanting her again and afraid that something might take her from him. For a man who considered himself to be strong, she made him weak. He could never trust his judgement of her.

With a soft cry that he couldn't contain, he pulled himself from her body and struggled back into his trousers. A contented smile curved her lips as she turned over on to her back to look at him, but alarm quickly set in when she saw that he was getting to his feet.

'Don't go.'

He shook his head and she made to rise, but he held out his hand to ward her off and said, 'Nay!'

His voice was harsh to his own ears and it startled her, but it only made her pause briefly before getting to her knees to beseech him again. 'Rolfe, let us talk. I don't want you to go—'

The door closed behind him as he made his way out into the frigid night air. The woman consumed him without even trying. He had to get away from her before he did something foolish like forget his anger or even the reason he was angry. One entire night with her and he was certain he'd forget all about her treachery.

Damn it all—he loved her.

* * *

Elswyth passed a fitful night and finally gave up attempting to sleep when the grey light of dawn shone through the edges of the door. For the very first time she allowed herself the absolute despair that her marriage with Rolfe might be over. For a few moments last night she had made herself believe that a future was possible.

The truth was that he despised her. She'd throw another pot if she had any anger left within her, but there was nothing left. He'd wrung it all out of her last night. Instead of behaving like a child, she'd dressed in her winter clothes and doled out a bowl of pottage for herself with the first morning light. There was nothing to do but wait until Lord Vidar arrived and then she could finally tell her story. She didn't know what would happen after that and she couldn't bring herself to care.

Then something extraordinary happened. After she had finished her meagre meal, a man opened the door. He was the Dane who had been sent to guard her on a previous day. The man she had attacked with her blade when he'd refused to summon Rolfe, to be exact. He stood inside the door and gave her a wary stare.

'What do you want?' she asked with very little patience.

He bristled, looked out the open door as if he didn't like what he'd been tasked with doing, and then glanced back at her. 'I'm to take you to visit a grave,' he mumbled.

The hope bursting through her heart brought her to her feet. Rolfe had sent him. He'd remembered her request from the night and sent this man to take her to see Osric. After everything else that had happened, she had assumed he'd forgotten the request. What did it mean? Did he still care? Was he merely attempting to assuage his conscience? Whatever it meant, he was thinking about her. Last night hadn't been some final goodbye. He might have meant for it to be, but he was still thinking of her this morning.

Biting back her smile, she hurried to find her cloak and in moments had joined the Dane at the door. He held up a rope made of hemp and she glared at him. 'I'll not be restrained. If you must, then you can go find your master and tell him that I won't be bound. Let him come do it himself if he insists.'

Shifting from one foot to the other, he sighed, clearly wishing to have any other duty than to deal with her. She crossed her arms over her chest, feeling very much within her rights to insist that she be treated better than a common criminal.

Evidently deciding that he'd rather have the deed over with quickly than to return to Rolfe and explain his failure, he glared at her and stepped outside, indicating that she should come with him. He wound the rope back up into a coil and affixed it to his belt as he led her around the house and to the path that would take them to the village.

Despite the morbid reason for the outing, she was happy to be outside again. The day was clear, if not blue, and there was no new snow so the path was easy to navigate. She'd nearly worn holes in the plank floor of the house, pacing with unexpended energy over the past several days. In the distance a man—though if he were Saxon or Dane she couldn't tell—put out hay for the sheep, their anxious *baas* making her feel more at home than she had since she'd arrived. How easy it would be to slip back into her old life, as if what had happened in Alvey had been a dream. But it hadn't been a dream and she still had the telltale body aches from last night to prove it. Rolfe had been real and he'd been hers.

Her eyes moved of their own accord to find him. There were men sparring in the clearing outside Cnut's longhouse, but he didn't seem to be one of them. Aevir seemed to be the one running them through their paces. As they approached the village, men, women and children were moving about their daily chores. Not one of them seemed concerned with the additional Danes in their midst. She shouldn't have been surprised. Without her father and the other agitators, there was nothing to keep life from happening as it should.

Lady Gwendolyn had been right. Everyone served someone and most people didn't care who it was as long as they could live their lives in peace. As long as there was enough food and work and time to enjoy life, what did it matter? The Danes were here, but they were not a hindrance and they were not malicious invaders. If only her father could have seen this, perhaps life could have been different.

What would have happened had her mother never met that Dane and run off? Would her father have been more willing to work with Lord Vidar? In the days since talking to Father, she'd not been able to stop thinking of Mother. Somehow knowing that she carried the Dane's child made the woman's decision more poignant. She hadn't simply left her family because she'd found a man more exciting than her husband.

She'd been forced to choose and she'd followed her heart. She hadn't left them so much as she'd chosen a future for her unborn child.

The knowledge gave clarity to Elswyth's own dilemma. If she was allowed to follow her heart, it would lead her to Rolfe. She only hoped it wasn't too late to choose him.

'Good morning, Elswyth!' They had walked close enough to the outskirts of the village that a few of the women paused to set their heavy baskets of laundry down to call to her.

She called back and smiled, happy to see familiar faces. She would have stopped and talked, but the Dane looked back at her. 'Let's go,' he grumbled.

Biting back a retort, she followed him and gave a regretful wave to the small group. Soon he led her to a grave, a fresh mound of dirt covering it. A wave of sorrow came over her. Though she'd had days to come to terms with his fate and she had, it still didn't seem possible that the boy she had known was gone. She wanted to laugh with him one last time, but she couldn't and that wasn't Rolfe's fault. She could accept that now.

Rolfe was no more to blame for Osric's death than he was to blame for the Dane presence in their lands. Osric had made his own choice and he'd been fully aware of the consequences. Even so, she found that she had to be angry with someone, because Osric wasn't here to bear the brunt of it. In the days she'd spent in that farmhouse, she had come to realise that if anyone should share the blame with Osric that it was her father. Father and his bitter sense of betrayal towards Mother had led them all to this. Osric had not been a warrior. He would've been content living his life in peace. Father must have encouraged him to meet the Scots.

The sharp whinny of a horse caught her attention. Sleipnir raced across the ridge separating the field from the village. Rolfe was on his back, leaning forward as the stallion ran beneath him. Her heart clenched with longing as she watched him and it was quickly followed by a surge of possessiveness. He was hers. They had taken vows and nothing could change that. His people might believe in divorce, but hers didn't and nothing he or Lord Vidar could say or do would change that.

Rolfe would always be hers.

She hadn't realised she'd started running towards him until the Dane guarding her called out. She'd caught him unaware as he'd left her to pay her respects in peace and watched some of the women in the village. His heavy footfalls came up behind her, but they only spurred her faster. Rolfe had reached Aevir and had vaulted from his horse to talk to him about something that seemed rather important.

'Wait!' The Dane grabbed her arm, tugging her to a stop. Jerking away from him, she nearly succeeded in running again, but he was too determined. 'You can't go there. I have to take you back to the house.'

'Nay, I need to see Rolfe.' She swatted at his hands in a way that might have been comical had she not been so desperate. She opened her mouth to tell him in no uncertain terms that she wouldn't be returning without speaking to her husband when a great roar sounded from the forest north of the longhouse. Men on horseback flooded the valley, spilling in from the forest as if they had no end.

Scots! That's why Rolfe had been moving with such urgency. He must have seen them from the rise and come to warn everyone.

'Go to them!' she yelled when the Dane seemed intent on dragging her away from the sight in the opposite direction.

'I can't leave you!' His voice was stern, but he wasn't looking at her. He stared at the coming violence as if he itched to join in.

'Rolfe needs you more. I need to lead the

women in the village to safety.' One look showed her that the villagers were aware of what was happening. They ran for the forest to the south, prepared years ago by her father for the eventuality of invasion with peace with the Scots and Danes being so uncertain. Something must have happened with her father's truce with the Scots to make them invade. Or perhaps they only came for the Danes and planned to leave the village in peace. Either way, someone needed to make sure they all hid in safety.

'Nay, they'll be fine. Jarl Vidar arrived with his men late last night. We've more than enough warriors.'

Relief overcame her. At least there was that. 'But what if they need you?'

The Dane wavered, but his youth eventually won out. It was clear that he'd much rather fight with the men than hide with the women, so he shoved the grip of his dagger into her hand. 'Run!' he ordered. 'Do you know where to hide?'

'Aye, the rise in the forest.' She indicated the direction in which the villagers were fleeing. Father and the warriors had made certain everyone knew to hide behind the rise. It was difficult to see for anyone who didn't know the landscape and it would give the villagers a safe point from which to view the battle. It would also give them ample time to see any attackers who might approach.

He gave a curt nod. 'Go then!' But as he ran towards the battle, he didn't even look back to make sure she followed his orders. Why would he? She was a woman and she was meant to obey.

Only she wouldn't.

She ran as fast as her legs could carry her into the village. By the time she reached it most everyone had gone. A few of the men stayed back with weapons to guard their houses should the Scots get past the Danes. Sliding the dagger into her belt, she picked up a short-handled axe that had been left carelessly by the woodshed. Taking it in hand, she hurried towards the battle. Already the sounds of steel on steel could be heard ringing out as warriors clashed.

The echo only made her legs pump harder. Her only thought was to get to Rolfe, to make certain that he was safe. She could make out his head and shoulders at the edge of the sparring field. She couldn't see clearly from the distance, but he moved fast, striking with his sword as it seemed one Scot after another came at him. She lost sight of him for a moment as she was forced to run around the forge, the tall stone wall blocking her view.

When next she saw him, he had two men coming after him at once. Blood dripped from his sword as he stepped over the bodies of the slain enemies at his feet. Aevir was across the way, fending off his own attackers. A man sneaked around the longhouse, walking silently but briskly into the open to approach Rolfe from behind. She called out, but her voice seemed to be lost in the noise of battle.

Bracing her feet against the dirt, she pulled back the arm with the axe. Excitement and fear ran through her entire body, but she forced a calmness she was far from feeling and breathed in. On the exhale she let the axe fly. It whooshed through the air and somehow that sound was louder than her own cry had been. The weapon was a blur as it sailed, coming to a rest with flawless accuracy in the back of the man who would have attacked Rolfe.

The attacker let out a startling cry as he fell to his knees. Having dispatched the two men he'd been battling, Rolfe turned, his eyes finding her before landing on the man at his feet. 'Get down!' he yelled.

It was only at that moment that she realised she was standing in the middle of a field, the battle swarming around her, with only a dagger in her belt for a weapon. Her heart too frozen in fear to pound, she looked for a place to hide as Rolfe finished the man off. The longhouse was farther away than the forge, so she turned back to it, hiding herself behind the solid stone wall and drawing her dagger.

She could hear Rolfe's voice calling to Aevir, but she couldn't tell what he said. By this time her heart had resumed its pounding and seemed to have taken up residence in her ears. All she could hear was the blood rushing through her veins. It might have been only moments or maybe it was hours that she stayed there, but Rolfe came around the stone wall. His eyes found hers and he rushed over.

She rose to her feet just before he caught her in his arms and pulled her against him.

'Elswyth,' he whispered against her ear, his hand going to the back of her head to hold her tight. 'You're safe.'

'Is it over?' she asked against his neck. He smelled of sweat and horse, but it was the most glorious scent ever. He was safe and whole.

'Aye.' His voice was little more than a hoarse croak as he tightened his arms. 'Why didn't you run to the forest?'

'Because you needed me.' She pulled back just enough to glare up at him.

He grinned, his arms still so tight that she could barely draw breath. 'Aye, I did. You saved me.'

She'd been prepared to battle it out with him, not thinking that he'd relent and admit that her axe had taken the man down before Rolfe could handle him. So she stood stunned, not certain what to say. Rolfe seemed to know what to do because he kissed her deeply, his tongue plundering her mouth with determination. When he pulled back to take a breath, he said, 'Thank you.'

She shook her head, wondering how he could ever think she could do anything less. 'I would give my life for you.'

He looked stricken, as if her words pained him. Dropping his forehead to rest against hers, he said, 'Nay, never do that. I love you too much. I couldn't live without you.' He took a deep, wavering breath. 'I'm sorry, Saxon. For ever thinking that I could live without you. For doubting you. For believing that you were anything less than you are.'

She laughed, though it sounded rather like a sob. 'I forgive you as long as you spend the rest of your life making it up to me.'

His deep laughter moved through her as he swung her up into his arms. 'You can count on that. I love you.'

Chapter Twenty-One

It was evening before Elswyth was brought before Jarl Vidar to explain her crimes. The Scots had been soundly defeated, thanks in part to the arrival of the Jarl and his fleet of warriors. As before, this attack seemed to be a test. It wasn't the whole of the Scots horde, but enough to check their weaknesses. It had been a foolish ploy, because far more Scots had been cut down than had escaped—though Domnall hadn't been among either group, much to Rolfe's displeasure. They had even taken a few for questioning. The whole of the afternoon had been taken up with dealing with the battle's aftermath.

Now Elswyth sat at the long table in the hall with Rolfe at her side as she recounted what her family had called upon her to do. Her chestnut hair was pulled back, but left to flow down to her waist, the fire picking up streaks of red and gold. She was beautiful as she fearlessly answered the Jarl's questions. Rolfe was proud to see that she didn't shirk her own responsibility—she *had* after all agreed to spy—but neither did she deny how she had been misled by Galan and, ultimately, her own father. She would never have stolen the jewel without the threat of Baldric's safety spurring her on.

He believed that now. A strong thread of honour ran through his wife, guiding her actions and judgement. It had been there all along, which is why he'd been called to her from the beginning. Perhaps she would have opened up to him earlier had he shown her that he loved her, instead of allowing Hilde to cast her shadow on their union. He stroked a hand down Elswyth's back as she finished her story and sat silently awaiting Vidar's judgement. She seemed to take strength from his touch, notching her chin a bit higher as she met Vidar's harsh gaze head on.

'Do I understand you to claim that you never actually gave your family any beneficial information?' Vidar asked, his brow furrowed as he looked down at her.

'Nay, my lord. After seeing Alvey with my own eyes, I came to the conclusion that peace would be best. Your forces were too strong to fight, but more than that, I saw how peaceful it was there. With Lady Gwendolyn's help, I came to believe that we could find that peace here in Banford if given the chance.'

Vidar took in a deep breath as he stared at her, his expression still fierce and hard. 'Then it appears your only crime is that of theft.'

He raised a brow and she nodded. 'Aye, my lord. Again, I am very sorry for that. I only took it because—'

He held up his hand, palm out, to stop her. 'I understand what prompted the theft, Elswyth. I cannot fault you for your intentions, but neither can I ignore the outcome.'

Rolfe clenched his jaw and gently pressed his palm into her back, reassuring her. He didn't believe that Vidar would treat her harshly, but he had no idea what his friend intended. If he set out to make an example of her... He couldn't even allow the thought to finish in his mind. Knowing how her family had used her and forsaken her was punishment enough.

'Aye, my lord. I understand.' She stiffened under Rolfe's touch, steeling herself for the punishment.

'You stole from Rolfe, so I will remand you to your husband for him to mete out a suitable punishment. However, I would urge you in the future to come to us should you or your family need assistance.'

She nodded, but relief was postponed at the mention of her family. 'What will become of my family?'

No one had seen her family since Rolfe had confronted them outside Alvey's walls. In the rush to find Elswyth and deal with the impending Scot threat, they had slipped away. Yet with several of the villagers missing along with her family, it could only be assumed that they had wilfully left. Perhaps to join with the Scot cause, perhaps not. The next few days would tell. Rolfe burned to get hold of her father and tell the man what he thought of him and his treatment of his daughters.

'It's good that your father and brothers were not with the Scots who attacked. I won't leave Banford until this problem is dealt with once and for all and that includes finding your father and brothers. I'll give them the same chance I gave you to answer for their crimes.'

She nodded and Rolfe took her hand in his, giving it a squeeze. She hadn't given up hope that her family would turn up soon. 'What of Ellan? She never entertained our father's hatred.'

Vidar nodded. 'I've already sent for her to

join us here. I'll question her, of course, but if that's true then she'll be free to do as she'd like. She can return to Alvey or stay in Banford.'

Unable to wait another moment to be alone with his wife again, Rolfe rose to his feet and pulled her up with him. Murmuring his thanks to Vidar, he put an arm around her waist and ushered her from the building. She smiled up at him when he tucked his fur cloak around her shoulders and let the door close behind them.

'Where are we going?' she laughed. 'We should at least check on Aevir.'

Aevir had been wounded in the battle, but had been tended to hours ago. Rolfe shook his head. 'You already made him a poultice and he's resting. It's time to discuss your punishment, Wife.'

She pulled a face, but he could tell it only hid a smile. 'I knew you wouldn't let that go.'

'Of course not. Jarl Vidar specifically said that I was to punish you. I can't defy an order.' He swung her up into his arms and ran with her through the cold to the farmhouse, her laughter floating behind them. The housemaid had left the fire burning in the hearth with a pot of stew bubbling over the flame before she'd left for the night. His stomach growled at the aroma, but it would have to wait. He had another hunger to assuage first and it was for something far more important than food.

After he set Elswyth on her feet, she hurried to the hearth to warm her hands as he secured the door closed behind them. After hanging up his cloak, he walked up behind her, putting his arms around her and drawing her back against his chest.

'You forgot your gloves in Alvey.'

She shook her head. Her voice was soft when she said, 'Nay, I left them on purpose. At the time I couldn't keep them. They were your first gift to me and it hurt too much to look at them.'

He breathed in her sweet scent and ran his lips along her temple. 'At the time...but not now?'

'I'm sorry I left the way I did. It was wrong.' She turned in his arms as she spoke and looked up at him, her hands cupping his face. 'I want us to always talk going forward. I know that there will be things you have to do that I won't like, but we can't allow that to come between us. We can't forget that we are better together than we are apart.'

Lacing his fingers with hers, he kissed down the tender inside of one slender wrist, smiling when she sucked in a breath. 'I'm sorry for what happened with Osric. And more, I am sorry for not telling you and being honest with you from the beginning.'

She nodded. 'I love you, Dane. I love you far more than I could ever hate you, no matter what happens. Please believe that. Always.'

His answer was to press his lips to hers and hold her close. With the bitter winter wind raging outside, treachery and heartache was forgotten as they explored the love that burned between them.

* * * * *

MILLS & BOON

Coming next month

HIS CONVENIENT HIGHLAND BRIDE
Janice Preston

Lachlan McNeill couldn't quite believe his good fortune
when he first saw his bride, Lady Flora McCrieff,
walking up the aisle towards him on her father's arm.
Her posture was upright and correct and her figure was...
delectable. The tight bodice and sleeves of her wedding
gown—her figure tightly laced in accordance with
fashion—accentuated her full breasts, slender arms and
tiny waist above the wide bell of her skirt. She was tiny,
dwarfed by her father's solid, powerful frame, and she
barely reached Lachlan's shoulder when they stood side
by side in front of the minister. True, he had not yet
seen his new bride's face—her figure might be all he
could wish for, but was there a nasty surprise lurking
yet? Maybe her features were somehow disfigured? Or
maybe she was a shrew? Why else had her father refused
to let them meet before their wedding day? He'd instead
insisted on riding over to Lochmore Castle, Lachlan's
new home, to agree the marriage settlements.

Their vows exchanged, Lachlan raised Flora's veil,
bracing himself for some kind of abomination. His chest
loosened with relief as she stared up at him, her green
eyes huge and wary under auburn brows, the freckles
that speckled her nose and cheeks stark against the pallor
of her skin. His finger caught a loose, silken tendril of

coppery-red hair and her face flooded pink, her lower lip trembling, drawing his gaze as the scent of orange blossom wreathed his senses.

She is gorgeous.

Heat sizzled through him, sending blood surging to his loins as he found himself drawn into the green depths of her eyes, his senses in disarray. Then he took her hand to place it on his arm and its delicacy, its softness, its fragility sent waves of doubt crashing through him, sluicing him clean of lustful thoughts as he sucked air into his lungs.

He had never imagined he'd be faced with one so young…so dainty…so captivating…and her beauty and her purity brought into sharp focus his own dirty, sordid past. Next to her he felt a clumsy, uncultured oaf.

What could he and this pampered young lady ever have in common? She might accept his fortune, but could she ever truly accept the man behind the façade? He'd faced rejection over his past before and he'd already decided that the less his wife ever learned about that past, the better.

Continue reading
HIS CONVENIENT HIGHLAND BRIDE
Janice Preston

Available next month
www.millsandboon.co.uk

LET'S TALK
Romance

For exclusive extracts, competitions and special offers, find us online:

- facebook.com/millsandboon
- @MillsandBoon
- @MillsandBoonUK

Get in touch on 01413 063232

For all the latest titles coming soon, visit
millsandboon.co.uk/nextmonth

COMING SOON!

We really hope you enjoyed reading this book. If you're looking for more romance, be sure to head to the shops when new books are available on

Thursday 21st March

To see which titles are coming soon, please visit **millsandboon.co.uk/nextmonth**